GRINDYLOW AMBUSH

GRINDYLOW AMBUSH
THE ORIGIN STORY OF MONSTERS™ BOOK FIVE

MARTHA CARR
MICHAEL ANDERLE

DON'T MISS OUR NEW RELEASES

Join the LMBPN email list to be notified of new releases and special promotions (which happen often) by following this link:

http://lmbpn.com/email/

This book is a work of fiction. All of the characters, organizations, and events portrayed in this novel are either products of the author's imagination or are used fictitiously. Sometimes both.

Copyright © 2023 LMBPN Publishing
Cover Art by Jake @ J Caleb Design
http://jcalebdesign.com / jcalebdesign@gmail.com
Cover copyright © LMBPN Publishing
A Michael Anderle Production

LMBPN Publishing supports the right to free expression and the value of copyright. The purpose of copyright is to encourage writers and artists to produce the creative works that enrich our culture.

The distribution of this book without permission is a theft of the author's intellectual property. If you would like permission to use material from the book (other than for review purposes), please contact support@lmbpn.com. Thank you for your support of the author's rights.

LMBPN Publishing
PMB 196, 2540 South Maryland Pkwy
Las Vegas, NV 89109

Version 1.00, May 2023
ebook ISBN: 979-8-88541-163-9
Print ISBN: 979-8-88878-366-5

THE GRINDYLOW AMBUSH TEAM

Thanks to our JIT Readers

Jackey Hankard-Brodie
Dorothy Lloyd
Diane L. Smith
Jan Hunnicutt

Editor

SkyFyre Editing Team

CHAPTER ONE

"Think you can handle this?" Halsey Ambrosius extended a hand toward her cousin with a haughty smile.

Half-propped on his elbows in the middle of the quiet, empty main street of Coningsby, England, Brigham stared at his mission partner and laughed without humor. "If you're about to tell me healing an unhealable barghest wound with that creepy magic ball of yours is only the beginning, Hal, I think I'm better off hanging out here."

She cocked her head in a wordless gesture for him to accept the boost after he'd already accepted the magical help neither one of them had expected. Especially not when that help came from the copper orb Halsey had transmuted from a pile of leftover magical sand in the Ambrosius Clan's acquisitions warehouse in Dublin.

After wrinkling his nose in consideration, Brigham finally grabbed her hand, and she hoisted him up to his feet. His sneakers scrabbled against the pavement as he briefly fought to regain his balance. The last time he'd been on them, the slash across the side of his lower abdomen from the barghest's claws had drained the life from his body by the second, spreading with alarming speed as its unique poison had coursed through him as if he'd been injected with enough venom to kill a horse.

Now, though, he stood steadily beside his cousin as he dragged a long, deep breath through his nose. He could obviously speak coherently again now that he wasn't on the verge of losing consciousness. Or worse. More than that, he *looked* stronger, and the color was back in his cheeks.

As if the last twenty minutes had never even happened.

But they did happen, Halsey thought as she released his hand and looked him over from head to toe. *The barghest got him. I got the barghest with Pappy's shotgun. Florence's healing potion didn't do a damn thing, but I healed my cousin with a kind of magic that isn't even...*

She had to brush that thought aside before she could finish it. She'd wanted to convince herself the magic inside her copper orb was foreign. Outside of her, belonging to someone else, unfamiliar and unknown.

Yet the truth was harder to look at head-on.

When she'd used the orb to heal Brigham's wound, she'd been using her own magic. Maybe it had been boosted by the copper ball. Maybe the use of the strange artifact had affected her magic or given it a new flavor that didn't fall into the category of traditional elemental magic. Not for the Ambrosius Clan, anyway. Not for any other Clan she'd heard of, either.

Brigham had felt the same thing, which meant they now

had one more mind-boggling mystery on their hands and not nearly enough time to work it out right now.

It's not my magic. It can't be my magic. I'm an Ambrosius elemental all the way, and that was...

While she tried to both wrap her head around the new puzzle and keep her thoughts from writing themselves all over her face, her cousin took that moment to double-check what they both already knew to be true.

Now that he'd steadied himself on his feet, he grabbed the hem of his blood-stained t-shirt and lifted it a few inches above the waistband of his jeans to take another look. Smears of dried blood covered his belly and coated the top of his jeans, but where the wound had been openly bleeding no more than three minutes ago, now it had stopped.

The mark from the barghest's slashing claws was still there. A slightly raised stripe of brand-new scar tissue, shiny and pink, as if he'd sustained the wound weeks ago instead of minutes. At least the supernatural necrosis was gone, the black streaks that had coursed under his flesh up to his neck had disappeared, and the wound was healed.

"You know, for a moment there, I really didn't think I'd be getting back on my feet," he murmured as he lightly brushed his fingers across his skin below the scar.

Halsey snorted. "Yeah. A moment that felt like an entire lifetime."

"Oh, it was long for *you*?" He raised his eyebrows, still pinning the hem of his shirt against his ribcage to expose the proof. "Next time you almost forget your own name, come talk to me again about long moments." The bottom of his t-shirt dropped from his hands, and he gave it a light tug to make sure the scar was fully covered. "You didn't answer my question, by the way."

"You didn't ask a question."

"Fine." Brigham fixed his cousin with a knowing look. "You're *not* gonna tell me healing an unhealable barghest wound with that creepy magic ball of yours is only the beginning, right?"

"Well, seeing as I was about to rip up one of your shirts for a DIY bandage you don't even need anymore…" Halsey gestured flippantly toward the blood on his shirt. "No, Brigham. I'm not gonna tell you that." Her gaze fell on the copper orb in question, which she'd all but forgotten in the relief of seeing her cousin well again and the dizziness that had hit her like a train after performing a spell she hadn't known she was capable of until it became the last option at the last second.

It rested on the pavement where she'd previously knelt beside her wounded cousin, glinting under the muted English sunshine. The sphere looked harmless, like a small toy that regular, sane people would let their small children play with and not think twice about it.

Now that the orb had their attention, she felt an overwhelming need to get the thing out of sight. To secure it, keep it close, protect it. She took a quick step toward it, scooped it off the pavement, and casually slipped it into the pocket of her dark green canvas jacket.

Only then did she realize how strange the urge was.

Protect it from what?

"Good." Brigham sighed in relief, then pointed weakly at the same jacket pocket. "So you're done with that thing."

"Yeah. Totally. I'm done with it." Scanning the empty street but paying far more attention to the cold, smooth, reassuring weight of the sphere beneath her fingers than to anything she saw with her own eyes, Halsey cleared her throat. She finally removed her hand from her jacket pocket and absently zipped up her jacket as if that would somehow conceal everything she was hiding beneath it. "For now."

"What?" Her cousin clicked his tongue and rolled his eyes. "Aw, hell, Hal. Don't say that."

"Say what?"

"*For now*. Like you've got some kinda catch-all plan for that thing brewing away upstairs." He leaned toward her and twirled a finger at her forehead. "Should've listened to me when I told you to lock it up and throw away the key."

"Yeah, and if I had, we would've been torn to shreds and burned to a crisp by the chimera. Or I'd have watched you get eaten alive by barghest poison until you actually *did* forget your own name. Who knows? Maybe even in that order."

He tried to stare her down like he didn't believe it. Then he shrugged and muttered, "I guess it's good for something…"

"Exactly. Even if we haven't figured out exactly how or why yet." *Even if the thing's starting to seriously creep* me *out now too.*

Spinning on her heels, Halsey headed across the pavement toward her hastily opened weapons bag stuffed full of all the gear she'd brought for the barghest hunt that had been a hell of a lot easier than they'd thought. Even the

Council had made it sound like a bigger deal during Cavanaugh's first and only briefing for this mission.

Minus one crunched English rental car and both cousins' things scattered across the empty street, getting rid of the barghest had been the quickest and easiest part of this entire assignment. One shot to the chest with their grandpa's old bolt-action shotgun, and the monster had disappeared forever.

Everything *after* the actual hunting part had Halsey more on edge than she would have liked. The healing potion given to them straight from the Council and their aunt Florence's personal herb garden should have done the trick with a barghest wound like it always did. That part obviously hadn't followed the rules and regulations of How to Hunt Monsters and Clean Up a Village of Civilian Witnesses.

Neither did the fact that so far, this village of civilian witnesses had turned up no civilians and no witnesses. Since the second Brigham had driven them onto the village's main road and past the "Welcome to Coningsby" sign, the cousins hadn't found a shred of evidence that anyone was left for them to save. Or, at the very least, to reassure that the little supernatural problem they'd been dealing with for the last few days had been taken care of by a team of top-notch professionals who knew what they were doing.

Halsey nestled her grandfather's old shotgun back into her weapons bag, zipped the whole thing up tight, and hauled the bag's strap over her shoulder. There still wasn't a speck of life to be found. Not human life, anyway.

Somewhere in the distance, a pair of dogs barked

tiredly at each other. Their voices bounced off all the cobbled stone and the thatch-roofed buildings lining the street that might or might not have only held the same structural design from hundreds of years ago in an attempt to maintain the village's quaintness.

It sounded like a whole pack out there when we first arrived. So where did all the other dogs go? Not to mention the people.

She stopped searching the empty street when her gaze fell on Brigham's weapons bag next. It was right where she'd left it after pulling the thing out from under a villager's car parked on the side of the street, the flap hanging chaotically open as a testament to how rushed she'd been. Halsey had wasted precious time pulling the leather purse of healing potions from her cousin's bag, but only her copper orb had saved the day. Again.

"How do you feel about carrying heavy things?" she asked, still staring at his bag and the jumbled collection of monster-hunting weaponry within it.

"You mean in general, or…"

"I mean are you cool carrying your own bag around, or do I need to go search somebody's farm for a pack animal?"

With a snort, Brigham stooped toward the ground, quickly straightened when he got dizzy, then bent over again at the waist, this time to retrieve the purse of healing potions. "The barghest got me in the gut, Hal. Not my arms."

"They're all connected one way or another."

"I got it. Thanks." He approached her with a crooked smile, though it must have already occurred to him there might still be some residual side effects from the monster's slash against his belly neither of the cousins could predict.

Because now it wasn't only the monsters who were changing in form, behavior, and magical ability. Now, a barghest scratch could take down one of the Ambrosius Clan militia's best operatives in a matter of seconds, and all traditional methods of cleaning up, stabilizing a supernatural mission site, and getting rid of unwanted side effects were null and void.

Neither of the cousins voiced this real possibility or the additional burden it placed on their shoulders, though. They were professionals, even at twenty-three years old with only five years of active monster-hunting under their belts.

Whether or not monsters and magic had now officially broken all the rules of monster-hunting engagement, professionals didn't leave behind evidence. And the mission wasn't successfully completed until they made sure they'd mopped up any and all potential evidence. Including the memories and imaginations of "normie" civilian humans who had correctly assumed their whole world had been turned upside-down by a real-life barghest.

Despite having been on the brink of death or something much worse, Brigham moved with ease as he stooped to grab his duffel bag. The gear thumped against his hip when he slung the strap over his shoulder. He'd made sure to carry everything on his left side, away from the wound on his right hip and belly that had already sealed itself up beneath healthy scar tissue. He glanced at the purse of potion vials in his other hand and clicked his tongue. "Guess we won't be needing these anymore, huh?"

"Guess all you want." Halsey took the purse from him

and delicately buried it in his open bag under his gear. "Until we know for sure, we're not getting rid of anything."

"Even your magic ball?"

After fixing her cousin with a pert look, she brushed past him to head down Coningsby's main street in the direction they'd been heading before they were almost run off the road by a giant black hellhound from British lore. "Come on. Something tells me there's more to see here before we call this a job well done."

"Yeah, yeah. Sure." Brigham turned slowly to stare at the place in the road where he'd fallen to his knees before crumpling into a pile of semi-lucidity not that long after. A frown flickered across his features as his right hand reached absently for the wound that wasn't even a proper wound anymore. Then he sucked in a sharp breath and spun toward his cousin, who walked steadily away from him down the street. "Wait, what do you mean one of *my* shirts?"

Halsey smirked but didn't look back or stop to wait for him. "Hey, if you packed the magical first-aid kit, you should say something next time."

"Magical first-aid… There's no such thing." He hurried off after her, slowing every few seconds to scan the narrow alleys between buildings as empty and silent as the open road ahead of them leading into the heart of the little village. "But seriously. If you're gonna save a guy's life with a homemade tourniquet or bandage or whatever, at least let him keep his clothes."

"If I'm gonna save a guy's life, the last thing he should worry about is what's happening to his shirts."

Finally catching up to her, Brigham slowed from his jog

until their footsteps echoed together in perfect rhythm across the pavement. "I have a 'one ruined clothing item per mission' limit, Hal. Max," he muttered before picking at the hem of his blood-stained t-shirt again with a scowl. "And you clearly have no idea how much I spend on these things."

CHAPTER TWO

The sound of their own footsteps seemed to grow unbearably loud in the early-evening silence of Coningsby. Despite everything they'd been through, Halsey and Brigham were trained to stay calm and keep their heads about them in the presence of "normies" and potential eyewitnesses to the monsters they hunted. That was a lot easier to do when not a single person showed their face, and the farther the cousins walked through the village, the more Halsey wondered if the Council had been too late in sending them out here to rural England.

Finally, she couldn't take the silence anymore. "Where *is* everybody?"

"Packed up? Moved away? Got the hell outta Dodge?" Brigham shrugged, then shot her a curious frown. "Hey, is there a British saying for that? 'Cause if there's not, we could make one right now. Get outta Coningsby. Doesn't have the same ring to it, but this is what we're working with."

Halsey scanned the side streets as the main street took

them deeper into the heart of the cozy little village and slowly shook her head. "That's not what happened here."

"It's a *saying*, Hal. Sayings don't literally happen."

She ignored her cousin's attempts to avoid reality with humor, which in this particular instance was flat-out poorly timed. "If everyone had gotten up and split in a hurry, there'd at least be some sign of it. Front doors hanging open. A dropped suitcase. A few personal items left behind in the rush. And anyone in their right mind trying to get away from a barghest wouldn't leave their car parked out in the street."

He snorted. "We left *ours* in the street."

"You know what I mean, dude."

"Yeah, you're right. It's a rental."

Somewhere up ahead, more dogs barked, though it sounded like four at the most and nowhere near the insanely large numbers they'd heard right before the barghest had attacked.

The dogs' exact location was hard to pinpoint with all the echoing between buildings and all along the side streets, but Halsey pointed ahead up the street anyway. "And *nobody* leaves their dog."

"True." Brigham cocked his head in consideration, then tried to find where the barking was coming from. "You know, I honestly thought we were gonna have to fight off a pack of rabid strays when we first got here. It sounded like a hundred of 'em. Not that I know what a hundred dogs at once sounds like, but that's about as close as I'm likely to get. I hope."

"That's part of the barghest lore, though. The giant black dog with hellishly red eyes showing up as an omen of death. Sometimes with a pack of dogs acting all nuts around the thing. Sometimes with a pack of other barghests, but those are generally way smaller. Two or three. *Maybe* four, tops. And a barghest doesn't sound like an actual dog."

"It doesn't T-bone your international rental, either," he muttered. "Or stand up on its hind legs like some kinda groomed werewolf that missed out on its rabies shot. Or slice a poisonous hole in your side that even the world's best elemental herbalist can't get to heal the way it's supposed to. But hey. It's the twenty-first century now, right? *Everything's* a damn experiment."

Halsey shot him a sidelong glance, then quickly looked away.

Now's not the time to pick apart his logic and reason when it's all pretty much gone out the window anyway. He's blowing off steam. Let him cycle through, then he'll be back on his game. This is how he works.

"I don't think the dogs had a whole lot to do with it this time, though," she added slowly, making it sound as if she were thinking out loud for both their benefit in case her cousin was ready to take what he wanted and leave the rest. "If at all."

"You said the dogs are part of the lore, Hal."

"I know what I said. But all the lore covers dogs walking around the towns and villages *with* the barghest. Or a pack of them if it's a particularly auspicious day for deaths in the local population."

"Mm. They really knew how to have fun back then, didn't they?"

Halsey fought not to roll her eyes as they continued

along the empty street, now rising up a gently sloping hill. "This one came out of nowhere. Without the dogs."

"Not without the dogs." Brigham pointed at her without taking his eyes off all the dark, secret places where plenty of supernatural threats could still be lurking. "Fido and all his buddies were going nuts right before the barghest went all Superman, and you and I hit the deck."

"That's right... Wow." She finally looked at her cousin long enough to catch his gaze and shoot him a quick, surprised smile. "Your memory's almost as good as mine right now."

He shrugged. "Hey, I just got a mega-boost of seriously freaky magical...whatever-the-hell. And probably hit my head a few too many times in the last half-hour. Don't worry. It won't last."

That was the first thing she could let herself at least chuckle about since they'd figured out Halsey's magic, combined with the magic inside her copper orb, could do things no other elemental on the planet could do. The cousins were starting to loosen up after a multitude of shocks, one right after the other.

Keep him talking. We'll stumble on the right answers eventually.

"Okay. So the dogs were barking *before* the barghest attacked us and not the rental." She wrinkled her nose, trying to catch the connection in her mind as if it were floating right there in front of her on a lazy August breeze. "That puts a different spin on things. Almost like...they were trying to warn us?"

"Or call for help. Too bad pets can't talk. Actually, strike that. Rupert has some kinda weird mutt now. You know, the one he picked up down south last year? Jesus, if that dog can talk, I'll never be able to look at my own brother the same way again. I don't wanna know."

Halsey released another wry laugh as they walked and kept scanning the main road and all the intersecting little side streets. "I have no problem leaving your brother and his dog out of all our missions."

"Yeah, that's probably for the best…"

"So what happened to all the dogs, then?" The second the question had left her lips, the barking they'd heard echoing through the village stopped.

The abrupt silence filling Coningsby was even worse than the last time, and it made the cousins pause in their investigatory trek.

Brigham sniffed, looking around without moving a muscle, and lowered his voice. "Probably the same thing that happened to all the people."

"Which would be…what?"

"I don't know, Hal. We were sent out here to tackle a pack of barghests tearing the place apart and terrorizing all the villagers. Not too far out of the question that the last living things here got snuffed out the way *we* almost did." He nodded slowly up the road in the general direction of the previous barking and now the utter lack of it.

"Great theory, cuz." Turning in a slow circle toward the way they'd come, Halsey studied the empty streets they'd already passed and shook her head. "There's one *tiny* little hole in it, though."

"You mean besides the weirdly empty village that was supposed to be swarming with terrified normies on the verge of losing their minds?"

"Nope. That *is* the hole."

He looked over his shoulder to shoot her a confused look with a wordless prompt to explain further.

"I think we can scratch the idea that the people who live here packed up, ran away, and left all their furry friends behind to fend for themselves. But if the barghests tore through the whole village and attacked every local and all their pets…" Halsey gestured toward all the empty streets in general and shrugged. "There would be a lot more bodies in the streets."

"Huh." Frowning, Brigham tilted his head in thought and pursed his lips as he searched the same empty streets, shuttered windows, and tightly closed front doors all over again. "Yeah, that part's weird. And I can tell you right now, getting hit by *these* barghests doesn't leave a whole lotta room for getting up and walking away afterward."

"Yeah, I noticed."

"Right." He ran a hand through his shaggy auburn hair and sighed. "So what's behind door number three? If you tell me a couple of hundred people vanished into thin air overnight, I gotta tell ya, cuz. I'm not buying it."

"Should I be insulted you actually think that's what I'd come up with next?"

With a crooked smile, Brigham readjusted the strap of his weapons bag on his shoulder. "I don't know if *insulted* is the right word here, cuz. But if you have something better and way more possible in mind, feel free to—"

"Shh." She set a hand on his shoulder to stop him and leaned slightly forward, listening. "You hear that?"

"I hear my own blood rushing in my ears right now."

"Something's coming." Thinking only of the version of

her cousin that had been almost entirely incapacitated and incapable of holding his own, Halsey hauled Brigham after her toward the side of the main road. There weren't many places they could hide at a moment's notice, and they weren't fast enough to avoid being seen out here in the open.

The light *click* of claws across the pavement echoed closer, and before the cousins had even reached the closest building to attempt to find shelter, the owner of those claws trotted into view.

Halsey's hand dove into her jacket pocket to clamp around the cold smoothness of the copper orb there. Before she could pull it out again or make any other move to engage the threat she'd expected, Brigham ripped his arm from her grasp and headed right back toward the road.

She almost dove after him, but her cousin's relieved chuckle made her stop. "Brigham."

"Relax, Hal. It's not the big, bad hellhound." He turned to shoot her a playful smile, then kept walking into the street. "Only one of its way less deadly little cousins."

It took another second for his words to sink in as Brigham approached the only other living thing they'd seen here besides the barghest, which was now unequivocally out of the picture. She sighed and rolled her shoulders back to collect herself.

It's just a dog, Halsey. A regular, non-magical, non-poisonous dog trotting around the village and probably looking for its master. Or food.

She released her grip on the copper orb in her pocket, glad she hadn't pulled such a powerful weapon on such a helpless and relatively harmless creature. But she didn't follow her cousin to go greet the thing. Somehow, that still felt like a bad idea.

"Aw... Look at *you*, little buddy," Brigham cooed as he gently headed toward the dog.

The hound clearly wasn't surprised to see them there and had probably known their whereabouts for quite some time before deciding to show itself. Panting with its tongue lolling from the side of its mouth, the animal stopped six feet from the stranger in the street and stared at Brigham with wide, glistening eyes.

"Okay, fine," Halsey called, trying not to raise her voice too loud but wanting to make sure her cousin heard her. "It's only a dog."

The animal spared her a glance, then returned its attention to Brigham.

"Hey, don't listen to her," he added with a gentle laugh. "Sometimes she says things she doesn't mean. *I* know you're not *only a dog*. You and all your pals were trying to warn us about what was coming, weren't you? That's a good dog."

When he stooped and held out a hand toward the undecided pet, Halsey finally took an urgent step back into the street. "Brigham, I don't think it's a good idea to—"

"To what? Pet a dog, Hal? Come on. That's literally what they're for."

"That doesn't mean *you* need to touch it."

"Wow." He shot her a condescending look and laughed again. "I didn't know you had a thing against dogs."

"I don't have a *thing*." She looked around them again, unable to help thinking there was still so much buried here in this village that looked like it had nothing to hide on the surface. "I just think we should keep our heads in the—"

"Oh, hey. Good boy." Their new furry friend stole Brigham's attention when the pup trotted hesitantly toward him, its tail wagging intermittently in hopeful wariness. "Yeah, that's right. I'm not gonna hurt you. He's wearing a collar, Hal."

"Good for him. We need to keep moving."

"Yeah, sure. Let me get a few good pets in first. Maybe a nice little ear-scratch, huh? What do you think? Would you like that?" Her cousin's voice rose in pitch as he started up again with the cooing dog voice bordering on baby talk. "We'll take a look at your collar, and maybe we can take you back home to your house. How 'bout that, buddy? Are you looking to go home?"

The dog took another tentative step toward him, ears perking up as it hopefully licked its chops.

Brigham went down on one knee in the middle of the street and reached even farther toward the dog. "I'm not gonna hurt you, pup. I promise. Me and my cousin over there? We're here to help."

It looked like the animal was finally about to give in to its obvious desire for affection in the midst of everything that had happened in this village. Then it stopped short and whipped its head toward Halsey's side of the street. Its ears flattened as it released a low whine, then the dog spun away from Brigham and took off. In seconds, it had disappeared down one of the narrow alleyways.

"Well, hell." Brigham sighed, pushed back to his feet, and shot his cousin a disappointed frown. "Happy now?"

Halsey spread her arms. "I didn't do anything."

"You know dogs can smell fear, right?"

"I'm not—"

"Also aggression. And a bunch of other stuff, probably." Dusting off his hands, he scanned the empty streets one more time, then shrugged at his cousin. "You could've at least *tried* to be friendly."

"Seriously? This isn't an animal rescue mission, Brigham."

"Well, maybe if you hadn't been so prickly, Fido over there might've been able to show us a few—"

A loud, metallic clang ripped through the air, echoing deafeningly against all the houses and the pavement.

The cousins abandoned their argument and spun toward the source of the noise with wide eyes. Brigham's hand went to the zipper of his weapons bag. Halsey's eased back inside her jacket pocket.

A metal trashcan lid rolled out from between two buildings up ahead, wobbling in its own path before it inevitably slowed right there in the middle of the street.

Great. Frozen, Halsey scanned the area where the lid had appeared and could have kicked herself. *Here we are, arguing about* dogs *while there's clearly something else out there.*

CHAPTER THREE

"See anything?" Brigham whispered.

Halsey slowly shook her head. "I'm seeing what you're seeing, cuz."

"Okay, then what the hell was that?"

"Another dog?"

He shot her a quick look of disbelief, and she would have shrugged it off if they hadn't been interrupted yet again.

"Psst!"

Frowning, Halsey tilted her head and searched the empty street and closed-up buildings ahead of them. "Did you hear—"

"Psst! You lot." The harsh whisper sounded like it could have come from everywhere and nowhere at the same time. "Over here."

Brigham shook his head. "It wasn't…ow!"

He stumbled forward and hunched under the sharp smack to the back of his head. A small stone toppled down his back before clattering to the pavement. Rubbing the sore spot on his skull, he scowled and turned around.

Halsey did the same, readying herself to face another barghest because that was what they'd been told to expect when they got here.

Instead, they found a woman poking her head out from one of the narrow alleys between houses and shops. Dressed in a loose skirt and bulky woolen sweater, she appeared somewhere in her early to mid-fifties, her washed-out blonde hair cut short away from her face. With wide eyes, the woman leaned slightly farther out of the alley and waved the Ambrosius cousins toward her.

Brigham chuckled. "Well, that's *one* way to get somebody's attention."

"Shh." The woman peered up and down the street again, then waved them fervently toward her one more time. "This way. Hurry."

Halsey met her cousin's gaze and nodded toward the woman. "Signs of life."

"Yeah, and she's got one hell of an aim."

"Oh, for the love of..." Rolling her eyes, the woman pushed herself away from the walls on either side of her and scurried across the street toward them. "Have you both lost your minds? You can't be standing out here in the middle of the road, loves. Come with me." She stopped a few yards away, took in the sight of both cousins lugging obviously stuffed duffel bags over their shoulders, then waved them forward again. "It's not safe here."

"But you know somewhere that is?" Halsey asked.

"Aye. But hurry, now. This way."

The cousins exchanged another quick look before

heading toward the only living human soul they'd seen in Coningsby since the moment they drove into the village in their now-crushed rental car.

"Come, come. There you are. Right through here." She kept waving as if she were ushering a bunch of children at a crosswalk after school. Halsey and Brigham each received a tight smile as they passed her to enter the narrow alley she indicated with an open hand.

When they were safely out of the open, the woman paused, turned to scan the street one more time with wary, terrified eyes, then spun after the village's two newest guests, who clearly didn't have a clue what was happening here.

"Quickly now. Keep going," she called after them. "Turn right at that next opening there."

As Brigham took the lead, Halsey couldn't help but look over her shoulder at the woman, hoping this wasn't Coningsby's sole survivor. "What happened here?"

"No time, love. No time. We need to get you off the streets and *inside*, understand? Keep you far away from that unholy demon."

"Unholy what, now?" Brigham stopped before the right turn their new friend had indicated, frowning at her in disbelief. "Did you say *demon*?"

"Aye. Come straight from the fiery pits of hell, it did. No matter what anyone says, that barghest could have come from nowhere else."

Halsey and Brigham both stopped dead in their tracks at the end of the alley, where another opening split off to the right between buildings. The woman had turned back to make sure no one and nothing else had followed them this far off the street, and she almost ran right into Halsey before noticing the strangers she'd saved were no longer following her directions.

"Oh!" She squeaked in surprise, then stepped back and smoothed down the front of her sweater. Both the strangers under her care were staring at her. The surprise vanished from her features, replaced by a stern, no-nonsense frown. "No need to look at me like *that*. I know it sounds like the ravings of a woman gone mental, but I've seen the beast with my own eyes, I have. As real as either one of you."

"We don't think you're…mental," Brigham muttered. "Trust me."

"We're surprised to hear you call the thing by name," Halsey explained. "We don't see a lot of that."

"Aye, well, I've seen more than enough. If you know what's good for you, you'll save the chit-chat for later and follow me."

"Lead the way." Dipping her head, Halsey gestured for the woman to squeeze past both her and her cousin down the narrow alley. She received a dubious frown in return, but their new guide through the village of Coningsby accepted the offer anyway.

Brigham cleared his throat and pressed his back against the closest alley wall so she could brush past him. Then he shot Halsey another knowing look, and she nodded.

Yeah. We're not dealing with a little town of normies who can't fathom what's been happening to them here. This woman knows what a barghest is, and she's not afraid to call it by name. Which might end up making things more complicated than we want.

"Keep moving along, loves," the woman called over her shoulder with another wave. "The Hall's not too far off. Do put some hustle into it."

"Sorry." Brigham cleared his throat again. "How do *you* know about the barghest?"

"How do I..." She stopped at the end of another alley, peered out to scan the smaller street ahead of them, then turned to meet his gaze. "All the way out here in the countryside, love? I grew up on the stories, I did. The proper ones, mind. The terrifying ones. Never thought I'd see *this* much proof with my own two eyes, but that demon's right here in this village. *That's* what's been tearing Coningsby apart, and every soul here knows it. Though I may be the only one saying it."

"We believe you." Halsey nodded, trying to look as earnest and reassuring as possible. "We've seen one too."

"Oh, aye? Well then, you must know how lucky you both are for having gotten away from the beast before it had its way with *you*."

Brigham shrugged, his fingers absently moving toward the healed scar on his hip and lower abdomen. "I don't know if I'd say *that*, exactly."

"What is that supposed to mean?" The woman scanned him, then finally noticed the blood staining the bottom half of his t-shirt. A hand flew to her mouth. "Oh, dear. It's already gotten you too. It's a miracle you're still walking around on your own two feet! Quickly. Quickly, now. It's only a bit farther. Then we'll get you settled and—"

"Hey, I'm fine." With a bashful smile, he dipped his head and tugged at the hem of his shirt but didn't pull it up to reveal his new, magically healed scar. "Really."

"You're a horrid liar, love."

"What? No. It's...an old shirt."

"What we want to know is where we can find the others," Halsey added because now their guide seemed to think they were far enough out of danger that they could speak without whispering.

The woman's eyebrows shot up in surprise. "Others?"

"More barghests. That's why we're here. We found the first one—"

"More like the first one found *us*," Brigham muttered, rolling his eyes.

"—but we still need to find the rest of them," she continued without missing a beat. "As quickly as possible."

"The rest of 'em." The woman stared back at her with wide eyes, blinked once, then barked out a high-pitched laugh. "And *I'm* the one folks've taken to calling mad. Not anymore, though. I can tell you that."

"You seem perfectly sane to me," Brigham added with an attempt at a genuine smile. "You know, given the circumstances."

"And I truly wish I could say the same for you, loves. Truly. But after everything you've said, I'm more inclined to believe one, if not both of you, already had your run-in with that demon. Did you get any scratches? Bites? Even if it's only a bit of a sting—"

"We're fine," Halsey insisted tersely. "Thank you. But if there's anything you can tell us about where we can find the other—"

"I'll stop you right there, love." The woman smiled, but it still held a tinge of fear and hardship and something else neither of the cousins could quite place. A sort of grim determination mixed with triumph, however strange a combination that might have been. "You think you can show up in this village, say a few things about a barghest, and frolic off after it with…what? An intention to put it in its place? I can tell you right now it's not worth the effort or the headache. That demon's as unkillable as they come. Believe me. Plenty of folks have already tried."

The cousins exchanged another glance. *If I push this too hard, she'll go right off the deep end. Still, we can't keep sneaking through the village with who knows how many other barghests out there. We have a mission. End of story.*

Halsey dipped her head in concession but still had to keep trying. Hiding out wherever the locals deemed "safe" with monsters nearby and on the loose wasn't how the Ambrosius Clan militia did things. "I know you're trying to help us, Miss…"

"Miss?" The woman laughed. "No, thank you. Mauve will do."

"Mauve. I'm Halsey. This is my cousin Brigham."

"Aye, of course." Mauve's smile flickered wider as she looked between the young people. "Saw the family resemblance right away, I did."

"And we appreciate all the warnings," Halsey continued. "Really. It might help to know we're a little more… prepared than most other people who might've tried to take down the barghest on their own."

"It's kind of our job," Brigham added with a smirk, puffing out his chest.

"And we're here to take care of *all* of them before anyone else gets hurt."

"Anyone else?" Mauve tossed out another laugh. "There

isn't anyone else *to* get hurt, love. Did you not notice the silence?" She spread her arms and paused to further cement her point. "Oh, sure, a few of us are still make the rounds and keeping things running. Yet we've gotten ourselves and everyone else off the streets. That's what I mean to do with the both of *you*—"

"Wait." Brigham cocked his head. "You mean *everyone* in Coningsby was attacked by the barghests?"

"*Barghest*, love." Mauve thrust a finger in the air. "There's only ever been one."

"Well, I know it might seem like one," Halsey replied. "But we—"

"How long have you been here, love?" Mauve crossed her arms and raised an eyebrow.

The cousins shared a hesitant glance, and Brigham scratched the back of his head. "Maybe an hour. Tops."

"An hour. Well, that's quite long enough not to have gotten yourselves killed out there. Or worse. But I was born and raised right here in Coningsby, and when I say there's only one of those demons skulking about, that means there's only one. More than that, and the rest of us would never have made it."

There's no way a regular human can be that *sure how many monsters are running around their own town. Unless it's the truth. If it is, the Council got pretty damn lazy with their intel and decided it was impossible for a single monster to rack up this much damage in one place by itself...*

Halsey nodded slowly, trying to figure out the best way to keep the conversation going without disregarding what Mauve had told them. That ran the risk of insulting their one and only host so far in the village, and by the sound of it, plenty of people here still needed a lot of extra outside help.

Since he was much faster in recognizing the need for diplomacy, Brigham beat her to it. Serious determination replaced his smile. "If there really was only one of them here, nobody has anything to worry about anymore."

Mauve didn't look very convinced. "Well, now. Why might that be?"

"Because we killed it," Halsey answered quickly. Her cousin shot her a sharp look of disapproval, but she kept her gaze on the older woman and lifted her chin. *She's obviously a straight shooter. We can't tell her everything, but we can at least say we took care of the problem. Or the biggest problem with teeth, claws, and nasty magical venom, anyway.*

Mauve blinked, then her gaze dropped to the bulging weapons bag hanging at Halsey's waist. "What's in the bag?"

"Weapons."

"For hunting monsters only," Brigham clarified.

"I see." The woman battled between wanting to believe these two young foreigners who'd shown up out of nowhere to traipse through this little English village and the knowledge of what she'd already seen with her own two eyes. "What did it look like, then?"

"Really?" Brigham's chuckle died instantly under her warning glare. "Okay, uh... Big black dog-looking thing. Red eyes. Claws like knives." He held a hand up in front of his face as if his own nails were tipped in the same razor-sharp edges that had split him open and almost taken him out of the game entirely.

"Aye. Sure." Mauve nodded coolly. "You've heard the stories, then."

"But this one stood on two legs," Halsey interjected. Mauve's eyes widened as her cheeks flushed. "Almost like a human. Not a regular barghest anymore, either. We know that much."

"Hmm." Mauve lifted her chin and studied Halsey, then Brigham. Her brown eyes narrowed. She stuck her hands on her hips and asked, "Do you have proof?"

Brigham shot her a crooked smile. "That we killed a barghest?"

She nodded. "That sort of thing would go a long way around here."

"Yeah, except it's impossible to get when the damn thing up and disappeared on us right after *she* fired the final shot."

"Well, I knew I heard *something* fire. But you?" Mauve pointed at Halsey. "You want me to believe such a tiny little thing took down the demon that turned our quiet little village topsy-turvy in only a few days?"

Halsey reached for her weapons bag and unzipped it enough for the woman to get a glimpse of the old bolt-action shotgun sitting on top of her gear. "That's what happened, but Brigham's right. We don't have proof. A dead barghest doesn't hang around for long afterward."

"Well." Mauve blinked quickly, then licked her lips and made her final decision on the matter. "Be that as it may, if you don't have proof, you'll forgive me if I don't drop everything *I* set out to do because you say you've done something we couldn't."

"It's all hard to believe. We know."

"Aye, that's one way to put it. Seems none of us have all our ducks in a row, so I'll say this. You come with me. My only concern now is getting you two somewhere safe and out of harm's way. Then we'll carry out the rest from there."

The woman turned briskly around to face the open side street at the mouth of the alley, checking both ways one more time to make sure the coast was clear again.

"Mauve," Halsey urged gently. Their host paused. "What happened to this place?"

When Mauve turned again, her dark gaze settled intently on Halsey, and she nodded. "It's better if you see it with your own eyes, love. That seems to be something of a theme lately. Otherwise, it's fairly hard to explain and bloody near impossible to believe."

She didn't give the cousins another second to ask any more questions before she slipped into the street and hurried across, waving them after her yet again.

Halsey and Brigham looked at each other, and he shrugged. "Nothing we haven't seen before, right?"

She sighed. "I sure as hell hope not."

CHAPTER FOUR

For the next fifteen minutes, the Ambrosius cousins followed their unexpected guide along the twisting, turning path she blazed between houses and shops and business fronts. Occasionally, Mauve stopped and lifted a hand in silence for them to wait while she scuttled ahead to search other alleys, passageways, and side roads. Then she'd wave them forward again, and Halsey and Brigham had no other choice but to follow along until they managed to get their answers.

If this woman wasn't willing to tell them everything up front, maybe she would lead them to someone else who could explain what had happened here without teetering on the verge of superstition.

That's gonna be hard for a whole village of normies who've been dealing with the supernatural for days out here all on their own. But we're not going anywhere until we have the whole picture.

Finally, Mauve ushered them up the front steps of the largest building they'd seen in Coningsby so far. A sign hanging over the front door read "Community Hall." All the windows were shuttered. The door was shut tight. There was still no sign of any other living thing besides two Ambrosius elementals and one middle-aged woman brave enough to go out to the main road to get them.

When all three of them stood on the front landing, Mauve turned toward the cousins and lowered her voice. "Plenty to see inside. If I were you, I'd keep my questions to myself for a bit. The chairman will want to have you both checked over for any…injuries you might have missed on your own. Play along while you can, won't you?"

Brigham tried not to frown too deeply at the woman. "Is the chairman handing out personal frisking these days?"

Mauve clicked her tongue. "Well, *acting* chairman, anyhow."

"What happened to the official major?" Halsey asked.

"Same thing that happened to everyone else." With that, the woman spun around and rapped out a series of rhythmic knocks on the building's front door.

Five seconds later, the door swung inward with a groaning creak, and the Ambrosius cousins were ushered inside.

The front vestibule was so much darker than the slightly overcast day outside, but the grim-faced man standing behind the open door didn't seem bothered by letting a little sunlight in. He did, however, seem bothered by the sight of two unfamiliar faces following Mauve inside.

"Who's them?" he grumbled, jerking his chin at Halsey and Brigham.

"Standing about in the street, they were," Mauve replied

as she pushed the door shut behind her. Its heavy click echoed through the front room. She turned toward the man at least a decade older than her, who wouldn't stop glaring at the cousins. "So I brought them in."

"Doin' what?" His squint deepened. "Bringin' even more trouble to our front door?"

"They say they're here to help, Willard."

"Fat chance of *that*. Either one of 'em got the sick?"

"Not as far as I've seen or they've shown me." Mauve gestured toward the other end of the vestibule, which was closed off from the room beyond by a set of double doors that looked like they belonged in an old middle-school cafeteria. "But that's not all for us to decide, is it?"

Willard sucked on his teeth, his nostrils flaring as he glared at Halsey and Brigham. Then he grunted and nodded toward the other closed doors. "Eh…"

That one noncommittal word said more than anything else the man could have told them.

He doesn't think there's anything anyone *can do right now. But he sure doesn't want* us *here. In a village this small, there's no way we won't stand out like two American sore thumbs.*

Halsey nodded at the man as she passed him. His dubious scowl remained unchanged, even when Brigham walked past and shot him a friendly smile.

Mauve had clearly already written off Willard's bad mood, which very likely could have been his only mood. She was far more focused on reaching the closed double doors and the small sliver of warm light showing through the crack between them.

By the time Halsey and Brigham reached her, their vision had adjusted to the darkness, and now a low murmur of voices, footsteps, and shifting movement made its way through the doors. Mauve widened her eyes at them, then turned to push open one of the double doors and lead Coningsby's unexpected visitors into what had recently become the heart of the village.

The low sounds the cousins had been able to hear from the other side of the door in no way matched the sight that greeted them when they stepped inside. The room beyond was enormous, probably used for village meetings or even a few small local plays. All the regular furniture that would have filled a space like this, rows of chairs and side tables, had been cleared away.

Now, dozens of cots, sleeping pads, mattresses, and beds took up the floor space. In almost every makeshift bed was a human body, a citizen of Coningsby, lying prone or curled into a ball. Some of these people looked like they were only sleeping. Others could have been mistaken for dead as they lay there motionless, skin gray and pale, breathing shallow.

Only a few moaned, shifted on the beds, or tried to sit up and speak. When they did, they were eased back down by others around the room who were in much better shape. The healthy folks shushed their wards, patted wet cloths on foreheads, offered small sips of water, or knelt by the beds to take an injured person's hand and sit with them.

Yet there was only about one unaffected villager strong enough and healthy enough to tend to the incapacitated for every six people who'd been injured and brought here.

Worst of all was the smell.

Halsey fought down a gag and forced herself to breathe

through her mouth. *Jesus. They turned this place into a combat hospital. Or a refugee camp, but all these people are refugees in their own village.*

Brigham hummed in displeasure and pressed his lips together, fighting not to clap a hand over his nose. "Looks like we found all the villagers."

"And neither one of us guessed correctly."

Mauve finished closing the double doors behind them, then returned to the cousins' side again. "This is the only place we have big enough to fit everyone who needs a bit of tending to and all those willing and able to do the tending. We figured it was better to keep everyone together all in one place. Only until the danger's passed."

"Right." Halsey nodded and headed slowly after the woman on autopilot. She couldn't stop looking at the frail, weak, groaning, intensely uncomfortable "patients" laid out in all the makeshift beds. Her heart sank.

They all look like Brigham did before I healed him. Shit, does that mean every single person in a bed here got hit by the barghest?

Mauve led them across the room, keeping to the perimeter along the wall and allowing herself to glance at the poor folks laid out in bed who could hardly turn their own heads, let alone keep their eyes open. About a dozen people milled around, stopping to offer water or a word of encouragement to less fortunate neighbors. A handful of those caught sight of Halsey and Brigham moving along after Mauve, and while everyone who noticed the newcomers fixed the cousins with suspicious looks, none of them left their post in caring for the mortally wounded coating the floor of the main meeting room.

Brigham sucked in a sharp breath and subtly nudged his cousin's arm with an elbow.

"What?" Halsey looked at him, then followed his gaze toward one of the men in a makeshift hospital bed on her other side.

The man couldn't have been much older than his mid-thirties, large and muscular, with an enormous beard covering most of his face. This was exactly the kind of person Halsey had imagined when Mauve had told them plenty of people had already tried to take the barghest down on their own.

Coningsby might have encountered any number of situations in which a man like this would be perfect for the job. A pack of wild dogs or foxes stealing off with their farm animals, or maybe a gang of young troublemakers from the closest city rolling through for a little aggressive fun with the country locals. The man was big enough, looked intimidating enough, and might have been smart enough to lead the charge in protecting the village from more natural threats.

However, against a barghest, this man was as vulnerable and helpless as the others. Especially *this* barghest, and especially at this point in the history of monsters and the magic-wielding elementals who hunted them down.

The man's deathly pale skin, the dark circles under his eyes, and the shallow rise and fall of his muscular chest made that clear. He was in bad shape. Worse was the giant gash splitting the flesh of his muscular forearm. His sleeve had been rolled up to keep the wound exposed to fresh air, which seemed the best tactic these people had come up with for treating barghest wounds.

No amount of antibiotic, ointment, or fresh wrappings could heal the gaping tear surrounded by black, deadened flesh. It wouldn't have done anything to lessen the stink of rotting meat and death. It wouldn't have done anything to ease the man's pain, which was most likely what kept him on the verge of unconsciousness, even if these people had pooled together enough resources for the kind of painkillers capable of providing any relief from an injury like that.

Damn. Add twenty years to him, and he almost looks like my dad...

The thought of Aiden Ambrosius—her bear of a father who'd been the Clan militia's best monster-hunter before his daughter had taken his place—brought to his knees by a scratch made Halsey want to run from this room and hightail it out Coningsby.

She didn't, of course. She couldn't.

Even if there hadn't been dozens of injured locals lying about with horrifying necrotic wounds worming their way deep into living flesh, Halsey and Brigham still had a job to do. Their mission wasn't complete until they were certain they'd taken care of all the monsters here and helped restore as much normalcy to the village of Coningsby as possible. That meant ensuring the safety of the locals, talking them down into accepting what had happened but not letting the secret of their new supernatural reality slip into the greater public sphere for everyone to hear.

It also meant healing anyone who'd been affected by the monster the Ambrosius militia operatives had been sent to eliminate.

They weren't going to successfully complete that final

objective using the healing potions the Council had sent them off with on this last-minute mission.

Bad intel, lack of preparedness, and the wrong gear. Either they panicked and threw us into the wind, or they can't even fathom what's really going on out here in the world. Or the Council still doesn't want to admit that monster-hunting's gonna take more footwork now that the Blood Matriarch's out of her prison and walking around on dry land...

"Hal." Brigham nudged her again with an elbow, but this time, he was looking at her in concern. "You good?"

"In the middle of all this?" she murmured, sweeping her gaze around the room. "Rainbows and unicorns, cuz. Why wouldn't I be good?"

"Yeah, no reason I can think of," he replied blandly. "Other than, you know, the fact that you're starting to look pretty pissed. Then there's..." Brigham nodded at her jacket pocket.

Halsey hadn't even realized she'd let her hand slip right back into the pocket holding the orb, which only bulged slightly farther than the opposite pocket. She slid her hand out and gave him a quick but firm nod. "I'm good. Promise."

"Good. I trust you." He glanced at her pocket one more time, but as long as his cousin didn't pull out that magical ball and start flashing it around, he was willing to let the whole thing go for now. There were slightly more important things on their plates here.

Great. If I'm feeling feelings, I keep going for the orb. If I stow it with my gear, that's gonna be the exact second I need to use it the most. Keep your hands out of your pockets, Halsey, and we'll all be fine.

Even if the cousins had more to say to each other right now, they didn't have any privacy for an open conversation. And Mauve had finally led them to the very back of the room before she gestured toward the small stage against the center of the far wall and started talking again. "These are all the supplies we managed to pull together at the very beginning. That was…oh, boy. Four days ago. Perhaps five. Hard to tell how much time passes during a thing like this. But what we've set up there on that stage has managed to get us through the worst of it. So far."

Brigham widened his eyes. "Doesn't look like you guys have a whole lot left."

"Aye, and when we run out of this, we'll send another small group out there to gather what they can. Quietly. Without looking for trouble." Mauve turned to meet the cousins' gazes one at a time. "I imagine that's rather a far cry from what you two say you're doing here."

"Thank you very much, ma'am," Brigham replied through a fake grin as he batted his eyelashes at her. The woman still wasn't amused by his humorous antics, so he wiped it all away and tried a different approach. "So everyone's homes and farms are being raided by their neighbors to save each other's lives. I get that part. Great way to keep all this contained. But what happens when all the homes and farms run dry?"

Mauve's puckered lips popped open as if she had an immediate response waiting right there on the tip of her tongue. But then she closed her mouth again and sighed. "I'm a bookkeeper, lad. Best if you broach those more complicated subjects with someone who knows how to answer them, aye?"

Then she turned and walked swiftly past the end of the small stage toward another door on the far side of the room.

Halsey leaned toward her cousin and murmured, "And the award for Friendliest Out-of-Town Weirdo goes to…"

"Oh, come on." He rolled his eyes. "It's a legit question."

"For sure. Now you get to ask it of a super-legit village leader in a totally legit hospital ward for even more legit barghest bites and scratches keeping all these nice people legitimately in bed."

"Don't do that." Shaking his head, he started after Mauve again, who now stood beside the closed door, patiently waiting for them. Halsey followed, trying her best not to grimace at the overwhelming scent of death and decay that wouldn't let up. "So sue me if I need more time to get over the weirdness of hearing a normie talk about monsters like she's one of us, okay? I wanna help these people as much as you do, Hal."

"Yeah, I know." She clapped her mouth shut after that because this wasn't the kind of conversation they could have around witnesses yet. Even if those witnesses had all the proof they needed that barghests were undeniably real. Not to mention the fact that at least one of them had ripped through Coningsby like the plague, leaving behind a debilitated population and a whole bunch of physical wounds that refused to be treated the way normal wounds could typically be treated.

They're doing the best they can with what they have. A little village in the middle of nowhere, all the supplies they could pull from their kitchen cabinets, and legends about the omen-of-death hellhound and the unhealable wounds it leaves on its victims.

Only the legends are twisted now. The barghest didn't come to kill anyone. I don't think any of these people are actually going to die. Not like this. They'll just...stay in these beds forever until the whole town and everybody in it drains themselves of everything they have left to give. And then what?

"Here you go, sweetie." A young woman turned toward the stage to grab a fresh bottle of water and paused when she met Halsey's gaze. They were probably the same age, though the other woman looked haggard, exhausted, horrified, and hopeless all in one seconds-long glance. She quickly broke away from the look to turn toward the cot set closest to that part of the stage. The crack of the water bottle's plastic seal breaking filled the air. Then she handed the open bottle to the tiny form nestled in a pile of blankets in the center of the cot.

A pale, trembling, alarmingly tiny hand reached out from the pile of blankets to take the water bottle.

That was when Halsey realized this wasn't a small person who'd been too starved or too sick by the magical injury to keep any real bodyweight on them. It was a child.

The little girl couldn't have been much older than six or seven. Her long, dark hair was matted and greasy-looking, her lightless eyes made even larger by the dark circles around them and the hollow cheeks beneath. Wherever her barghest wound was, Halsey couldn't see it, but the amount of silent strength and acceptance shown by a child that young almost broke her.

No complaining. No crying. She probably doesn't even have the energy for it.

When the young woman had to help the little girl raise the water bottle to her lips, Halsey had to look away, blinking back the sting of oncoming tears. Then she quickly scanned the other dozen cots in the same row of makeshift patient beds. Each one of them held a much smaller form than the other beds, only a few stirring in their wounded state that left them somewhere between unconscious and dead.

They were *all* children.

Fuck? How are all these people so calm about the whole thing? If it was Ethel or one of Cliff's kids lying in a bed like that, I'd be burning shit down and staging a coup.

It briefly occurred to her that was what she'd already done. Only it had been Brigham lying in a hospital bed at the Ambrosius Clan estate, nearly crushed to pieces by his failed mission against a gang of corpse-eating ogres driven insane by blood magic that wasn't even supposed to exist in the world anymore. Halsey hadn't literally burned anything down, but if there had been enough Ambrosius elementals on her side at that point, she probably would have been able to stage a coup against the current acting Clan Council. Instead, the best move she'd had was to dump half a dozen severed ogre hands at the Council's feet and shove it in their faces that they should have listened to her the first time.

With all this racing through her mind, she almost walked right into Mauve standing beside the closed door at this far side of the room. "Wait here a pinch, loves. And don't…touch anything."

The woman's gaze flickered one more time to the blood-stained bottom half of Brigham's shirt, then she knocked twice on the door and twisted the handle before slipping quickly inside.

Brigham glanced at his shirt and sighed. "She has a point. Covered in blood doesn't exactly scream, 'Trust us, we're professionals.'"

"For anyone else, maybe," Halsey murmured. "The way things have been going lately, Covered In Blood might as well be the official Clan uniform."

CHAPTER FIVE

Fortunately, Mauve and whoever else she'd gone to talk to in the other room only made Halsey and Brigham wait outside in "the recovery center" for around two minutes. That was more than enough time for the cousins to get a good, long look at the issue the entire village faced now, even without the threat of a barghest chasing down all the other healthy survivors.

I seriously hope she's right about there only being one. This is enough of a mess all on its own.

Standing beside her with one hand on the strap of his weapons bag and the other thumb hooked through his beltloop, Brigham shook his head. "This is insane, Hal. All these people. I don't even know…"

"Well, we're not going home until it *is* clean. I'm not screwing up my perfect mission record *now*."

He turned toward her and wrinkled his nose. "Yeah, good for you. Keep it up. But how the hell are we supposed to sweep something like *this* clean?"

Raising an eyebrow and fixing him with a pointed look

was all she had time for. Telling him that he already knew how they could help these people was on the tip of her tongue, but she didn't have a chance to say anything before the door opened again, and Mauve poked her head out.

"You can come on in now, loves. Mr. Hornbull's ready." The woman disappeared into the room but left the door open.

Halsey shrugged. "Don't wanna leave *him* waiting."

The wry humor that usually got her cousin going went over Brigham's head this time. He stared at her in disbelief. "No. Hal, tell me you're not thinking what I think you're thinking."

"Meeting time, cuz." Halsey turned toward the open door and eased inside.

"*Hal*," he hissed before taking off after her. "I'm serious. That's not even a plan. That's a shot in the dark. We don't even know—"

Brigham's mouth clamped shut when he stepped through the doorway to find what looked like a massive conference room on the other side. In fact, the whole layout looked disturbingly similar to the briefing rooms at the Ambrosius Clan estate. A long, wide table lined with chairs dominated the space. Enough seats for a dozen, maybe more if everyone crammed together. A refreshment table on the far side of the room held a pitcher of water, a kettle nestled in a tea cozy, plenty of teacups and glasses to go around, and a sad-looking plate of cookies with more crumbs on it than actual cookies.

"Here you are, loves." Mauve closed the door behind them and nodded. "Chairman Remus Hornbull."

"*Acting* chairman," the man corrected as he stood from

behind the far head of the table. "Just for now, anyway. Thank you, Mauve."

The woman dipped her head pertly, looking thoroughly disappointed in the fact that the village's current chairman wouldn't accept his role in an official leadership capacity. "Anything else I can get you, sir?"

"Nothing for me, thank you. Perhaps for our guests?"

"No, thank you." The words tumbled from Halsey's mouth with a lot more urgency than the situation warranted, but the thought of eating or drinking anything right now after what they'd seen in the last room was unfathomable. Then she cleared her throat and plastered on a tight smile. "Thanks, though."

Hornbull dipped his head in acknowledgment and leaned forward over the head of the table, tapping his splayed fingertips lightly on the surface. An awkward silence followed, then the acting chairman cleared his throat. "Well, then. I suppose we—"

"Oh." Mauve released a self-conscious chuckle before grabbing the doorhandle again. "Then I'll just...hmm. Excuse me."

The woman slipped from the meeting room, and the door clicked shut.

Hornbull stared at it, then heavily exhaled. "You'll have to excuse the woman. She's eager to treat all this as a legitimate undertaking. Perhaps with a bit more enthusiasm than is warranted, given our...situation."

"Doesn't look like there's much to be enthusiastic about," Brigham suggested with a shrug.

That made the man look at him, and a sardonic smile

flickered at the corner of his mouth before disappearing. "I agree."

"What about *you*, Chairman?" Halsey asked.

"Please." He gestured toward the multitude of open chairs around the table and nodded. "Call me Remus."

The cousins accepted his wordless offer to sit, each of them taking one side of the conference table and walking toward the town's newly appointed official. Halsey took the chair on the man's left, Brigham took the one on his right, then the acting chairman finally sat back down and scooted forward. He folded his arms and sat back in his chair, gazing intently at Halsey. "I'm sorry. Mauve failed to properly introduce us, Miss…"

"Halsey Ambrosius." She reached out to shake the man's hand, and he willingly obliged. "My cousin Brigham."

"Pleasure." The men shook hands, then Remus looked between the cousins with a deepening frown. "So, Miss Ambrosius. What *about* me?"

Halsey raised her eyebrows as she held his gaze. "Do you *not* want to treat this as a legitimate undertaking?"

"Ah." Remus blinked furiously and ducked his head to stare at his knees, almost hidden by the edge of the table. "I'll be perfectly honest with you. I'm a businessman, Miss Halsey. Not a politician. Certainly not qualified to fill the position of chairman. But I happened to be staying in one of the rooms at the inn down the street. Passing through at the same time as… all this." He gestured toward the closed door and the horrors of magically induced wounds on dozens of villagers right on the other side. "Now I find myself in an impossible situation."

Brigham cocked his head. "Just passing through?"

The man's tight smile flickered again. "I'm not...from around here."

"Well yeah. You do stand out a little." Brigham huffed. "Maybe slightly less than we do."

"Yes, with those accents of yours, I have no doubt."

"And I'm guessing Coningsby's former chairman was one of those hit first by this...disaster," Halsey added. "Right?"

"That sums it up fairly well, yes. He was on the front lines against... Well. You've seen the damage."

Big-city businessman traveling through the middle of nowhere can't even say the truth out loud, huh? Because it goes against everything he thinks he knows. His rational world separated from the irrational rantings of all these country folks who grew up on terrifying bedtime stories. Sorry to burst your bubble, Remus, but you're in deep now.

Halsey nodded her understanding, but she wasn't finished prying. "That kinda begs the question, though, doesn't it?"

Remus fixed her with a genuine, openly curious look. "What might that be?"

"Obviously, there aren't many people left fit enough for the job right now. Even as *acting* chairman. Still, of all the folks who could've stepped up to sit where you're sitting now, how did an outsider only passing through manage to make himself temporary chairman while the old one's... laid up? For lack of a better term."

"I've been asking myself the same for the last three days since it happened, Miss Ambrosius." Remus spread his arms, drew a deep breath as if he were about to launch into a long explanation, then paused. "The only answer I have is a simple one, actually."

Brigham scooted his chair closer to the table and leaned toward the man. "Which is?"

"Apparently, I have a startling capacity to keep my head during the most inexplicable crises. After Chairman Brudge was brought into the…recovery center with his very own set of injuries, I believe that particular ability made me stand out. And the locals took a vote."

"Cool as a cucumber." Brigham bobbed his head, his smile growing. "Nice."

Remus choked and jolted forward in his chair before clearing his throat again. "That's hardly the word I'd choose to describe it."

Halsey continued. "Regardless, you're the head honcho around here now. I hope you stuck around out of *some* altruism and not only because the village basically put itself on lockdown to keep everyone off the streets."

Remus caught her gaze again and briefly pressed his lips together. "So do I."

"Great." Brigham clapped his hands and leaned forward before folding his hands on the table. "Then, first things first, Mr. Chairman. How many barghests are *actually* out there?"

The man barked a nervous laugh, but when he realized neither of the Ambrosius cousins was smiling, seriousness overwhelmed him again. "I-I'm sorry. How many *what?*"

"Barghests, Remus." Halsey gestured toward the door and the room of intensely sick and injured people beyond. "The mythical black dog, omen of death, hell of a lot of bad news if you or anyone you know gets so much as a glimpse of the thing."

"Sure. But..." He chuckled again, though this time, it didn't sound nearly as tickled. "That's all codswallop. Bedtime stories for children. Country superstition." Remus regarded the cousins with a growing expression of dread. "It's not *real*."

"You know," Brigham replied, "usually we'd tell you you're right and leave it at that before we move on. But we're all in deep now, Mr. Chairman. We're here to tell you that the mythical hellhound ain't all that mythical."

After another long moment of staring at them in disbelief, Remus shook his head. "This is insane. Absolutely bloody mad..."

"So is an unhealable wound that looks like death and smells even worse less than ten minutes after getting hit." Halsey shrugged. "But that's what we're dealing with right now. I'm sure you've walked through that recovery room plenty of times since these people moved the whole operation here to this building, yeah?"

"Of course." The man's frown deepened, and he looked genuinely saddened by the thought of how many men, women, and children were stuck in those beds. "It's terrible. Just terrible."

"Yes, it is. And it's real." She leaned forward to catch his gaze, and Coningsby's newly elected chairman looked at her like a small child caught with his hand in the cookie jar. "All of it, Remus. The wounds on all those people out there. The fact that it won't kill them but only make them weaker and farther gone to unconsciousness, hallucinations, or whatever might come next. The threat of draining this village and all its resources dry in a matter of days is also very real. So is the barghest."

He stared at her, frozen for long enough that Halsey wondered if maybe she'd broken him by laying out all the truth like that.

Cool as a cucumber, huh? Right. So cool that he doesn't even know where his own line is between what he can mentally handle and what's gonna send him running for the hills. Barghest or no barghest.

When the man still didn't say anything, Halsey and Brigham looked at each other across the table. He shrugged and shook his head a fraction of an inch.

Okay. We'll try a few more things here. This is new territory for everyone.

Halsey leaned toward him again and extended her hand to pat the tabletop in front of him. "Remus?"

"I know." He drew a long, shuddering inhale, then sighed and nodded. "I saw it. The...that *thing*. Stalking down the street right outside the inn. I was having tea in the front tavern, and at first, I... I don't know *what* I thought I was seeing. But as soon as it looked at me, as soon as I saw those *eyes*..." The sound of his thick swallow filled the room. "I knew what it was. I simply didn't want to admit it to myself."

"Well, hey." Brigham spread his arms and grinned. "That's a good start, right? Little sit-down with us fixed you right up, my man. And we're outsiders, too, so you don't gotta worry about saving face and putting on a good show for *us*. Go ahead, bud. Let it all out."

Remus fixed the young elemental with a dubious look. "I'm not sure *your* enthusiasm is entirely warranted."

"Okay, maybe not. But when we get all this cleaned up and fixed for good, you won't hear *me* coming down on you for celebrating too hard. Promise."

"I don't follow…"

"What my cousin's trying to say is that we're here to help," Halsey explained, shooting Brigham a tight smile that he returned with his signature grin. "In order to do that, we need as much information as we can get about the situation. How many villagers are here. How many left. How many stayed. How many were injured by a barghest. Or by *the* barghest, and that's only assuming that Mauve told us the truth and there really was just the one."

"*Was*?" Remus' mouth opened and closed in wordless shock as he looked between the young American strangers who were even more coolheaded and level about this whole thing than he was. "Who *are* you people?"

"Who are *we*? Well." Brigham popped his lips and glanced at his cousin. "We're—"

"That's classified," Halsey interrupted, forcing her expression into what she hoped was the same stern, don't-fuck-with-me look she'd gotten so many times from her father and most of the current Council members in the last few months alone.

Brigham cleared his throat but had clearly gotten the picture.

We can come out here to kill a few monsters and help these people clean up afterward. We can't *start a bunch of rumors in the English countryside about two young Americans claiming they're magical monster hunters sent to kill demon dogs and pick up the pieces.*

Under different circumstances, the thought of gossip

like that spreading anywhere through the world of normie humans would have made her laugh. Right now, though, it was a very real possibility. They needed to make sure it never became a reality. The Ambrosius Clan elementals already had enough problems on their plate as it was.

After another thoughtful moment of silence, Remus nodded and muttered, "I see."

Brigham shot him a thumbs-up. "Glad you get the picture, man."

The man turned toward Halsey again and sat up straighter in his chair. "Though I must say you both look far too young for your professions."

"Our professions?" Brigham chuckled, looking flattered. "We didn't say anything about our—"

"You didn't have to, Mr. Ambrosius." Remus nodded, looking more composed and in control of himself now that he'd put the pieces of the puzzle together on his own. They simply happened to be the wrong pieces to the wrong puzzle. "I've seen plenty of moves. Read plenty of books. CIA, FBI, DND, D2, MI6. Though you *would* be hard-pressed to pass as military intelligence for the British Crown. Far too young."

"Military *intelligence*," Brigham mused as he turned toward Halsey with wide eyes, fighting not to crack up laughing in the man's face.

Remus continued. "Whatever your agency or organization, I understand. I won't pry any further. However, if possible, I would like some reassurance that when this *is* all over, I will be allowed to return to London. My home. The country air doesn't agree with me, and I've already been here far longer than I can normally stomach."

If he wants to think we belong to any of those organizations, fine. Better, actually. He can add to the rumors about all the secrets any number of governments are keeping from the general public, and our kind of magic stays in the shadows where it belongs. Might be time to get the whole militia a new cover story like this one, come to think of it...

A slightly awkward silence followed, then Brigham shrugged. "Misery acquaints a man with strange bedfellows and all that, am I right?"

Halsey and Remus both gawked at him in surprise.

"Wow, cuz." She failed to hide a chuckle behind one hand. "I'm impressed."

"Hey, thanks." He grinned, shifted in his chair, and rolled his shoulders back. "I, uh...can't remember exactly who said that one—"

"William Shakespeare," Remus replied dryly.

"Yeah, yeah. Sweet. Shakespeare."

Then again, Brigham could blow our secret-agent cover at any second. As long as we get this whole thing cleaned up and the little village set back on track again, whatever.

"All right, Mr. Chairman." Halsey turned toward Coningsby's new and hopefully temporary leader and dipped her head. "If it's all the same to you, we'd like to get down to it."

"Of course." He nodded, trying to keep a straight face but still looking pleased with himself for coming to a logical, though incorrect, conclusion about who these strangers were and why they were here. "I'm happy to help."

CHAPTER SIX

Drawing information from Remus Hornbull was a lot easier after that. For such a mind-bending situation as this one, the facts were simple and relatively straightforward. The first barghest attack was five days ago. The victim of that attack, a local farmer named Matthias, had been laid up in the recovery center since one of his neighbors found him the next morning and brought him in.

After that, the frequency of attacks had grown exponentially until over three-quarters of Coningsby's population had either been attacked or was directly related to someone who was. A number of healthy, brave men and women dedicated to protecting their community had gone out after the creature, and every single one of them had returned bloody, weak, stumbling, and otherwise on the verge of death.

Until their caregivers realized that nothing would make them stronger, nothing would heal them, and wounds like theirs wouldn't kill them, either.

The number of those infected with the barghest's

venom grew overnight. By the start of the third day, the village had banded together to bring all the injured into the Community Hall building in the center of their small, quiet little community. Neighbors, friends, and family members had pooled what little resources they had in their homes and businesses for dealing with something like this, and no one else attempted to hunt the barghest down on their own.

That didn't stop the barghest from hunting them, though.

A few phone calls from terrified villagers had gotten out. Calls to friends and family in other parts of England to share the mind-blowing news of real-life monsters right here in their very own Coningsby. After that, the original chairman and several villagers with enough foresight to predict the oncoming giant shitshow went ahead and made the necessary serious changes. Phone lines were cut. Cell phones were confiscated. People were told to come to the Community Hall or, if they couldn't make it, stay indoors at all times unless stepping outside was absolutely necessary.

In a small town that had been fairly self-sufficient for quite some time, reliance on communication with the outside world was practically nonexistent. Nobody argued. Nobody tried to rebel against the new rules set in place. Most of the folks here led simple lives and were ready and willing to do whatever they were told, as long as someone was in the position of telling them.

Which was how Mr. Remus Hornbull found himself in the position of acting chairman. The man was suddenly and without warning caught between a rock and a hard place. He wanted to get out, he wanted to go home, and he'd also been suddenly put into the position, however temporary, of being responsible for the entire village of Coningsby and all its inhabitants, injured or otherwise.

Once Remus started talking, he didn't seem to have any trouble continuing the momentum until the end. Clearly, he'd wanted to unload the unexpected burden he'd taken on. Yet as the person who'd taken over for the currently wounded chairman, he felt a certain responsibility not to spread that burden among the villagers who trusted and looked up to him solely because he'd remained calm and collected.

Now that Halsey and Brigham were here, though, Remus had an opportunity to lay all the information out at someone else's feet for a change.

In twenty minutes, he'd gone through everything he could think of to share with the two young people he truly believed worked for a government agency. When he'd finished, he sat back in his chair, straightened his shirt collar, and nodded. "There. I...I believe that's everything. But if you have any additional questions, I'll do what I can to drum up a few more answers for you."

"Thank you, Remus." Halsey met her cousin's gaze, and he dipped his head to offer her the first crack at finding out what they needed to know. "I think the most important question, to start, is one I'm going to circle back to real quick."

The man looked drained after the ordeal of recounting his nightmarish stay in this part of the countryside. Yet he nodded anyway. "Of course."

"Can you say, with any level of certainty, how many

barghests were here in Coningsby within the timeframe of this whole…debacle?"

Brigham almost snorted, then managed to choke it down before covering his mouth with a hand and sternly nodding in agreement.

He thinks it's funny to hear me talk like that? Sure. It's even weirder spitting the words out of my mouth.

"How many…" Remus blinked numbly at her.

"How many barghests, Remus." She breathed in deeply and put on her best patient smile. It wasn't particularly convincing because patience wasn't exactly something at which Halsey Ambrosius excelled. But apparently, it was enough to get the wheels in Mr. Hornbull's head turning again.

"Right, right. Yes. Well, um…I can't say I'm certain of anything other than the fact that I saw one of them myself."

"Yeah, I think we've already established there was at least one."

"Oh. Yes, of course."

He's fried. Looks like the new chairman needs a little hand-holding.

Smiling politely, Halsey tried again. "Personally, you only saw the one. But what about others in Coningsby? What do they say?"

"Ah. Well, um… Let's see. I'm…not entirely sure, to be honest."

"Have you heard anything about a potential second barghest?" Brigham asked, timing it perfectly to keep the man from feeling like he was being grilled extra hard by only one of the presumed "agents."

"I…I don't think so. No."

"Nothing about multiple sightings? Different locations? Impossible attacks occurring simultaneously in more than one location?"

Halsey pursed her lips to keep herself from smirking at her cousin. *Now who's taking the super-official language to a whole new level?*

"No, no." Remus shook his head. "Nothing like that. Good God, if I'd heard about more than one of the bloody bastards, I'm not sure the locals would have given me the job. *This* one, I mean."

"Sure." Brigham nodded professionally. "One is terrifying enough."

"Actually, though, now that I think about it…" The man wagged a finger at absolutely nothing in the center of the long conference table. "I'm quite sure there is only one. Quite sure. And that's what Mauve told you, isn't it?"

"That's exactly what she told us," Halsey confirmed. "But aside from you, she's the only other person we've spoken to so far. We like to get our information from as many dependable sources as possible. You understand."

Remus scoffed. "All the way out here where a beast like that runs rampant in bedtime stories, old drunkards' tales, *and* real life? I should bloody well hope so!"

The conference room fell silent as the cousins gave their normie contact another moment to compose himself.

A normal reaction from a normal human. He's no threat to either of us, but he might be if we take too long to finish this. The guy's about to blow.

When the new chairman realized he'd let a not-so-levelheaded outburst get the better of him, he readjusted the collar of his button-up shirt and cleared his throat.

"Please excuse the shouting. I, uh... I don't quite know what came over me."

"Everything you're feeling is totally normal, man." Brigham sounded far chummier than an official government agent. "We know this shit is weird. Takes a bit to get used to, and after we're out of your hair, you'll never have to try getting used to anything like this ever again."

"Good. Yes, that's good."

Halsey shot her cousin a warning look. *Ease up on the promises, cuz. If he stumbles into a werewolf or boggart den, that unravels all our credibility. Hopefully, way after the fact, if ever.*

"So," she continued to steer the conversation back on track before Remus Hornbull ran out of steam. "If we were to talk to any of the other villagers here, you think they'd tell us the same thing? About there only being one barghest, I mean."

Remus widened his eyes and looked like he was about to cry. "Are you saying you think there's more than one?"

"Definitely not."

"Actually, that was our assessment as well," Brigham cut in. "It doesn't hurt to cover all the bases, though. Makes the whole thing more efficient and the paperwork a hell of a lot easier."

That seemed to calm their ad-hoc village official right back from the ledge again. "Yes, I can imagine."

"From the second I walked into this room, Remus, I knew you were a reasonable man. Logical. Respectable. Someone we could depend on."

That made the man's lips twitch into an uncertain smile, but Brigham's conversational skills had done their job.

Laying it on thick, isn't he? That's exactly what this guy needed.

"Well, then." Remus took a breath, nodded, then exhaled slowly. "How can I help get this over and done with, Agents? What's next?"

Both Ambrosius monster hunters had a hell of a time containing their amusement at being called "Agents," but that struggle only lasted until Halsey was able to find her voice again without letting it waver.

"Right. First things first. Now that we're sure there was only one of the damn things—"

"I'm sorry. Excuse me." The man lifted a polite finger, frowning in confusion. "You keep saying *was*. Apologies for my ignorance in these matters, but is that part of your protocol, or are you...referring to the beast in the past tense for some other reason?"

Brigham chuckled politely, a sound much like the half-amused, half-condescending laugh a much older, less monster-huntery high-society person would offer in the presence of commoners. Halsey almost expected him to say how cute Remus' question was.

Instead, her cousin folded his hands again in a very businesslike manner on the table and looked the new chairman directly in the eyes. "The past tense *is* the most accurate way to address something that *was*, but no longer *is*, right? Or did the rules of the English language change, and everybody forgot to tell me?"

"I... Well, it's..." Remus blustered incoherently, and Halsey had to step in again.

"My cousin's a big fan of wry humor."

"So am I most of the time. When I'm not, well, in a place

like this, having conversations like this one." The man swallowed and shrugged. "It's quite British."

Great. Let's try getting out of this thing without being adopted by our new normie friends, huh?

Halsey tried to squeeze the thought into another warning look aimed at her cousin, and Brigham lowered his gaze to the table, still working hard to contain his laughter.

Remus, however, was far more in control of himself to let his unanswered question slide by. "For the sake of clarification, Agent, would you mind indulging me with something more…concrete?"

Halsey nodded. "Sure. We're talking about the barghest in the past tense because the truth comes more naturally. As in, that creature no longer exists and won't be causing any more trouble than it already has."

That made the man perk up quite a bit. He looked quickly between them, trying to gauge the authenticity of their reassuring smiles. "Truly? It's gone?"

"Very, *very* gone," Brigham replied.

"Well, that's…that's wonderful! When did this happen? How on Earth did you manage to chase it off? How do we keep it *away*?"

"That won't be a problem, Remus." Halsey swallowed sharply, already hating the way the words would sound on her tongue before she'd spoken them. "The barghest is dead."

"Dead." Remus blinked. "As in…"

"Deceased." Brigham counted synonyms on his fingers. "Expired. Departed. Nonexistent. Bereft of life. *Dead*, Mr. Chairman."

"I..." The man looked like he was about to start choking, and Halsey tilted her head to watch him from the corner of her eye.

Yeah, the whole militia's trained in basic first-aid and CPR, but that doesn't mean I wanna have to use *it.*

Finally, Remus stopped blustering about and surprised them all by slamming the heel of a solid fist down on the table. "What the hell are we still doing here, then?"

His shout echoed through the room again, and it took him a moment to realize how heavily he was breathing.

"We'll get this whole thing sorted out soon, Remus." Halsey chose to tread carefully since they'd had two pieces of evidence in the last thirty minutes suggesting this man wasn't nearly as held-together as Coningsby's citizens seemed to believe. "With the barghest out of the picture, I'm sure the folks here would more than understand your decision to end your extended stay and be on your way out of here—"

"No." He took another deep breath and met her gaze. "I can't do that. I will not."

"That's very brave of you, Mr. Chairman," Brigham added with a nod. "So you know, we won't force you to stay."

"No, I'm sure. But my conscience will." Remus' gaze darted all over the room as his mind worked desperately to weigh the pros and cons of making this particular decision. "I've already come this far with all these people. The...*monster* may be disposed of, but there are still dozens of people lying out there in the next room, injured, in pain, exhausted, and terrified. Those they trusted to lead them before this horrible nightmare began are not yet in a position to do so again. Until they are, I will stay. Whatever you need, Agents, I'll see that you have it. To the best of my limited abilities, of course."

"Yeah, totally."

"We appreciate that," Halsey added.

The man was looking more and more pleased with himself by the minute, which probably had quite a lot to do with the exciting news that the barghest would no longer be terrorizing the sleepy little village in the English countryside. But that was only the first obstacle here, which the Ambrosius cousins had known from the beginning.

"Which leads us to the next step here," she added, nodding at both men sitting with her at the table. "We're not leaving until every single one of the victims in the recovery center is back to their normal selves again. Healed. Healthy. Like this whole thing never even happened."

It was the truth. Their mission wasn't successfully completed until they'd cleaned up the barghest's entire mess, which now consisted of leaving no stone unturned and no possible shred of evidence behind. There would always be the villagers' memories of the last five days and the two young foreign "agents" who'd shown up out of nowhere to end the short-lived reign of supernatural terror. However, those memories would quickly become nothing but speculation, hearsay, and the farthest thing from proof of monsters they could ever possibly get.

Despite her optimism and the fact that now the bulk of the danger was far behind them, Remus' renewed confidence and self-assurance deflated instantly at the mention of healing all those who would remain perpetually wounded unless somebody did something about their barghest injuries. Someone like Halsey and Brigham Ambrosius, but the poor city businessman from London couldn't have possibly known that.

He nervously licked his lips and shook his head. "That's impossible."

"Oh." Brigham sat back in his chair and put on a good show of looking thoroughly surprised. "Mind telling us why?"

"Whatever that...*thing* did to them," Remus continued slowly, as if he were finally afraid to continue talking about any of this out loud, "their injuries are impossible to treat. And yes, we have tried everything. Several of the people here have had extensive medical training. I've personally spoken with three nurses and one doctor who are all included in this...lockdown, as it were. The medical supplies and medication were all brought straight up here from the local pharmacy, and none of it did a thing. Those wounds..."

He nervously licked his lips again and couldn't look either of the cousins in the eye.

This is the part where whatever's left of his sanity starts breaking. It's one thing to have proof that monsters exist. Or at least one *monster, at the very least. But it's something totally different for any of these people to wrap their heads around wounds that don't heal, Western medicine being useless, and the possibility that anyone might actually have a way to solve the final impossible problem. And there's no way in hell we can tell them* magic *is the reason we can do what we do. So what* do *we tell them?*

CHAPTER SEVEN

"We know what those wounds are," Brigham explained in an attempt to assuage the acting chairman's doubts. "We know normal medicine and healing procedures won't do a thing to help all those sick people in all those beds out there."

Remus grunted in acknowledgment, but that seemed all he was capable of for the time being.

"And we *do* know how to heal them," Halsey added.

The man sighed heavily before looking up at her again with one of the most forlorn expressions she'd ever seen. "I'm sorry, Agent. I understand the two of you are specifically trained to handle situations like this, however that may be. But I don't see how what you're talking about is even possible. Or how either of you can be so…bloody certain of yourselves."

"That's easy." Brigham fixed the man with an easy, crooked smile. "Personal experience."

"I'm sorry?"

"That's what it boils down to, Remus." Halsey nodded,

hoping the amount of reassurance coming from both her and her cousin at the same time would help refortify the man's composure, if not a good portion of his confidence. "We fought the barghest and killed it. Since there's only one, that's a done deal. *And* we've already healed a wound sustained from that beast, so we know it can be done, and we know exactly how to do it."

Her cousin shot her another quick look of disapproval from across the table, and she knew what that look would have said if it could talk. *Don't say anything else because we seriously need to talk about this first.*

Relax, Brigham. I'm not gonna spill all our secrets.

Halsey returned his intent gaze and raised an eyebrow. They'd have their own private talk after this little meeting with the village of Coningsby's most recent chairman they'd appointed to steer them through these times of immense community upheaval. That was when the cousins would talk about exactly *how* they would heal everyone in the recovery center.

That was also when Brigham would try his damnedest to convince her that what she wanted to do here was a bad idea.

But it was an even worse idea to do absolutely nothing and let all these poor people continue to suffer under their unending wounds for who knows how long.

Get back to the present, Halsey. We're not done here yet.

Remus took longer and longer to fully integrate and accept what these two young foreigners had been telling him. The man stared blankly at the surface of the table for several long seconds that felt like they stretched on forever. His lips moved without sound as he tried to work out the information being presented to him, then it finally seemed to sink in. He swallowed thickly and shot a wide-eyed look at Halsey. "That's impossible."

Brigham chuckled softly. "Again, man, this whole thing is impossible in the scheme of things. It might make all this easier if you throw out what you think you know about possible, impossible, fact, and fiction, okay?"

"Then tell me how that's possible because I don't understand." Remus shook his head. "How did you do it? *Whom* did you heal?"

The cousins shared another look across the table. This time, Halsey was the one prompting her best friend and mission partner to offer a bit more insider knowledge to this terrified man than they usually shared with normies. It was a lot to ask, sure, but if they didn't get the okay from Coningsby's acting chairman, they wouldn't get it from any of these people. The villagers were terrified enough as it was. Adding a lot more magic to a mind-numbingly supernatural situation would only stir the pot if they tried to force it.

Yeah, and there's a fine line between nudging somebody into doing the right thing and forcing it on them. If you don't tell the guy, Brigham, I will.

Her cousin clearly got the message, though he didn't seem very happy about it.

With a sigh, he leaned back in his chair and nodded at Remus. "The *how* is more complicated than we have time for right now. But the *who*? Also easy. It was me."

Slowly turning his head to stare at Brigham now, the man simply gawked at him, blinking slowly. "You?"

"It's not *that* hard to believe, is it?" Halsey's cousin

offered a crooked smile. "Well, maybe it is, but that just goes to show how well it works."

Remus shook his head like a man not quite able to wake himself from a bad dream. "I still don't…"

"Go ahead." Halsey nodded at her cousin. "Show him."

"Show me?" The man's voice cracked as he echoed the question.

"Really?" Brigham tried to laugh it off, but his mission partner wasn't giving him any room to argue about it. So he sighed, rolled his eyes, and scooted his chair back to stand from the table. "Okay. Didn't know it was Bring Your Battle Scars to School Day."

Remus turned a baffled, disoriented frown onto Halsey again, blinking furiously. "Battle scars?"

"One of many." She nodded toward her cousin, hoping the man would follow her lead and look in the right direction. "Comes with the job, believe it or not."

"I see. With the…job."

Great. We drove him right into copycat mode. Either this'll drive our point home and seal the deal, or it'll break Remus Hornbull into so many pieces that all the king's men won't be able to put him back together.

The thought made her smirk, but fortunately, the acting chairman had already turned to watch Brigham's show-and-tell and didn't notice her amusement.

Clicking his tongue, Brigham stared at his cousin as he reached for the bottom hem of his t-shirt.

"Good God, man!" Remus lurched in his chair. "Your shirt!"

"Hey, trust me. I hardly feel it." Brigham's joke didn't land very well if it had even landed at all. He laughed at it anyway and grabbed the hem of his shirt before looking down at himself with curiosity and apprehension. "Guess that's our proof right there that I *was* injured. You'll take my word that it's all my own blood, right?"

"I..."

"Never mind. I guess we could always order a fun little DNA test from the local constabulary if anybody needs extra convincing."

Constabulary? Halsey almost burst out laughing. *Nice. He's so nervous that he's using all the weird old-people words again. Or maybe that's a British thing...*

Her musing on the etiology of various words her mission partner chose in times of higher-than-usual stress was interrupted by Remus' gasp when Brigham finally lifted his shirt to expose the dried blood smeared across his lower abdomen and the shiny, puckered scar stretching from below the bottom of his right ribs toward the waistband of his jeans.

Wrinkling his nose, Brigham thumbed down the waistband of his pants with the other hand and looked at his newest battle scar. "Yep. Still there. Look at that."

"You..." Blinking furiously again, Remus leaned toward the young elemental to get a closer look, then squinted. One hand went to his face as if he intended to push a pair of glasses up the bridge of his nose before the absence of any eyewear reminded him he was not wearing any. After blustering for a few seconds, he craned his neck to look at Brigham and murmured, "You're covered in blood."

"Oh, *that*." Brigham snorted. "Tends to happen when you get your guts sliced by a barghest claw. Or by anything, really. Don't worry, man. That part's totally natural."

The man didn't seem to notice the high levels of wry humor being tossed into the mix of unbelievable impossibilities. Instead, he wrinkled his nose and leaned away, troubled all over again. "And how long, exactly, have you been walking around with all that blood on you?"

"Years." The word flew effortlessly and stoically from Brigham's lips, and he chuckled when the acting chairman paled in horror. "Kidding, man. I'm just kidding. No, this…" He regarded the giant scar splitting the otherwise fairly smooth skin of his abdomen and gently brushed his fingers along it before sucking in a deep breath. "This happened…what, Hal? A few hours ago?"

"Something like that." She pressed a knuckle to her mouth to hide a smile that wouldn't go away, but Remus wasn't looking at her anyway. The man couldn't stop staring at the scar shining through all the streaks of smeared, dried, flaking blood on her cousin's belly.

"Right. Something like a few hours." Brigham dropped the bottom of his shirt, then spread his arms. "I know, I know. A thing like this usually comes with a change of clothes and a shower, right? If that was something I had on me between the main street out there and this room right here, trust me, I would've used 'em. But, uh… Okay. Series of events in a nutshell." He pointed at Halsey and dropped back into his seat, but she already knew it wasn't a cue for her to pick up his summary of their last few hours.

Good to see he's finally warming up for a little storytelling, I guess.

"We passed the 'Welcome to Coningsby' sign," Brigham continued. "Looking for a bunch of people running around screaming while a few barghests crunched through the place like tiny black Godzilla-dogs."

"I'm sorry." Remus cleared his throat. "Godzilla-dogs?"

"It's a metaphor, Mr. Chairman. Kinda. Anyway, pretty much before we even had a chance to assume we'd driven into a ghost town, that bastardy barghest T-boned our rental car, if you can believe it."

"Oh my…"

"I know, right? No injuries from that one. At least, not any that I'm feeling right now, but who knows what tomorrow brings, huh? We got out and grabbed our barghest-hunting gear because that's our job. Took a look around, then here comes Growly McGlowy-Eyes, headed straight for us."

Remus gasped and raised a hand to his mouth with perfect timing as if he'd had absolutely no idea that the village had been terrorized by an abnormally venomous supernatural creature for the last four days.

Brigham wiggled his eyebrows at the man. "Oh yeah, man. I know. Pretty scary shit."

"To say the least," the man murmured, captivated by the story the Ambrosius cousins hadn't exactly planned to tell anyone but Cavanaugh when they finally got home for their mission debrief.

Halsey looked quickly between her cousin and the acting chairman watching him with rapt attention, still trying not to laugh. *Oh yeah. He's* loving *this.*

"We hit the thing with everything we had, Remus." Brigham pointed at the man and nodded. "And I know our bags might *look* like regular bags with nothing too special inside, but I can tell you right now, we brought one hell of an arsenal for this little beasty."

Remus didn't move, staring at the young man with a hand pressed to his lips and fully captured by the tale. Which was more or less what any elemental would have expected from a normie getting the full rundown of a monster hunt, so at least the man wasn't dishing out any surprises there.

"And man, that thing could *jump*," Brigham continued, raising and lowering his hand in a wide arc onto the tabletop. "Like a pounce, right? A flying pounce. Took my cousin to the ground at least once—"

"*No…*" Remus turned toward Halsey, and she quickly had to wipe the smile off her face so she could nod with all seriousness to back up her cousin's very true recounting of facts.

"Oh yeah. Listen, Mr. Chairman," Brigham continued, "Halsey Ambrosius is a badass, okay? You don't wanna mess with her. And she held her own against that sonofabitch with nothing but her bare hands and a throwing axe."

"Good God…"

"Just until I managed to hit that thing with a few fireballs, you know?"

Remus straightened in his seat, finally knocked out of the storytelling spell, and cocked his head. "Fireballs?"

Brigham looked at Halsey with wide eyes, effectively hiding his reaction from anyone who didn't know him as well as she did, but not from her.

Careful, Brigham. Sticking as close to the truth as possible is fine, but diving into an elemental's ability to manipulate fire from one of your fancy lighters is seriously off the table.

She raised her eyebrows at him, wordlessly prompting him to figure out how to take his own foot out of his mouth.

"Yeah. Fireballs." Brigham cleared his throat. "You know, uh…"

"Simple tactical flamethrower," Halsey added before turning to give Remus a curt nod. "More or less."

The man's frown only deepened. "Tactical—"

"Super high-tech stuff, my man." Brigham rapped his knuckles on the table and continued as if he hadn't come way too close to blowing the magical lid directly through the window. "Disassembles for easy transport and everything. Anyway, we get in a few blasts of fiery vengeance on the thing, give it a little of the ol' one-two, then Hal grabs up this dinosaur of a bolt-action shotgun—"

"It's not *that* old," she insisted through a stifled laugh.

"And *bam!* Barghest shot, right here." Brigham thumped a fist against his chest in demonstration and nodded.

A massive sigh escaped Remus Hornbull because, apparently, the man had been holding his breath. Then he blinked as if waking up again and lifted an index finger to signal a pause. "A shotgun?"

"That's right, Mr. Chairman. You better believe it."

"*That's* what it was." The man looked at Halsey again in complete bafflement. "We heard the shot from here. Right inside this building."

"That was me." She fixed him with a tight smile. "Disturbing the peace wasn't initially part of the plan, by the way. Or whatever peace was still hanging on a few hours ago, anyway."

"Long story short," Brigham cut in without giving their audience of one an opportunity to continue waylaying the tale. "The barghest goes up in smoke. Or dust. Ash, maybe. I don't know. It disappeared. It's gone. There's no body, so sending out a search party to bring that thing's head back on a spike'll be a waste of everyone's time. Trust me. So it's Monster Down, party time everywhere, you know? Except for when the thing was jumping at us, it got its hooks into me during a fly-by. Literally."

"That scar on your stomach." Remus' gaze dropped to where the scar would have been on Brigham's lower abdomen if it hadn't been blocked from view by both the blood-stained shirt and the edge of the table. "That was from *today*..."

"Ding, ding, ding! We have a winner!" Brigham pointed at him again and winked. "Now you're gettin' with the program, Remus."

"But *how*?"

"We healed it," Halsey cut in again. This time, she said in a way she knew Brigham would understand as wrapping this fun little story up. "Just like—"

"Come on, Hal." Her cousin grinned at her. "No need to be so modest about it. Now's not the time. Listen to this, man." Then he leaned toward the awestruck Remus and pointed flippantly at Halsey like she was nothing but an afterthought. "She says *we*. But the truth of the matter my friend, is it was all her. *She* healed it. Me. She healed *me*."

"That's..." Fighting desperately to make sense of the

new information, the man looked all over the room before settling on Halsey's face to ask, "So, you're a doctor?"

"Uh." She drew a deep breath, momentarily stunned by his hilarious, far-off-the-mark conclusion. "Well, that's not exactly—"

"I'll be the first to admit I'm not well-versed in the available specialties out there, but I would *love* to know what yours is."

"That's classified too, pal." Brigham knocked on the table again without missing a beat. "Sorry."

"I see. Well then, can you at least tell me how you managed to heal a debilitating wound from a...creature like that?" Remus released a nervous, high-pitched laugh. "Not to mention how the scar looks like it was sustained weeks ago instead of mere hours. Which I'm sure goes without saying, doesn't it?"

"It sure does, Remus. Sure does." After shooting the man a raised finger in a signal to wait, Brigham leaned over the side of his chair before the harsh zip of his weapons bag opening filled the conference room. "And that's an excellent question. Of *course* you'd want to know how all this is actually possible. Totally reasonable request. Hey, you're the guy who gets to decide how we do this thing moving forward, right? Fate of the entire village in your hands and everything. For now, of course."

"Yes." Remus tried to peer below the table to see what the young elemental was doing, then gave up when he realized snooping like that would have been much too obvious. "Merely a temporary arrangement."

"That's right. And until 'temporarily for now' becomes 'over and done with in the past...'" Brigham grunted as he rifled through his weapons bag. "You're the man with the plan, aren't you, Remus?"

"Brigham," Halsey warned, already knowing what her cousin was looking for. "Maybe we should…"

"It's all good, cuz. All good. The man's got a right to know."

"Absolutely." The word almost hurt coming out, but Remus wasn't in any fit state to pick up on a little white lie coming from the mouths of two young elementals who hadn't bothered to correct him in assuming they were secret government agents from an undisclosed organization. "I'm only wondering if protocol might dictate—"

"Protocol, shmotocol. Am I right, Remus?" Brigham whipped his head up from his weapons bag to grin at the man from an incredibly awkward angle. Remus merely dipped his head in agreement, entirely confused as to what exactly that agreement contained. "That's right. These are strange times. And strange times call for weird-as-hell measures, know what I'm saying?"

"Brigham."

"Nah, we're good, Hal. I got this." Finally, he straightened in his chair and whipped his hands into his lap to hide them beneath the table. Then he wiggled his eyebrows at Remus Hornbull and inhaled deeply. "Mr. Chairman. You asked how we managed to heal one agonizing, debilitating, majorly effed-up slice in the belly from a creature that technically shouldn't even exist. And now I'm going to give you an answer."

Remus nodded eagerly. "Yes. Thank you. I appreciate that."

"Of course you do. Good man." Brigham winked at him, then let the suspense draw out a few seconds longer.

Halsey rolled her eyes. *Note to self. Don't let Brigham handle the summaries with normies. And I never in a million years would've thought that's something I'd have to remember for the future.*

Finally, Brigham lifted both hands from beneath the tabletop for his grand reveal, and the one thing Halsey thought was a bad idea to bring into this. The leather purse Cavanaugh had handed over during their mission brief came down onto the table, resting between her cousin's hands.

Remus bit his lip, looked hesitantly up at the young elemental, and leaned slightly forward. "With *that*?"

"Ah." Brigham reached into the purse and drew out one of the vials that still contained the glowing green liquid of Florence's ineffectual healing potion. Then he lifted it up toward the light like it was Coningsby's very own holy grail and exclaimed, "With *this*."

CHAPTER EIGHT

"Remarkable," Remus breathed as he gazed up at the glowing green liquid in Brigham's upraised vial. A smile of awe and wonderment passed across his lips, then he cleared his throat. "What is it?"

Brigham gazed at the man like a prophet looking upon his devout believers and nodded. "The answer to all your problems here, Mr. Chairman. That's what this is."

"I see. Well, that's...that's wonderful."

"Indeed it is."

While Brigham stuffed the vial back into the purse with a smug twitch on his lips, Halsey glared at him. *Nice one, cuz. So much for sticking as close to the truth as possible without breaking the whole thing wide open. Or digging ourselves into a ditch where no one will ever find the bodies.*

"Then let's get started." Remus slammed his hands on the table, finally recovering his air of leadership now that he felt he'd been saved by the two "secret agents" who could do what he couldn't for the village. Then he pushed himself from his chair with renewed vigor. "Right this instant. If that's the cure, we need to get it into the hands of everyone in the recovery center and end this nightmare once and—"

"Actually, Remus, this is gonna take a little time," Halsey interrupted.

The man stiffened, then slowly turned his head to look down at her as his smile wavered. "I wouldn't necessarily say that, Agent. These people here are *very* efficient when they have a plan."

"Yeah, I'm sure they are." She cleared her throat and shot her cousin another warning look. Brigham wiped the joyous smile off his face and settled the leather purse of vials back into his lap. "We still have a few…bugs to work out, though."

"Bugs." Remus shook his head, lost again.

"With the cure." Halsey gestured toward her cousin and nodded. "Brigham and I need to discuss how we're going to handle it moving forward so that everyone gets what they need."

"Bit of a detour," Brigham added, nodding sagely.

That seemed to deflate the acting chairman even more. He stiffly lowered himself back into his seat, flummoxed and stunned with all the fervor drained out of him again.

"Not really a *detour*, though. No." She shifted in her chair to face the man they still had to convince to give them more time before administering this "miracle cure" and reached slightly toward him before putting a reassuring hand down on the tabletop in front of him. "More like a workaround."

"A *workaround*," her cousin echoed. "Exactly."

"Well, what...seems to be the problem?" Remus asked.

Halsey gestured offhandedly toward her cousin. "I'd say the first hurdle we need to jump over is the fact that right now, there are only five vials in that bag. And there are a lot more than five people out there who need our help."

The man deflated farther in his chair, his shoulders slumping. "Oh, dear."

"We *can* find a solution, Remus. That's what we do. We only need time to figure out what that solution is." Brigham frowned at her, and she returned it with full force when the chairman turned toward her cousin instead for more explanation.

Quickly plastering on another smile under the village leader's attention, Brigham nodded. "That's right. More time. You know, to walk through our protocols again, assess our assets, and do a little math."

"Math?"

"Arithmetic, Mr. Chairman. Plus a dash of chemistry, just for fun."

"Oh. Oh, I see. You want to split effective doses."

"We want to make sure everyone in the next room over gets what they need to heal from this." Halsey nodded firmly. "Physically speaking, of course."

"Yeah." Her cousin snorted. "We can kill monsters and heal wounds all day, but we don't shrink heads."

Oh, come on. Seriously?

Despite Brigham putting on an act to the point where it almost felt like he was treating this whole thing as a joke, Remus ate it up without question. He nodded in contemplation, then folded his hands on the table. "Yes. That's something that can be handled here by the locals, I'm sure. After this is over. For now, let's focus on helping those who can't help themselves right now."

"Excellent idea, sir," Brigham chirped. Then the conference room fell into contemplative silence as both Ambrosius cousins waited for their last-minute host to take the hint. But Remus was so lost in the deep well of his thoughts that he probably wouldn't have noticed a barghest racing right through the room and onto the table. So Brigham clapped his hands with a startling crack and shouted. "So!"

That jolted Remus out of his own head, and he blinked furiously, looking around.

Halsey's cousin grinned. "No time like the present, Mr. Chairman. Am I right?"

"What? Oh yes. Absolutely. No time…" The man pushed his chair away from the table with a loud screech of metal chair legs across the floor, then stood. "I'll leave you to it, then, Agents."

"Very good."

Halsey wanted to smack her cousin for acting more like a normal person. Instead, she smiled at the acting chairman gathering enough of his faculties to reach the door at the opposite end of the room without crumpling into a heap. "Thank you, Remus. When we come up with the best solution for everyone, we'll let you know."

"I'll be waiting." On wobbly legs, the man crossed the room, grabbed the doorknob, then paused before turning to look at the two young people who'd shown up out of the blue to save one very bad day. "And do let me know if you require any additional supplies or…what have you. I don't personally know where everything is being stored at the moment, but I do know the right people to set to the task. Should you find yourselves in need of anything."

"We'll let you know that too. Thanks." Halsey's smile faded as she gave the man a final nod of dismissal and hoped he'd get the picture.

And as soon as he leaves, I get to rip my cousin a new one for making this way more complicated than it needed to be. Total bullshit lie or not.

"Wonderful. Then I'll just…" Remus offered an awkward half-bow at the waist, then stiffly jerked open the door and slid into the recovery center's main room filled with all the wounded citizens of Coningsby for whom he'd become responsible, including his predecessor.

The door shut again with a soft click, and Brigham burst out laughing.

Halsey fixed him with a deadpan stare. "Nice."

"Oh, *man*! That was awesome."

"Not sure I'm with you on this one, cuz."

"Aw, come on, Hal. That was *gold*." He laughed again and clapped his hands together. "You saw that, right? I had him eating right out of my hand."

"Bordering on emotional torture, but yeah. Sure. You sure did."

"You know, I think I'm starting to like this whole 'normies on the inside' thing. Right?" Sitting back in his chair, Brigham drew a deep breath and ran a hand through his messy auburn hair. "Whew. Never thought I'd say *that*.

But for real. They can handle a lot more than we give them credit for. Case in point."

"Sure. Until they can't."

Her cousin chuckled, still enjoying the part he was proud of playing in their pseudo-explanation given to a man who didn't even officially hold the position of the right man for *his* current job, however temporary. When Brigham saw how unamused she was by the whole thing, though, his smile dampened. "What?"

She folded her arms and sat back in her chair. "You went a little overboard, dude."

He clicked his tongue and stuck a thumb out toward the conference room's door. "Remus handled it like a champ. Don't undervalue the guy's integrity, huh?"

"I'm not talking about his integrity. Only yours."

That finally got him to stop laughing about the whole thing. Brigham's smile disappeared, and he sat back in his chair to engage in the staring contest his cousin had started. "Mine?"

"You took it too far."

"I was lightening the *mood*, Hal. No harm, no foul, yeah?"

"Okay, so explain to me how it was a good idea to pull out the healing potions and start waving *those* things around. 'Cause I can't figure it out."

Pausing, Brigham cocked his head to think, then looked at the leather purse in his lap. "It's a black sheep."

"A what?"

"Or red herring. Scapegoat. Whatever they call it. I don't know."

"Nice. Really professional, cuz. Objective, analytical way to go about the last part of *our mission*…"

"Jesus, Hal. Did you want me to explode the poor dude's head by telling him it was actually your *magic* that cleared away the boogeyman's virus and saved my life? 'Cause the way I see it, that was the only other option."

"There are always other options," she intoned. "You didn't even give us a chance to throw a few more things at the wall."

When she didn't continue to explain why she wasn't particularly happy by the way he'd commandeered the most delicate part of their conversation with Remus Hornbull, Brigham set the leather purse gruffly down on the table, the glass vials clinking together inside. "Go ahead, then."

"Go ahead what?"

He flippantly tossed a hand in her direction, his good mood now thoroughly cowed under his cousin's scrutiny. "You obviously had a better idea for proving to these people that we actually know what we're doing. So let's hear it."

With a sigh, Halsey shook her head. "That's not what I meant."

"Well, I know you well enough to know that it's along those lines, Hal, so come on. No bullshit."

She gazed at the leather bag on the table with all their useless healing potions inside and drummed her fingers on her thigh. "Obviously, we couldn't just tell the man that I healed you with the orb and some weird new magic I didn't even know I had."

He grimaced at her mention of the copper ball and snorted. "Obviously."

"Plus, the potions don't actually work, dude."

"Also obviously."

After taking a long, slow inhale to calm her frustration as much as possible, Halsey shrugged and shook her head. "So now I can't help feeling like you've dug us into a deeper hole that's gonna be even harder to climb out of."

"Oh, come on." Brigham lurched forward in his seat and gestured sharply toward the conference room door. "It's called improvising, Hal. I had to say *something*."

"Then maybe you should go join an improv group and save the last-minute ideas for that. Figuring out how we're going to help all those injured people was bad enough without adding a bunk potion to the mix."

He stared at her, his mouth hanging open, then shook his head. "What's your point?"

"My *point*," she replied as she slid her hand into her pocket to wrap her fingers around the cold metallic curve of the copper orb inside. "Is that we needed to come up with a way to heal those people that didn't give away anything else about our world. Magic, monsters, all of it."

"Yeah…"

"And now we have to figure out how to heal everybody the *real* way while making them think it was a vial of glowing green crap from two complete strangers instead."

At first, when her cousin didn't do or say a thing, Halsey wondered if he was still so caught up in the whirlwind of his own storytelling that he simply didn't get it. But then he looked slowly down at the purse of vials in front of him, wrinkled his nose, and murmured, "Shit."

Well, at least he gets it now. This just got a lot harder than it had to be, and we're still not done until every single person in that recovery room is up and walking around and showing off a fresh pink scar like his.

When he looked back up at her, Brigham's eyes were wide with realization. He chuckled uncertainly and spread his arms. "So…brainstorm session 2.0?"

CHAPTER NINE

They stayed in that conference room for another two hours, uninterrupted by the chairman of Coningsby or any other citizens healthy enough to check in on the American strangers who'd appeared without warning and claimed to have far more answers than any of the locals. Fortunately, none of those locals used that good health to interfere with the intense brainstorming session Halsey and Brigham had essentially locked themselves up to perform. At the very least, it meant the cousins didn't have to plaster smiles on their faces or put on a show of complete confidence for anyone who wanted an update on their progress.

Pretending that everything was fine and they had it all figured out would have been too difficult for the Ambrosius cousins, anyway. Their current round of brainstorming revolved around Brigham's disgust and fear of the copper orb.

At first, he'd tried to wrap that distrust up in a package of concern about Halsey's wellbeing instead. "Look, we both know something freaky happened out there when you used that thing to…bring me back to life or whatever."

"Yeah, we covered that." Halsey sat in her same chair on the opposite side of the long conference table, staring at the sphere as she slowly turned it over and over in her hands.

"That freaky ball." He nodded at the orb, then studied her face and didn't particularly enjoy the fact that she hadn't met his gaze since she'd pulled the thing from her jacket pocket. "And something else."

"Yep."

"Something that *kinda* felt like your magic but not."

"I said we covered that part, Brigham. So now we're brainstorming for *new* ideas."

"And it doesn't…" He sat back in his chair, crossed one leg over the opposite knee, and leaned sideways in barely concealed discomfort. "It doesn't worry you that we have no idea what that was or how it's even possible?"

Pressing her lips together, Halsey stopped turning the orb in her hands and finally looked at her cousin. "I don't think figuring out *what it is* should be at the top of our priority list right now. Knowing isn't gonna help those people any faster. I'd go so far as to say it's one of the best ways for us to waste our time here. And everyone else's."

"Right. I mean, sure…"

"So it can wait 'til we've finished our mission here and get back home."

"Probably, yeah." Brigham waited a few seconds, then sucked in a sharp breath and straightened in his chair. "Except we don't know shit about that thing, Hal. Or what it's doing to you. What if you get through half of those people out there and find out it's killing you or something?"

The tense pause after that made them both extremely uncomfortable, especially when Halsey's attention was focused on her cousin while he only seemed able to stare at the copper orb in her hands with something close to hatred behind his eyes. "You don't want to involve this thing at all, do you?"

"Of course I don't."

"Brigham, this is the only way to do what needs to be done."

"Yeah, I get that. But I don't..." He shifted uncomfortably in his chair again and shook his head. "Can't you at least put it away so I don't have to look at it and think at the same time?"

"This?" Halsey lifted the ball from her lap and held it across the table toward him. Her cousin didn't exactly flinch away, but he did lean farther back with a deepening scowl. "This thing right here? You don't wanna have to *look* at it?"

"Jesus, Hal. Come on."

Staring at him, she deliberately placed the copper orb down on the table so they both had a much clearer view of the thing. Then she sat back in her chair and folded her arms. "The orb stays."

"That's... Seriously. Don't do that."

"Do what, cuz?"

"Don't be petty like that. Not with that thing."

"Oh, *I'm* being petty? Me?"

"Hal..."

She pointed at the copper orb and raised her eyebrows.

"This thing saved our lives. And it saved yours more than once."

"Yeah, I know, but—"

"With all the craziness lately, I'm not even sure we'd be able to do our jobs at the most basic level if I hadn't kept this orb around to use when it was our only option."

Brigham stared at the object of the cousins' long-standing disagreement since the day she'd formed it. His nostrils flared, the lines of his jaw worked over and over as he clenched his teeth, and everything he hated about what that sphere had done to his cousin and what it might still do flashed through his mind in seconds before he finally found something else to say. "The chimera was one thing, sure. But this whole healing-magic bit…"

"Oh, so using it to slice an evolved and incredibly intelligent monster into three different mindless beasts is all well and good, huh? And the fact that it was the only way for us to actually survive that mission is a bonus. No harm done. Slap it on the necessary-evil list."

"That's not—"

"But when I actually use the thing to *save your life*, you know, when everything else our family's done for generations to heal the kinds of wounds that would've left you in constant agony and on the brink of death forever without actually *dying*, it's not okay. Is that it?"

Brigham scratched below his ear and let his gaze drift across the tabletop. "Wow. You've reached a whole new level of taking this personally."

"Of *course* I'm taking it personally!" The sharp jab of her voice was louder than she'd intended, and Halsey drew another deep breath to calm the storm. "Sorry. I'm not pissed at you."

"Well, that's good." Her cousin snorted. "'Cause I haven't done a damn thing."

"Except try to convince me that what I *know* will work for us is some excuse I invented to rattle the status quo. You might as well tack on that I'm *crazy* if I think any good can come of using this orb and my new magic to get the job done so we can go home with one more successful mission under our belts. Right?"

That made Brigham look sharply up at her, and now his visible distaste for the copper orb had morphed into a pained frown. "I never said you're crazy, Hal."

She took another deep breath and had to break away from his gaze. "Not yet, maybe."

"Don't." After turning his chair toward the table again so he faced her fully, he scooted closer and leaned forward. Then he rested a hand on the table between them as if he'd meant to lay it over hers but was too far away to make contact. "Don't lump me in with the rest of the Council. After Turkey, then Meemaw finally spilling the beans, I told you where I stand. I'm behind you, Hal. I *believe* you. So don't turn this into an emergency Council meeting where we're the only ones who showed up, okay?"

Halsey's heart sank. *Don't jump the gun here, Halsey. This is your best friend, not Arthur or Beatrice or even Dad. If you need to be pissed, don't turn it onto the only person who's out here slogging along through the muck with you.*

"You're right." She closed her eyes and nodded with a sigh. "There's no reason for me to jump down your throat like that."

"Oh." Brigham scratched the back of his head again and fixed her with a self-conscious smile. "Thanks. And hey, it's fine—"

"Not really, man. I know that. You're not the Council, and you've been right here with me the whole time for every screwed-up mission, so…" She shrugged. "I won't do that anymore."

"Huh." Her cousin stared at her with such vapid surprise that it almost felt like they were about to get into a confession party right here in the conference room.

Hell, we have to have that conversation sooner or later. If he's been keeping a few things from me, too, that'd make me *feel a whole lot better about all the other little things I still haven't made the time to tell him. Talking werewolf alphas. Arranging secret meetings with Yusuf Aydem that never actually happened. And I'll tell him eventually. Now's not the time, though. We have at least half an English village to heal.*

"Brigham?"

He blinked before shaking off his surprise and trying to cover it up again with another chuckle. "Yeah."

"We good?"

"We're always good, Hal. A-Team. Water under the bridge, yeah? I'm willing to forget all about it if you are."

"Okay." Nodding slowly, Halsey looked back down at the copper ball resting in front of her on the table. "I still need you to be okay with this, though."

"With…" Brigham glanced at the orb, then immediately met her gaze again as if he'd been trying not to look at the sun.

"With the creepy magical ball." Using his personal phrase for it made her huff out a laugh. "I know you don't like it. I know it freaks you out. But I also know it *works*. It worked for the chimera, it worked on your barghest wound, and I don't think we have any other options if we wanna make this a clean sweep before heading home."

"Right. Yeah. Ending a mission with one dead monster and telling the Council we left behind a whole little village of normie civilians laid up with a near-deadly supernatural disease that won't actually kill them…" Brigham snorted. "Probably won't help our case from here on out."

"Yeah, my one and only suspension was already one too many for me. And honestly, if we screw up now when the Council's still way too tense about the Blood Matriarch being back and all the monsters changing up the rules, I'm guessing a suspension is probably the *lightest* punishment they could cook up for no real reason."

"Whew." He shook his head and playfully rolled his eyes. "Halsey Ambrosius would hate to have an unsuccessful-mission blackmark on her record, wouldn't she? The thought just…makes me shiver."

"All right, smartass. The point is they're still not totally on board. Not with everyone we know and what we might actually be able to *prove* sooner than later. But we can't go home again with any loose strings still left out here." When her cousin shot her a pointed look, she couldn't help another small smile. "I know. Even when *they* sent us out here with bad intel and a useless healing potion they fully expected us to use."

"I get it. Trust me." Brigham grabbed the leather purse, opened the flap, and drew one of the potion vials halfway out to study it. "But it's not only about a successful mission and keeping the slate clean until we can figure out a better way to, you know, handle all this. Right?"

He nodded at the copper orb again, but Halsey knew he was referring to all the changes in magic and the rules of supernatural engagement that had so quickly appeared with the Mother of Monsters' return.

Halsey spread her arms. "I may make a few decisions here and there that make me *seem* off my rocker, cuz. But I do have a conscience."

That made them both laugh, and Brigham nodded again. "Just another new thing to get used to without warning."

"What, that I have a conscience?"

"That a monster-hunter would need a conscience out in the field." He slid the ineffectual potion vial back into the purse, then pointed at her. "I know that was a big thing for *you* before Ireland 2.0 and the silverback alpha."

Halsey grimaced. She didn't think now was the right time to bring up all the reasons why her first monster-kill hadn't changed her mind about killing monsters in general. Especially when it turned out that a select few of them could actually talk. Or at least one of them could.

"You're the only person I know who ever had an issue with taking them out. You know, for good." Brigham shrugged. "I'm not questioning your morals, Hal. Promise. And I'm with you on this. We can't leave all these people behind and wash our hands of the whole thing just because I don't like that freaky bookend of yours that tears monsters apart and pulls magical sickness out of people. Not in the state they're in right now, anyway."

"Thank you." She fixed her cousin with a grateful smile,

but now that he'd brought up the orb again, he once more found it nearly impossible to look away.

"And I mean, I really, *really* don't like it."

"Oh, yeah. You've made that abundantly clear."

Brigham kept staring at the orb a moment longer, then sat back in his chair, folded his arms, and made a grand show of drawing his gaze up from the copper ball to his cousin's face. Then he tapped his lips thoughtfully. "So…" His voice cracked, so he cleared his voice and tried again. "So. How are we gonna heal all these people with your fun new abilities and make them think they're drinking some kinda state-of-the-art new medicine at the same time?"

"Good question. Which would've been helpful to ask *before* I had to point out what a giant complication that is—"

"Yeah, yeah. I went overboard and took it too far. Won't happen again." He waved her off, then stroked his hairless chin and gazed at the opposite wall. "Focusing on how bad the problem is never helped anyone, Hal. Time to look for *solutions.*"

"Right. Solutions." Halsey's gaze dropped to the leather purse of potion vials one more time, and she narrowed her eyes. "I think I have an idea."

"For real?"

"For real *maybe*. But we're gonna need a few more supplies."

CHAPTER TEN

The healthy, physically capable citizens of Coningsby were only too happy to jump into action when they heard their "new special guests" needed their help with gathering supplies. Of course, all the requests and instructions went through Remus Hornbull, who looked beyond relieved when Brigham finally emerged from the conference room to tell the man that the Ambrosius cousins were fairly certain they'd come up with a solution for the village's lingering-wound problem.

"But we'll have to test it first. So don't start telling people that we've got it all taken care of or that this is gonna work one hundred percent." Brigham peered around the corner of the open door to see several villagers fixing their intent and hopeful gazes on him. "Better yet, don't tell anyone this has anything to do with the cures, all right?"

"Of course." Remus swallowed several times and realized he'd been wringing his hands since the moment "Agent Ambrosius" had opened the conference room door.

He jerked both hands down by his sides. "Purely out of curiosity, though, Agent. Won't a full list of the supplies you require make that clear?"

The young elemental broke into one of his wide, cheesy grins and clapped the acting chairman on the shoulder. "That right there, Remus, is where you're letting your vast intellect and vivid imagination run the show for you."

"I-I'm sorry?"

"It means no. Because what we need delivered to this conference room is actually surprisingly simple. Now, I know what you're thinking. Two American agents requesting supplies from the local folks? It's bound to be difficult, over-the-top, and hard to fulfill. That's not the case, Mr. Chairman. I can tell you right now that any man —or woman—who asks for more than they need might not be able to get the thing done they're saying they need it for. Understand?"

"Sure. Sure." Remus amicably nodded as Brigham clapped his shoulder again, this time without letting go. He looked into the younger man's eyes and leaned closer, lowering his voice almost to a whisper. "So, then…what *do* you need?"

Still grinning, Brigham whipped a folded piece of lined paper from his pocket, the edges on one side lined with paper shreds from where he'd ripped the page from a ringed notebook. "Only what's on this list, my man. Also, have your people do a double-count of all the patients lying in these beds. Triple-count is even better. We don't wanna leave anyone behind when we divvy out their medicine, right?"

"Absolutely not. What a horrid thought." Remus took

the paper in a limp hand and stared at it without bothering to unfold it or read the list. "So I have this right, Agent. You and your cousin... You *do* believe you can replicate enough of this cure for everyone affected by it, don't you?"

"We're feeling optimistic right now." Brigham released the man's shoulder and pointed at the paper. "We'll feel even *more* optimistic when everything's been checked off that list the way we wrote it down."

"Naturally, yes." Only then did Remus realize he had an opportunity to read the actual list and ask any questions about it while he still had the "agent's" attention. He did so, scanning the contents as his lips moved silently.

But Brigham had already noticed that several of the villagers hiding out in their own makeshift recovery center were now staring at him. These weren't the same people who'd been casting him hopeful looks as he spoke with their chairman. These people were the ones who'd been tending to their friends and loved ones over the last several days. The looks they gave him now were devoid of hope and eagerness. In their place were suspicion, distaste, and condescension.

Yeah, if we don't make this quick, we're gonna have an angry mob on our hands. Even with half of 'em in bed, they could still do serious damage.

"This is...very simple indeed," Remus exclaimed before pointing at the list. "I see why *this* number has to be exact, but—"

"Make sure it's all *glass*. Or at least see-through, right? Unless someone can drum up medical-grade equipment for ultimate precision, we're gonna eyeball it."

"Are you sure that's wise? Only in dealing with dosage specifications, of course."

"Yeah, with this kinda thing, a good visual estimate does the trick. Plus, I never did say I was a doctor."

"True…"

"Just tell people to knock on the door when they're ready to drop it all off for us." With another nod, Brigham started through the open conference room door.

"About this last item, Agent?"

"Yeah?"

"Well…" Remus' face reddened. "It's just that four American-style cheeseburgers seems awfully irrelevant to the task at hand."

Brigham made a show of looking appalled by the man's suggestion. He took two steps out of the doorway so he could dip his head toward Remus and quietly converse with the man. "Irrelevant to the *antidote*, sure. But my cousin and I are the ones manipulating the recipe in as many different ways as it takes for us to get this right, Remus. Hard thinking and a village of scared, angry, hurting people all waiting on us tends to be a bit of an energy-drain, know what I'm saying?"

"Of course. But if we can't manage to *find*—"

"Go with the next best thing, Remus. Halsey and I haven't refueled since we got off the plane on this side of the pond, and that was this morning. Don't want either of us passing out on the job, do ya? Good man. I'm willing to sacrifice four American-style cheeseburgers for whatever your hospitable little community can rustle up for us."

Remus lifted his chin and eyed the younger man sidelong. "Meaning…you're hungry?"

"Meaning we're hungry." Grinning again, Brigham scanned the recovery center and caught sight of a woman in jeans and a puffy sweater staring back at him as she briskly weaved through the rows of beds that held all the barghest's victims of Coningsby. Not wanting to be caught in an open conversation with a high chance of turning into a question bombardment he couldn't possibly field, Brigham flicked the list in the acting chairman's hand and headed back through the door. "Ball's in your court now, Remus. The faster your people can bring us everything on that list, the faster all our lives can get back to normal."

"Which couldn't come too soon. Oh, Agent. In terms of—"

"We trust you, Remus." Brigham shot him a quick thumbs-up before slipping fully through the door. "You're the best man for the job. You got this."

"But…"

The door shut with a firm click, then Brigham spun around, pressed his back against the door, and heaved a sigh.

Halsey looked at him from her new seat in the room, which happened to be cross-legged in the center of the conference table instead of another chair. She raised her eyebrows. "Problem?"

"How hard is it to read a simple list and understand what it says? Check off the boxes, and you're done, right?"

"I thought you liked Remus."

"What? I did. I *do*." Still leaning against the door, Brigham ran a hand through his hair and sighed again. "I only hope the guy's as thorough in execution as he is in interrogation, know what I mean?"

"Uh-huh." Still watching him dubiously, she stopped studying the copper orb in her hands and set it in her lap instead. "I don't think Remus could interrogate a fly."

He snorted, and she waited for him to spit out exactly what had gotten him into such a rush after he'd sent for the chairman to hand over their supplies list.

"It's the people out there, Hal. The normies." Brigham raised too fingers. "Factions."

"Factions."

"You heard me." He turned to lock the door, then headed slowly across the conference room toward her. "A lotta folks out there want this to be over. By now, everyone's heard about us being here and having something to do with fixing this problem, and that's givin' 'em hope. Some of 'em, anyway."

"And the others?"

"Yeah, the others look like they're ready to kill something. Take things into their own hands and all that. Which is weird, seeing as I can't tell how many people in this village have actually killed *anything* in their lives other than wringing a few chicken necks for dinner or turning their favorite King of the Pigpen into tomorrow's breakfast."

Halsey choked back a laugh. "You know what that makes me think of?"

"I couldn't possibly begin to guess." With a sarcastic eye roll, Brigham pulled the closest chair from beneath the table and slumped down into it. "Enlighten me."

"We get all *our* information from legends about monsters and mythical creatures the world thinks will always be just that. Stories. Obviously, we're the only ones who see them as history and fact."

"Uh-huh..." He picked at the collar of his t-shirt, then waved it in front of his neck to cool off in what Halsey considered to be a pleasantly room-temperature room. "And?"

"I think it's ironic that nobody's ever taken a good, hard look at the way all the *normies* react. One would think the provincial village mob banding together to take out *the monster* is a little contrite. Bordering on overdone."

"Hal. Is there a point?"

She shrugged and picked up the copper sphere again with both hands, dipping her head in a failed attempt to hide a smile. "Just a new idea. I mean, if we're going with *factions* and everything. Want me to find the internet password and start looking up old legends and myths to get a read on *the mob* for you?"

"That's..." He sat up straighter in his chair, eyes wide in consideration, then scoffed. "No. That's ridiculous. You're not gonna find any elementals in those stories anyway, so it won't even help."

A chuckle finally escaped her. "No one's going to kill you, Brigham. Or try. Remus made it pretty clear to everyone out there that we're here to help."

"Yeah, and that's the problem. 'Cause I'm still getting those looks, and don't ask me, 'What looks?' I know you know what I'm talking about." After running another hand through his messy auburn hair, he spread his arms and looked genuinely confused. "I'm a pretty likable guy, right? Not intimidating unless I have to be."

"No, definitely not." Halsey pointed at him and winked. "Unless you have to be."

"Right? Thanks. So what is it, then?"

"Desperate times, maybe?" When her cousin rolled his eyes, she dropped the orb into her lap and cocked her head. "Look, sometimes people give weird looks. Sometimes their looks don't even match what they're feeling, either. I wouldn't read too much into it."

"I don't know about that, cuz. *You* haven't seen any of those looks." Brigham fanned his face a moment longer, frowning at the table's surface. "So…what? Is it the Southern drawl? My perfectly straight rows of pearly whites? The folks here don't like seeing or hearing it if it doesn't look like their everyday normal?"

Halsey snorted.

"Sure. I know plenty of people in other countries like to have a *thing* against Americans, but I didn't think it was that bad."

"Well, at least you didn't walk off a private jet and into the village of Coningsby with your alligator-skin boots and a flashing belt-buckle the size of my fist."

"Don't forget the Stetson." Brigham pointed at her and flashed a crooked smile. "Man, I miss Texas already."

"Right. 'Cause that's totally our part of Texas." Instead of laughing at the exasperated look he shot her, she absently played with the copper orb again. If he'd asked, she would have told him it gave her something to do while they were waiting for their ad-hoc supply order to come in. In truth, keeping her fingers on that shiny metallic sphere was the only thing that made her feel steady. In control. Safe.

Halsey wasn't ready to admit that part of her, the part that felt more strongly connected to the orb than ever, knew she'd been nothing compared to who she was now and what she could do with one little sphere of transmuted magic. Magic that belonged simultaneously to whoever had left all the strange sand behind and to her.

One thing at a time, Halsey. You don't know how or if that's even possible, so don't put all your eggs in one magical basket, no matter how good it feels. Focus.

"Maybe they have a thing against secret government agents," she muttered in an attempt to lighten the mood. Hiding her smile was a lot harder after that.

"Yeah, that's another thing that's rubbing me the wrong way. We let *one guy* draw his own conclusions, and now the whole damn village is calling me Agent. I gotta keep reminding myself to *respond* to it."

Halsey burst out laughing, and Brigham only managed to glare at her a moment longer before he sniggered. It was hard to deny the amusement of Remus Hornbull's unwitting cover story. She cleared her throat. "In all seriousness, though…"

"Oh, goodie."

"I don't think we have anything to worry about from these people. If we'd spent a week here and still hadn't managed to clear things up, maybe. Sure. We just got here, though. Whatever tension you're feeling out there, I don't think any of it is aimed at you. Some people get scared and compliant. Others don't care about anything. Some get pissed, and some wanna get even. You know, enact justice on those responsible." She looked at her cousin and momentarily forgot how much he despised her inexplicably helpful magical tool as she pointed it at him. "That's definitely not you."

"No, the damn *monster's* responsible for—" He grimaced and leaned away from her. "Can you not with that thing?"

"Sorry." Halsey dropped the orb back into her lap, then leaned forward to prop an elbow on one of her crossed legs before settling her chin in her hand. She settled her other hand in her lap across the copper orb because it made dealing with their first normie-inclusive mission easier. "You were saying?"

"Right." He cleared his throat, then leaned back in his chair and crossed one leg casually over the other. "No, you're right. Neither one of us is responsible for how much any of those folks out there are suffering right now. And trust me, I know exactly how much that is. It sucks."

"I'm gonna take your word for it, cuz."

"Uh-huh." Now, Brigham had turned his attention to the hem of his t-shirt and absently picked at the bloodstain that was still prevalent and visible. "The barghest takes the blame. A hundred percent. And if the folks out there have already heard that we're the ones who are gonna set things right for them, which I bet they have, you can damn-well believe they've heard we're the ones who killed the red-eyed bastard too."

Halsey nodded patiently. "Which would make us the effective *secret-agent* heroes."

"Sure. Maybe. But for folks looking to even the score, Hal, there's no monster to go after anymore. Nowhere to aim all that...I don't know. Thirst for revenge or whatever."

"Not a great feeling either."

"Yeah, that one sucks too. I'm just saying...they've got all this pent-up shit making them pissed-off and rarin' to go, and it's gotta go *somewhere*. They'd have a target if the barghest wasn't a pile of ash on the wind right now, but they don't. Because of us." Grimacing, he tugged down his shirt and gave up trying to pick the dried blood out of it, which would have been impossible anyway. "That makes us the next best thing."

She nearly choked again, this time on surprise instead of muted laughter. "To blame for their loved ones being bedridden? Hey, that's a big stretch, don't you think?"

Brigham shrugged. "Hey, I'm looking at this from a normie's perspective."

"And from that perspective, we're the ones helping them put their village and their lives back together again, but it's *our* fault half the town's lying at death's door without ever going through? That doesn't make any sense."

"No, not that they think *we* did this. But... Okay. Here. Let's speak your language for a sec."

"Oh, sure." She chuckled and leaned back, propping herself up with both hands against the table's surface. "I have my own language now too."

"Imagine you're out there on a mission. Halsey Ambrosius the badass, doing all the research and hunting like the best of them. 'Cause, I mean...you are."

"Points for flattery, I guess."

"Great." Brigham shot her a crooked smile, then dove back into his hypotheticals. "You put all this work into taking down some big-ass sonofabitch monster that really needed it. You get to the end, ready to do whatever it takes to keep doing what you do best. Then some asshole with new weapons and all kinds of crazy magic or whatever swooped down in his fancy fucking jetpack and takes the shot before you even had a chance. You can't tell me you'd call it good, pack up, and go home after that."

Halsey blinked at her cousin, trying hard not to laugh in his face again. *He's trying to step into a normie's shoes right now, isn't he? But he can't. He's an elemental. I'm an elemental. Everything we do is done differently because of who we are and why we even exist.*

So she inhaled sharply and clenched her eyes shut. "Brigham, I don't think that analogy works here."

"Sure it does."

"Except for the fact that neither one of us would react like a normie in *any* situation." After brushing strands of dark, wavy hair from her face, Halsey opened her eyes and met her cousin's gaze with a knowing smile. "If that hypothetical situation of yours actually happened, I'd be thanking the guy and asking all kinds of questions about where I could get myself one of those damn jetpacks."

That made them both laugh, and Brigham's worried frown finally smoothed away into his usual carefree expression. "Whatever, man. It was the best I could come up with. Close enough."

"I know what you're trying to say, though. Those people out there could meet us with any number of different reactions to this. The good, the bad, and the ugly, right?"

"You know, there's something unfairly skewed about that phrase." Brigham brushed invisible dirt, lint, or maybe flakes of dried blood off his jeans and scoffed. "I don't get why people use it all the time when two out of three feel like bad news. Kinda cancels out the good, if you ask me."

"It doesn't have to." When he looked at her again in curiosity, Halsey let her smile grow. Now was one of those rare occasions when her cousin needed an extra boost of confidence, and she was the only one who could give it to him.

Feels kinda nice to switch up those roles every now and then.

"Listen, everything about this mission is new," she continued. "The barghest acted like it was supposed to. More or less."

"Minus the standing upright on two legs, yeah."

"Right. Still, it was an easy kill that we were honestly overprepared for. Florence's potion didn't work, which is probably a first in the history of our aunt's potion specialty. That recipe's been the go-to for generations. Since we're already the ones rocking the boat for the whole Clan, it's probably best that we're the ones who took this mission, right?"

Brigham clicked his tongue in indecision and grimaced as he gestured toward the door. "Yeah, but the *normies*, Hal."

"I know. There's no precedent for talking about monsters and magic right out in the open with all the locals, let alone while we're right in the middle of doing our jobs. But hey." She shrugged and shot him the same kind of crooked smile her cousin wore when he was about to crack the same kind of wry joke. "If someone's gonna blaze a trail, it might as well be us. You and me. Super A-Team…"

Hearing her use the unofficial name he'd been trying to push for months against Halsey's refusal to accept it made Brigham perk up. He laughed, then paused when a new thought hit him. "Like you said, no precedent for it."

"Right."

"Like with everything else we've seen in the last few months. But what if…" He puffed his cheeks and exhaled a massive sigh. "What if it's not only this mission? With all the normies talking about monsters and us having to…you know. Pretend to be something we're not?"

The fact that he'd even voiced the question lent gravity to the situation on a much broader scale.

The Council wasn't anywhere near ready to talk about all the rules of monster-hunting as we know it changing right in front of their eyes. If they can't handle that, how the hell are they gonna prepare for any of this going public in the eyes of all humanity?

After spending another long moment in silence, Halsey slowly shook her head. "I honestly don't have an answer for that, cuz."

"Hell. Me neither."

"But I *do* know that if it ever comes to that, we'll handle it like we always do. One step at a time."

With perfect timing, Brigham's stomach released an enormous growl, and he pressed a fist against it before turning in his chair to face the door. "Our next step better be the closest thing we can get out here to two everything cheeseburgers."

CHAPTER ELEVEN

To both their surprise, the Ambrosius cousins didn't have to wait much more than half an hour after that before another knock came at the door to the conference room.

"Come in," Brigham called, grinning and batting his eyelashes as he looked over his shoulder.

The door slowly opened, and Mauve poked her head through the small opening to blink in surprise at the newcomers. "*Agents*, is it?"

"Hi, Mauve." Halsey had slipped off the table and started slowly pacing around the room about halfway through their wait. Now she quickly headed toward the woman who'd pulled them from exposure in the middle of the street and brought them here for safety.

"You might have told me *that* at the start," the woman replied, clearly in a huff about having been left in the dark. "I had to hear it from Chairman Hornbull hisself instead. Made me look a right emptyheaded fool, it did."

"Sorry about that." Halsey finally reached the door and forced herself not to look at her cousin still sitting in his chair. Otherwise, they'd both start cracking up. "It's not generally something we go around telling everyone we meet. And we had to be sure Coningsby's person in charge was aware of the situation and our roles here before we opened up a few more little details for discussion. You understand."

"Aye." Mauve scrutinized the younger woman, and though her disapproving scowl remained, it had at least softened. "But hear you me, Miss. I don't walk around my own village calling myself *just anyone*."

"Of course not, Mauve." Brigham stood fluidly from his chair and joined them, his toothy grin flashing in the overhead light. "You're the person who found us and brought us here. And I know for a fact that we never would've found this place in the middle of a beautiful though unfamiliar village like this one. So can I be the first to say thank you so very much, Mauve? We owe that much to you, at least."

"Aye. At least." The middle-aged woman gave him the same once-over she'd given Halsey. Even if she wasn't still thoroughly upset with Coningsby's newest strangers, she clearly still wanted to continue her dubious scowling to make sure her point hit home. Yet when Brigham finally reached their closed-quarters gathering, all grin and confident swagger, Mauve couldn't help but break into a proud little smile. "Be that as it may, I humbly accept your gratitude, Agent. Both of you."

"Great." Halsey smiled politely, waiting for the woman to explain why she'd approached them. Yet the dried bloodstain on the bottom of Brigham's shirt caught

Mauve's attention, and she couldn't stop staring. "Is there something we can help you with?" Halsey pressed.

"Hmm? Oh, aye. I stopped by to inform you lot that Chairman Hornbull has a team all pitched together to get you those items on that list. Cavalry should be here any minute."

Brigham snorted and dipped his head, pressing a fist against his mouth.

"That's fantastic, Mauve," Halsey replied for both of them. "And so fast, too. Thank you."

"Aye, well..." The woman's cheeks colored with a warm flush of pleasure before she flashed another genuine smile. "Anything we can do to help two distinguished agents such as yourselves, coming all this way to our little—"

Outside the door, someone shouted incomprehensibly, followed by the tinkle of glass knocking against glass and a communal gasp from several other voices.

"Oh! Those addle-brained..." Mauve's scowl returned, and she spun without another word, leaving the cousins standing there in the semi-open doorway.

The elementals exchanged a look of confusion before Brigham shrugged. "Should we go help them with whatever that is?"

"I mean..." Halsey paused when Mauve's voice took on a demanding, matronly tone as she shouted instructions. "Sounds like it's pretty much being taken care of, right?"

They listened a moment longer, then he scoffed. "Wouldn't want to run across Mauve's bad side when she's in her element."

"I guess not."

As soon as she'd said it, Halsey quickly backed away from the door swinging open in front of her.

"In here," Mauve called brusquely through the doorway, waving her arm in a circle like a traffic cop rolling drivers through an intersection. "Everything in those boxes goes right in here. That's it, Harold. Ethan, there you go. Right through here—no, no. Charles! I said *carefully*. I will come right after you for carelessness like that, I will. You'd best shape up before anyone else sees how roughly you've…"

The woman stopped when she noticed both Ambrosius cousins staring at her from inside the conference room, then broke into a self-conscious smile. "They do their best, Agents. Honest, they do. Can't blame simple folk for being what they are…oh. Right in there. Mm-hmm."

The first man to enter the conference room, presumably Harold, staggered under the awkward weight of a large cardboard box he could barely balance in both arms. He looked the same age as Mauve, though where she was talkative and boisterous, he was silent. Moving slowly, he headed past the cousins toward the conference table, glass clinking inside the box. He set the whole thing down as cautiously as if a bomb were inside. Then he lifted both hands as if telling the box to stay, sighed, and turned around. Brushing off his hands, he stepped aside and nodded at the cousins. "Agents."

Brigham returned the nod. "Thank you."

A line of three more men, two around Harold's age and the youngest in his early twenties, made their slow, careful way into the room to set down boxes that looked like Harold's. Each of them carefully ensured their cargo was situated on the table before clearing the room with a nod and a murmured, "Agents," directed at Halsey and Brigham.

As soon as they'd left, a boy of about thirteen tried to scurry into the conference room, though his haste was barred somewhat by the two five-gallon jugs of water he hauled along with him, one dangling by its plastic handle in each hand. The kid hurried as fast as he could across the room, huffing and grunting. His predecessors had filled the closest half of the table with boxes, so he was forced to slog to the opposite end before finally finding a clear spot to lug the water onto the table. Each jug made an echoing, watery *thump* when it came down, jostling the boxes and rattling the glasses inside.

"Connor May!" Mauve shouted from the other side of the doorway. "If you break a thing clomping around like that, I'm charging you double on your scones until you make up the difference."

"Yes, mum. Sorry." The kid backed away from the table, then tried to scurry out of the room without meeting anyone's gaze.

Brigham leaned toward Halsey and murmured, "Guess there was no point in telling him to leave it on the floor, huh?"

She elbowed him in the ribs, making him chuckle, and the Connor kid paused in front of them to look at the foreign newcomers with wide eyes.

"Are you *really* secret agents?" he asked with an eager hopefulness.

"Don't badger them to kingdom come, boy," Mauve barked, waving the kid urgently toward her. "These esteemed folks have important work to do. Leave them be."

Connor averted his gaze again and hurried after the woman who'd either been appointed the task or taken it upon herself to bark orders at everyone.

After he'd cleared the room, Mauve finally entered, wringing her hands. "That's everything you asked for right there, loves. *Agents*. Excuse me." A nervous giggle escaped her. "All of it clear glass, like you said. Or mostly clear. Some of those are even antiques!"

Brigham widened his eyes and turned toward his cousin with exaggerated surprise. "*Antiques*. Well, didn't we hit the jackpot?"

Halsey ignored him and nodded at Mauve. "Thank you, Mauve. This is perfect."

"Of course. Will you be needing anything else?" The woman looked between the cousins, eager to serve the two foreigners she'd previously thought of as fools for running around the village through the open, deserted streets.

Trying not to pat his still-growling stomach, Brigham wobbled his head and managed to look incredibly apologetic. "Well, there *was* one more thing on the list I haven't seen come through here yet."

"Oh. Oh, dear. What did I miss, Agent?"

"Four things, if we're getting technical."

"Oh! Of *course*. You two must be absolutely ravenous." Mauve spun and peered through the open door. "Katherine should be here with your meal in a quick shake. Oh, where *is* that girl? I told her to hurry it up with all the—Katherine! Over here!"

The woman waved her arms wildly, practically hopping from foot to foot in her attempt to get the other woman's attention. From across a room full of wounded, weak, near-death villagers not making much movement or noise, it was easy for young Katherine to find the excited Mauve hopping about. It would have been impossible to miss even if the older woman hadn't been so remarkably enthusiastic.

"Here she comes, here she comes," Mauve exclaimed, glancing over her shoulder at the Ambrosius "agents" without actually looking at either of them. Then she stepped through the door and leaned forward to hiss, "Hurry it up, girl. Don't make these good people wait like this. Did your mother teach you nothing?"

Halsey pressed her lips firmly together to keep from saying anything. Mostly because she had a strong feeling that speaking up on behalf of any of Mauve's appointed assistants would only make things worse in the end.

Finally, a girl around sixteen with long strawberry-blonde hair slipped through the doorway, carrying a large, sterling-silver serving tray in both hands and trying desperately not to trip. The dishes on top of the tray were each covered with domed lids of matching silver, and it was a lot more than one plate for each of the elementals.

"Go on, girl. Go on." Mauve ushered Katherine into the room, shooing her toward the table. "In and out. Be quick about it."

Katherine shot the "agents" a glance but paused when her gaze fell on Brigham. A deep blush rose up the sides of her neck, into her cheeks, and up to the tips of her ears as she blinked furiously and tried to look everywhere but directly at him.

"Oh, what is it now?" Mauve scuttled after her. "Did you get something in your eyes?"

"This looks great." Halsey stepped forward in an

attempt to relieve the girl of her heavy tray and the older woman's scrutiny. "Thank you so much. We'll take it from—"

"Nonsense!" If Halsey's hands had reached any closer toward the tray handles, Mauve would have made physical contact when she slapped the younger woman's hand away. "You're guests here, you are. And I won't have guests lifting a finger to do what plenty of us are perfectly capable of doing ourselves." She leaned forward to catch Katherine's gaze and widened her eyes in warning. *"Aren't we?"*

"Yes, mum." Katherine dipped her head, then bent her knees in an attempted curtsy that would have already been stiff and awkward even without the added burden of the heavy silver tray and the meal that was clearly much more extravagant than what Brigham had requested.

The room filled with an awkward silence, then Mauve practically shrieked, "To the table, girl! Where's your head?"

"Yes, mum." Walking as fast as she could, Katherine approached the table and tried to set down the tray but found all the available space blocked by either one of the large cardboard boxes or one of the five-gallon water jugs. For a long, painful moment, she oscillated between setting the tray down where it wouldn't fit and trying to find a better place where it wouldn't topple over the second it left her hands.

"You know what, Katherine?" Halsey called with a nod and what she hoped was a reassuring smile. "Why don't you set that tray down on the floor over there? Yeah, right there."

The girl looked baffled, bordering on horrified.

Mauve laughed harshly before shaking a finger at Halsey. "Quite the sense of humor you have there, Agent. Indeed you do." Then she snapped at Katherine, "Put down their food, girl, and let these folks get down to—"

"That's a great idea," Brigham piped up, still grinning.

Mauve spun toward him with her mouth hanging open and now looked as befuddled as the girl with the tray. "You must be joking."

"Naw, it'll be perfect." He nudged Halsey's shoulder with the back of a hand and headed across the room toward the blushing young girl who trembled so violently that the silver dishes rattled against each other on the tray. "We'll have a picnic!"

"A picnic?" the older woman echoed. "In *here*?"

"Sure. You ever eat a good meal on the floor, Mauve?"

"Well I... I don't... It's not..."

"Super beneficial for enhancing brain function. Haven't you heard? No? Ah, I read it in an article somewhere. Wish I could remember where 'cause I'd sent it straight your way."

While Mauve sputtered and tried to collect herself after such an apparently appalling shock, Brigham approached the girl with the tray, grinning the whole time. "We like picnics. Eating on the floor. Gives you a whole new perspective on the matter at hand and a whole new meaning to the term business-casual, am I right?"

Katherine stared at him like a deer in headlights, her blush deepening until the next shade in line would have started to look purple. Brigham reached for the tray, but before he got halfway there, the girl gasped, spun around, and hunkered into a squat to carefully set the rattling tray on the conference room's thin, worn commercial carpeting. Then she leapt to her feet and ran around the other side of the table so she wouldn't have to pass him again on her way out the door.

With a confused smile, Brigham turned slowly to watch her leave and called after her, "Thank you so much!"

"There!" Mauve clapped her hands together, rubbed them, and nodded at the cousins with a firm, businesslike finality. "All settled, then. Now, unless you lot have anything else you'll be needing from *me*—"

"This covers it, Mauve." Halsey returned the nod and gestured toward the door. "Thank you."

"For now, yes. Yes, of course." The woman looked at Brigham without taking the hint that she'd already been dismissed. "And you?"

"Yeah, Mauve, if we need anything, we'll, uh…we'll let you know."

"Yes. Do let me know. I'll be waiting right outside, should the occasion arise."

Halsey approached the woman and placed a gentle hand on her shoulder to guide her toward the door. "You don't have to do that, Mauve."

"I'm quite happy to, love. Any occasion at all." The woman looked over her shoulder to smile at Brigham even while Halsey laid on the pressure and haste to get the woman across the room. "I mean what I say, I do. Absolutely whatever you need, Agent."

"That's great." He chuckled and shot her a thumbs-up.

"We're probably gonna be in here awhile." Halsey exaggerated her cheeriness because it was a lot better than snapping at the woman to leave them the hell alone so they could get their work done. "Not sure waiting right outside the door is such a good idea."

"Well, I won't be listening through the crack in the door, love." Mauve giggled again. "What do you take me for? The village snoop?"

"Not at all. We would hate to take up any more of your time. You've been wonderful, we have everything we need, and if there's something we overlooked or we change our strategy, we'll send someone to find you."

"But..."

"You're an important woman around here, Mauve. I'm sure you've got plenty of other things to keep you busy until then."

"Oh." The woman's hand flew to her chest, and she grinned at Halsey, entirely flattered. "Well, as a matter of fact, I do have several—"

"I know Brigham would *love* to hear all about it when we're finished."

"I would?" When his cousin shot him a warning look over her shoulder, he cleared his throat and tried again with extra enthusiasm. "Of *course* I would, Mauve. You bet!"

"See? Straight from the horse's mouth." Halsey finally got the woman over the threshold and officially out of the conference room, though she half-expected Mauve to spin around and grab the doorjamb with both hands to further insert her authority. "Right now, we need to get to work in here. Quiet. Focus. Concentration. Doing what we do best, and all because you helped us by doing what *you* do best."

"Oh. Well." Mauve was over the moon to hear so much praise. She patted the top of her short, dirty-blonde hair before shrugging with one shoulder. "We all have our strengths."

"Ain't that the truth!" Brigham shouted.

"Thanks for everything," Halsey added urgently. "Time to get to work. We'll see you soon."

The woman was still standing in the doorway when Halsey swung the door shut in her face.

The young elemental stood there staring blankly while her mind tried to catch up with what had happened. Brigham's chuckle broke her from her stunned silence, and she spun to face him before slumping against the door. "Right?"

"Whew, boy." He ran a hand through his hair and chuckled again. "Dearest Mauve could give any of the older Ambrosius alumni a hell of a run for their money, that's for damn sure."

A bewildered smile broke across her lips. "I thought she'd never *leave*."

"I thought she was gonna start hitting people left and right." Shaking his head, Brigham made a beeline across the room toward the silver tray of food resting in the far corner of the floor. "Like Uncle Arthur or even Wallace smacking us around for years and calling it training."

Halsey shot another dubious look at the closed door, locked it, then joined her cousin for their pre-proclaimed picnic on the floor. "Honestly, I think I prefer Arthur and Wallace. Together, even."

He sucked in a hissing breath through his teeth and grimaced. "That's harsh." Brigham stopped in front of the tray and sighed. "That poor girl."

"Oh yeah. She was getting it from *both* sides."

"I'm pretty sure when Mauve's in the room, she's the *only* side." Laughing at his own joke, he lowered himself to the floor and crossed his legs beneath him before reaching for one of the domed lids keeping their meal platters hot.

"Yeah, but I was talking about you."

The silver lid he'd halfway lifted from the platter clanged back down again. "Me?"

Laughing, Halsey sat on the other side of the tray and adopted the same cross-legged posture. "You don't have to play dumb, cuz. It was clear as day. Not that any of it's your fault—"

"What the hell are you talking about?"

His genuine confusion made her stop, and she looked up from the food they hadn't even seen yet to study his face. Then she laughed. "Seriously?"

"Yeah. I mean, what? Do I have blood all over my face, too?" Brigham swiped a hand across his face, looked at it, then dropped his hand into his lap.

"Wow, dude. I didn't know you were this clueless." She reached for the domed lid of the closest platter to her and lifted it. The scent of meat pies and buttered steamed vegetables barreled out from beneath on a gust of steam. With her mouth watering and her stomach growling, Halsey shrugged casually. "Our sweet little Katherine's got it bad for Agent Ambrosius."

"Agent…" His eyes bulged from his head. "What, *me*?"

"Well, it wasn't me, cuz. I can tell you that."

"Hal, the girl's like sixteen."

She picked up a French fry and pointed at him with it. "Again, I *did* say it's not your fault."

"Aw, hell." Staring blankly at the tray, Brigham grabbed

one of the lid's handles but didn't remove it yet. "Now I feel even worse…" Then the heat of the silver handle got to him, and he flung the lid away from the tray with a yelp before shaking out his hand. "Damnit."

Halsey chuckled and unwrapped a set of silverware. "I don't think it's only the teenage girl, either."

"Aw, piss off."

"You didn't see the exact same expression on our friend Mauve's face too? With the blush and everything."

"Feel free to shut up, Hal. Anytime." Wrinkling his nose, Brigham grabbed another silver lid to peer at the food underneath. Metal clanged against metal while he agitatedly searched every platter. "Where's my burger?"

"Hey, they got the fries right." Halsey leaned forward to dip one of hers in a small glass bowl of ketchup. "Everything else looks great."

"Man, I said whatever was closest to a burger if they couldn't swing the real deal. What is this? Meatloaf? Pickled…" He scooped a forkful of the dish in question, then brought it up to his nose for a quick sniff. "Jesus. Pickled fish?"

"I think there's some blood sausage in there, too." She pointed at the right platter with her fork and grinned at her cousin's grimace of distaste. "Hey, *or*… I bet if you went out there and specifically asked Mauve to make you an everything cheeseburger, she'd head right out to slaughter the cow and everyth—"

"Stop talking." Brigham's hand darted across the tray to snatch up a handful of piping hot fries. Half of them fell right out of his hands again, leaving a trail of crispy golden potato cuts across the silver platter. The other half he crammed into his mouth and chewed furiously before his eyes bulged from his head again. "Shit, that's hot."

Halsey laughed and kept eating as her cousin scrambled to his feet in a panicked search for something to ease his pain. "Got a whole five-gallon jug on the table, cuz. Two, if you really need 'em. Good luck pouring it into a cup right off the table, though."

"Jesus, the universe ain't making this easy for us right now, is it?"

CHAPTER TWELVE

Halsey and her cousin ate every scrap of food the people of Coningsby had brought them, and they probably could've eaten more after the day they'd had so far. With nothing left to keep them from the important job of figuring out how to heal half the village with five vials of useless healing potion and the copper sphere, it was time to hit the experiment table.

If they'd stopped to think about it, that was all this truly was. An experiment. Despite not having a sliver of an idea how they would get this done or where to even start, Halsey still knew in her bones that this was something she could do.

It was something she *had* to do. To complete their mission, to responsibly clean up afterward, and to be a decent human being, whether or not she had magic and the entire village of Coningsby didn't.

The only problem was figuring out the mechanics of *how*.

Hoping it would come to her while she set her mind to

some other task, Halsey made an executive decision to empty all the supplies they'd been given and start setting up for one hell of a magical-chemistry experiment.

"And you seriously have no idea yet how you're gonna turn these all into…what?" Brigham finished unloading one of the cardboard boxes and tossed it over his shoulder. It thumped against the wall behind him, spun, and dropped to the carpet. "Carriers?"

"Carrier *solution*, if we're getting crazy specific." Halsey shot him a quick smirk as she pulled the last two tall, narrow glasses from yet another box and set them beside all the others in neat rows on the table. "But yeah, that's pretty much what I was thinking."

"You still don't know *how*, though."

"Correct."

"Which makes you confident in this whole thing because…"

She tossed the empty box under the table at her feet and fixed her cousin with a warning stare. "Because I just know."

He narrowed his eyes, and it looked like he would start questioning her all over again. However, Brigham Ambrosius knew full well the importance of keeping his word. He couldn't even consider making a convincing argument for having forgotten his promise to his best friend and mission partner. Halsey had been right all along about the Mother of Monsters' return, the surprising reality of the stories they'd grown up on that had turned out to be true, and the connection between those stories and the wacky changes in monsters over the last few months.

In return, he'd promised not to question the how or the

why of anything his cousin simply *knew*. Today, he was keeping his promise.

"Okay." With a casual shrug, he pulled the final box of glasses toward him and started to unload its contents.

Halsey turned her head slightly away from him and watched her cousin sidelong. "Okay?"

"As long as you tell me what you need me to do. Would I *love* to be in the know about every little step of the process? Hell yeah. But I can't read your mind or anything. Not yet, anyway. We'll see what happens."

With a light chuckle, she pressed her fingertips down on the surface of the table in front of her. "Brigham."

"Yeah." When she didn't immediately say anything, he looked up from his work to find her grinning at him. "What? What's wrong with you?"

"Thanks."

His eyebrows waggled as he searched her face, then he shrugged again and returned to his work. "If you want my help, you can't expect me to *know* what comes next. 'Cause *I* didn't get hit with the crazy-as-hell-new-magic bug. Open communication, cuz. That's always the key. You bark an order at me, I salute back with a crisp, 'Yes, sir,' then we throw this magical double-potion spaghetti at the sick villagers and see what sticks. Not our usual MO, I know, but it still has a certain *je ne sais quoi…*"

Snorting, Halsey twisted off the lid of the first five-gallon water jug with a *crack* and peeled off the plastic. "I don't bark orders."

"Not when it's calm like this. Only under duress."

She chucked the plastic top at him, and he ducked out of the way with a wild laugh. Then he nodded at the five-gallon jug and failed in his attempt to look instantly and perfectly serious. "You gonna try your hand with that bastard or what? Give it the ol' heave-ho?"

"I'll heave-ho *your* ass right outta here if you don't cut it out."

"Oh, so it's serious business time." He cleared his throat, rolled his shoulders back, and wiped all expressions off his face. "No jokes. No laughs. Work good. Fun *bad.* Got it."

Halsey gestured toward the mouth of the open jug and raised an eyebrow. "Just like New Hampshire, right?"

"Huh." Her cousin crossed his arms and stroked his hairless chin. "New Hampshire. Sorry, Cap'n. Remind me how that one went again."

"Okay. You made your point, and I've made a note of you blindly following me into something neither of us understands, with only unwavering faith in your favorite cousin to back us up. Can we cut the shit?"

Brigham released a noncommittal hum and scrunched up his face.

Rolling her eyes, Halsey ignored him and turned her focus instead on the water jugs.

Even before she'd finished stretching her hand toward the mouth of the plastic jug, her magic had surged ahead of her to search for the life force within all the water sitting there between the cousins. Faster, more eager, more powerful than she'd intended or even been aware of, Halsey's magic hooked itself onto the special elemental flavor of manipulating water, and only after she'd finished reaching toward the open vessel did she pause to consider how strange that was.

Damn. Okay. Either I've fooled myself into thinking I'm

calmer than I am, or something lit a fire under my magic without telling me. That's fun. And fine, I guess, as long as it doesn't grow a mind of its own and start doing shit without my permission.

The thought was both unsettling and highly amusing at the same time. She frowned, snorted out a laugh, and shook her head.

"Oh, so you're the only one who can make jokes, but I'm not allowed to hear 'em, huh?" Brigham folded his arms in mock insult, then noticed the strange look passing across his cousin's face. "You good?"

"What? Yeah." Her hazel eyes flicked toward his. "Just making sure you're paying attention."

Without waiting for his smartass response, Halsey flicked her fingers and called on the life force inside the first five-gallon jug. The water instantly responded, leaping out of the jug in a delicate arc into the closest empty glass on the table.

"Wow, look at that," Brigham droned in mock awe. "You know what? You're right. It's *just* like New Hampshire."

"Very funny." She drew another stream of water from the top of the open jug and began another wavering, shimmering arc of it into a second glass.

"Just trade out all these glasses for entrance tunnels into a giant boggart nest, and it's basically déjà vu. And you're a hell of a lot more graceful about it this time—"

"Okay, wait a min—shit!" The second Halsey's attention had diverged from calmly transferring water from jug to glass, her magic's hold on the water's life force diverged with her. The last bit of the water stream she'd almost dropped into the second glass shot toward Brigham instead. Except dozens of glasses stood in the way, so the straight shot wasn't all that straight and didn't make it to her cousin.

Three empty glasses toppled in different directions as the water surged across the table's surface, and she leapt forward in an attempt to somehow catch them all with her outstretched hands.

Before she had the chance, all three toppled glasses rose off the tabletop and hung suspended, each of them tilting at various angles. The rogue burst of water launched over the edge of the table and dropped with an anticlimactic patter onto the carpet at Brigham's feet. Halsey caught herself, pushed away from the table, and looked at her cousin.

Brigham's hand extended in front of him, palm up and fingers curled as if he were balancing all three glasses in his physical grip instead of within the grip of his magic. He stared back with surprised amusement, then laughed. "Sorry, cuz. Did I strike a chord with that one?"

"No. Come on." She scoffed and tried to stuff her surprise and confusion under humor, which was usually her cousin's thing. "Unless you wanna go into how much *you* talk when I'm trying to focus. In that case, I'd say less talk, more magic."

Sniggering, Brigham slowly lowered his raised palm, and the three glasses righted themselves and settled gently back onto the table again as if nothing had happened. "Well. I, for one, feel *very* focused right now. And quite magical, if we're being perfectly honest."

"Great. You're coming around." With a hidden smile,

Halsey reached out to the water's life force again and pulled another stream from the jug.

"It's just, you know... Now I can't help but wonder if New Hampshire is another one of your super-hot buttons I get to push from now on."

"It's not." Water streamed from the jug and wavered through the air under her command.

"Really? Well, maybe it should be. 'Cause hey, you're a hell of a lot calmer now than you were when we went after those boggarts. All collected and confident. Back then, you were just another militia operative, running around and screaming your head off while they popped out of those holes like a game of Whack-A-Mole—"

He stopped short when a blast of water struck him in the face, splashing into his hair and around his chin and neck before dripping onto his shirt and the floor.

Halsey laughed. "You're such a little shit."

With his eyes still closed against the gush of water, Brigham opened his mouth, drew a deep breath, and grinned. Water pattered all over the carpet. "Yeah, but I'm the little shit who *knows* he knows how to push your buttons."

"Are you asking for another, sir?"

"Are *you*?"

Outside the door to the conference room inside the Community Hall building, Mauve Connelly tried not to look like a woman snooping on the two very young, very secretive special agents who'd marched so confidently through her village to help the citizens of Coningsby with one major monster problem. At first, she hadn't wanted to believe Remus Hornbull's account of who these foreign newcomers were and why they were here. To Mauve's seasoned and experienced eyes, they practically looked like children.

As she'd listened to the acting chairman's story, which he'd shared only with a select group of trusted advisors and unofficial support staff during this grim interim, Mauve had come to believe that more of it was actually possible. Every person in Coningsby knew beyond the shadow of a doubt that a real barghest had come to their quiet little home, rampaged against the community, and put dozens of lives at stake.

After that, it was less difficult to believe two young people barely old enough to be university graduates had appeared on the main street intending to kill the foul demon and save the village from an agonizing and macabre fate. Perhaps they did know how to heal those strange, unhealable wounds that no amount of proper medical attention had affected one way or the other. If they were actually secret agents sent for what seemed to be a top-secret cover-up, surely they must have been new to the job. Mauve hadn't heard of any agents acting like *that*.

Then again, she hadn't met many secret agents in her quiet little life out here in the English countryside, and even if she had, she certainly wouldn't have expected any of them to be as good-looking as the grinning young man who'd been *so* polite to her since she'd stumbled upon them both in the street.

She'd done her best to get the newcomers exactly what

they needed, and for the most part, Mauve was quite pleased with the results. Of course, there had been a few hiccups. There always was with important work. She thought she'd handled those as gracefully as anyone could have, given the circumstances. Now, Agents Ambrosius and Ambrosius wanted their privacy to work with their materials and reinvent their poison-antidote. To heal the sick and restore Coningsby to full health and prosperity.

They told me to scurry off and do something else as if they wouldn't need me again right away. Pah!

So Mauve had stayed outside the door, standing at attention with her hands on her hips and overseeing the entirety of the recovery center as if she'd been appointed to that job as well. But she didn't pay attention to much of anything in the room filled with beds and all the wounded people lying in them. Because her focus was entirely centered on listening to whatever she might overhear through the conference room door.

Though she'd overheard the young agents diving into the meal she'd had specially prepared for them, so much better than *cheeseburgers*, it was impossible to make out anything beyond muted voices, laughter, and clanging lids. This made Mauve smile because she'd known all along these two young people would much rather enjoy a good home-cooked meal than what they'd requested on that list of theirs. There was no telling what kind of poor excuse for food they'd been sustaining themselves with during their travels. In any event, she had a strong feeling secret agents didn't get many home-cooked meals.

When the sounds of a thoroughly enjoyed meal faded away, Mauve kept her hands settled on her hips and sidled closer to the door. She wanted a sign that these young agents weren't as self-sufficient as they made themselves out to be. A shout, an exclamation of frustration or disappointment, perhaps a dash of hopelessness accompanied by a few tears.

Oh, Mauve didn't relish in the suffering of others, absolutely not. That was selfish and quite detestable. Rather, she prided herself on the ability to recognize the exact moments when her particular skillsets and talents were of the most use to everyone involved.

If tears were involved, that only expanded her opportunities to make herself indispensable. When tears could be wiped away, dried, and forgotten about because of *her*, all the sadness, grief, and hopelessness were worth it in the end.

This was what Mauve Connelly listened intently for, leaning sideways toward the door until she realized how strange it would look to anyone in the recovery center. *If* anyone in the recovery center had spared a sliver of attention for the middle-aged woman known for sticking her nose in all the places noses generally didn't belong.

Nevertheless, she straightened, patted her short hair, then returned her hand to her hip and scanned the recovery center. With no gazes currently fixed on her person, she lifted her chin and sidled closer to the door for better audio.

The only thing Mauve heard was the soft tinkling of glass, a few thumps, and the muffled murmur of the agents' voices without being able to distinguish a word of it for herself. It almost sounded like some of those glasses she'd worked so hard to curate for the village's foreign guests were being knocked carelessly about inside that room. The woman tensed, straining to hear anything else but only coming up with what she thought was laughter.

Certainly doesn't sound like two professionals hard at work on our cure. Never mind how *old they are.*

Frowning, Mauve concentrated so diligently on listening to the odd noises on the other side of the door that she didn't move a muscle.

She also didn't see David Mackleby approaching her until the man was practically standing inches in front of her face, though he stood a good six inches taller, at least.

"Mauve, dear?" The man spoke gently as he dipped his head to catch her attention. "I popped by to see if—"

"Shh!" She whipped a finger to her lips for emphasis, still frowning as her overly kind next-door neighbor stepped back. Then she gestured toward anywhere else in the recovery center that wasn't in front of her and taking up all her attention before shooting him a glance. "Later."

"Oh. I see. Well, I'll just…well…" With nothing further coming to mind, trusty ol' Dave turned and lankily stalked across the recovery center, making another supervisory round of the ad-hoc patient beds.

Mauve paid no attention to the man's shot-down confidence or the utter confusion racking his features.

She was preoccupied with the new sounds coming from the other side of the conference room door. The agents' voices grew louder. There was a loud smack that sounded like a bare handing slapping flesh.

Yet it was the shriek that sealed the deal for Mauve. Halsey's shriek.

How dare *he?*

Boiling rage fueled her, leaving no room for her tendency to curry favor with those holding top-priority positions. In this case, that included two young secret agents from who knew where. Mauve lunged for the door, grabbed the handle, and twisted, only to find it locked.

Luckily for her and for the young woman on whose behalf she was about to bravely intervene, Mauve made it a habit to copy every key those in Coningsby had lent her over the years. Even if that had only been once or twice. She'd done so for this exact reason, and she'd be damned if she stood outside this door and *listened* while the young woman inside was being terrorized in a locked room.

The keys jingled in her hand for a split second. She found the right key according to her incredibly organized key-coding system only she understood, then unlocked the door.

Mauve burst into the room, leaving the entire keyring in the lock and instead brandishing a warning finger. "Now see here, young man! It makes no matter to me in the slightest who you are or what you—"

Then she stopped, frozen in disbelief, because what she found inside the conference room was nothing like what she'd expected.

"Oh shit." Brigham lurched backward away from the table and whipped both hands behind his back. Lines of uncontained water trailed behind his hands as if he were holding streamers instead, and a split second later, a loud splash followed as all the water fell to the carpet behind him.

Halsey was subtler with her own hurried cover-up and brought the water she'd been manipulating up to her face with both hands before splashing her forehead, cheeks, and chin. Sputtering and breathing heavily, she blinked the water from her eyes and grinned at the woman who'd intruded on their private antidote-making session. "Mauve! You…have a key."

Brigham snorted, then tried to cover it up with a fake cough.

"Is there something we can help you with?"

The woman's mouth popped open. "I heard shouting. A-and of course I wanted to make sure everything was… was moving along smoothly for you and your work."

"We're all good in here, Mauve," Brigham replied happily. "Right as rain. Or…you know." His gaze flicked sideways toward a few straggling beads of water floating inches from his face. With his hands still clasped behind his back, he flicked his fingers toward the droplets and tossed his shaggy auburn hair from his eyes at the same time, hoping to distract her from the floating water. "Whatever."

"I, um…yes." Mauve cleared her throat. "I see. I believe I may be a…a bit overzealous at times."

"No problem." Halsey wiped a sheen of water off her face with her jacket sleeve and chuckled. "A nice cold splash to the face helps me think sometimes. Have you tried it?"

"I imagine there's…something of a…" Unable to finish her attempt at an excuse to get away, Mauve threw all polite caution to the wind and spun on her heels. Then she raced back toward the exit, skirted through the open doorway, and pulled the door shut behind her with a violently loud slam. The keys jangled in the lock, and it took her three tries before she finally yanked them from the doorknob and thrust them into the pocket of her long skirt.

It took another few moments for Mauve Connelly to get her bearings again. So she stood there by the closed conference room door, her face darkened by a scowl. Now, though, the woman was disconcerted not by her insatiable curiosity about everything that simply didn't concern her but about something else entirely different.

What did you see in there, old girl? Water flying through the air? A couple of children playing around with who knows what sort of flim-flam while good people are lying out here in their beds?

After taking a deep breath, she lifted her chin and scanned the recovery center once more, which remained entirely unchanged.

"So unprofessional," she muttered, then patted the top of her hair again and took off toward the building's front exit. The barghest was gone, the danger was over, and all she wanted was a good meal and some shuteye in her own bed.

Only after she'd made it there late that night would Mauve successfully convince herself that she'd seen nothing out of the ordinary inside that conference room. It was the stress of her self-appointed duties and the suffering of the whole village filling her imagination with suspicion-ridden fantasies. Nothing more.

The barghest she'd spent hours hearing stories about as a girl was undoubtedly real. Still, there was no such thing as magic.

CHAPTER THIRTEEN

"Think we're busted?" Brigham asked as soon as the startled Mauve had slammed the door shut without another word.

"I don't know..." Halsey stared at the door with an uncertain smile playing on her lips. "But maybe we should focus on, you know, getting this thing done before we do anything else."

"Roger that, team leader."

With a snort, Halsey turned back toward the table, swiped dripping beads of water from her forehead and cheeks again, then returned her attention to the task at hand.

Timing couldn't have been more perfect, right? The second Brigham and I start loosening up and playing around on a mission that's only half monster-killing, in comes a normie to see the whole magical water fight mid-splash.

Thinking about the woman's reaction made her stomach flutter against itself as she and her cousin continued to fill each individual water glass with a magically manipulated stream of water from the top of the giant five-gallon jugs. They worked in silence until she couldn't *not* talk about it anymore. "I feel like we handled that fairly well."

"Oh, for sure." Brigham cleared his throat, finished filling one glass, then stepped down along the table to start working on the next row. "That line about a brisk splash helping the old thinktank? Pure gold."

"Shut up." They both laughed, though she couldn't help but look at the door again. "You don't think she's gonna *tell* anyone about that, do you?"

"Who, Mauve?" He shrugged as another twisting stream of water burbled into a tall drinking glass. "Hard to tell with an old bird like her."

"Dude."

"Hey, I'm just saying. She told us she was the only one walking around calling the *barghest* by name. That she's always known about *that* thing while the others in the village tried to deny it or whatever. If there was ever a time in her life to spout a bunch of unbelievable shit about two secret agents caught in a magical water fight with each other and have someone believe her, it'd be now. You know, while the suspension of disbelief is still fresh in everybody's minds."

Halsey wrinkled her nose. "Kinda sounds like that could pose one more little problem for us."

"Naw, I wouldn't worry about it. Woman like her? She's on top of the world right now, feeling vindicated as hell 'cause a monster finally showed its face, and nobody around her can argue anymore that the ol' gal went a little cuckoo." When he finished filling his final glass two-thirds of the way, Brigham directed another stream out of the five-gallon jug, this time straight into his mouth. He gulped it down, then exhaled a contented sigh. "That means way too much to her right now. I think she's smart enough to know that as long as she doesn't tell anyone, nobody's gonna keep thinking of her as Off-Her-Rocker Mauve."

"Huh. You know, you make a good point."

"No shit."

"Well, look at *you*. Brigham Ambrosius and all his working knowledge of *people*."

He shot her a quick look and chuckled. "I always have a working knowledge of people."

"Except when they're twitterpated by you, right?"

"Nice, Hal. *Now* who's using the old-people words?"

After that, the mood between the cousins had lightened considerably. They were able to focus on their preparatory work, which would hopefully lead to Halsey having a miraculous 'Aha' moment before having to take their fake-healing-potion plan to the next level.

The lightbulb went off at such an unexpected moment that she almost dismissed it in lieu of being a decent person who didn't dirty other people's refreshments.

After they'd finished filling the exact number of glasses as sick Coningsby villagers with water, Brigham withdrew the remaining five vials of green-glowing healing potion from the leather bag. One by one, the stoppers were popped out, and the vials were slowly upended over each glass of water.

"Little bit for everybody," Brigham commented in a singsong voice. "Plenty to go around."

"You know this part is only for show, right?"

"Show and *glow*." He stepped back and gestured toward the closest glass he'd added a few drops of useless barghest-bite healing potion to. Though the green liquid was diluted, it glowed in a way that couldn't be confused for a trick of the light. "Kinda pretty, don't you think?"

"Sure. As long as everybody thinks it's *pretty* and not some kind of biohazard waste that's gonna turn everybody into superhuman mutants…" She leaned over the table to peer straight down into the closest glass to which she'd added a few more drops of the potion.

"You mean like us?"

Her gaze flicked toward her cousin, and she huffed out a laugh. "I guess. But we were born with our superhuman stuff."

"Details, schmetails."

Halsey glanced down at the glass in time to feel a wayward drop of water that had been clinging to her hairline trickle quickly across her temple, beneath her eye, toward the bridge of her nose. Then it was gone.

"Oh, crap." She lurched upright and reeled away from the table, wiping at her nose, but it was too late. The ripples of a single drop of water hitting the fake potion in question still moved in that one glass, and Halsey grimaced. "Awesome."

"What'd you do, cuz? Get too up close and personal with all this magic juice?"

"Very funny. No." She snatched up the glass and lifted it to the light for a closer look. "I dripped in the antidote."

Brigham burst out laughing, clutching the almost empty vial to his chest and furiously shaking his head. "You don't…you don't hear *that* one every day!"

"Yeah, okay. Seriously, the last thing we need is to start dripping water and sweat and who knows what else into these poor people's drinks. They're already trusting us for a cure." Rolling her eyes, Halsey walked down the edge of the table, meaning to set this particular glass aside behind the five-gallon water jugs so they'd know it was contaminated and separated under "Do Not Give To Normie Patients." Before she'd reached the other end of the table, a flicker of silver light illuminated the vaguely green mixture in her hand.

It could have been a trick of the light. It could have been something she only thought she saw because she wanted to see *something*. Anything that might help them make this last phase of their mission legit and successful.

Then again, there was always the chance that what an Ambrosius elemental saw with her own two eyes aligned with reality. Halsey had seen weirder things in her lifetime.

Regardless of what she'd seen or didn't see, that fleeting glimpse of silver had given her an idea.

"Or maybe it's exactly what we need…"

Brigham finally caught his breath with a deep, rasping inhale, then blew it out in another chuckle. "What, you mean the antidote? How astute of you, cousin."

"No, I meant the other part."

"Dripping water and sweat?" He wrinkled his nose. "I've heard a few things from people in food service. You know, once or twice. All hearsay and conjecture, obviously. That's not *our* job, though." When he noticed his cousin standing perfectly still on the other side of the conference table, holding a glass of glowing, potion-laced water up to the light, he realized she was being serious. "Ew. Are you for real?"

"Actually, yeah." Halsey finally turned toward him and lowered the glass so she could meet his gaze. "I think I know how to make this work."

"What, you wanna cut open your palm and squeeze a few drops of blood into every glass too?"

Another joke, but her cousin was getting remarkably close to her bright idea by using humor to hide his discomfort over the whole thing. She shrugged. "Something like that."

"Hal. No. That's disgusting."

"If I was literally considering your suggestion, you're right. It would be disgusting." She set the glass on the table again, reached into her jacket pocket, and slid her fingers around the smooth curve of the copper ball's metallic surface. "I'm thinking we go with something less blood and more…magic."

Brigham was entirely aware of his cousin pulling that damn orb from her jacket pocket to emphasize her point, but he refused to look at it all the same. "No."

"Come on, man. You haven't even heard my idea yet."

"I know. And I *still* don't like it."

"Brigham. You said you were with me on this. Without any available explanation from me, right?"

His gaze roamed all over the conference room, then he released a growling sigh and rolled his eyes. "Damn it, I need to stop promising you shit."

"You know I have to use this thing anyway." She gave the copper ball a shake despite it not being nearly enough to catch his gaze, even by accident. "It's the only way of healing these people that we both know will actually work. We have the proof. What we don't have is time."

Brigham tossed a hand toward the door. "Those wounds aren't gonna kill 'em, Hal. That's the point! That's what that kind of magical wound does. We literally have nothing *but* time."

"Uh-huh. And the more we use, the more we're tempting fate with all things in our secret little world that've gone topsy-turvy in the last three months. So would you rather we do this sooner with a creepy magical ball you don't like and don't have to? Or do you wanna hold off, wait around to figure out a different solution that *hasn't* been proven yet, and give the barghest's poison a lot longer to show us what fun new mutations it can spit out in the next twenty-four hours?"

"Oh, please. Mutations?" Her cousin scoffed, but his confidence had dropped well below its usual reserves again. "We're talking monsters and magic, Hal. You can't throw in a little mutation whenever you feel like—"

"Dude, the chimera grew wings overnight," she replied flatly. "Literally."

His face paled, then he clamped his mouth shut and sighed through his nose. "Shit. Fine. Option A, I guess."

"Which is…"

"Doing this sooner. Now. With that asshole disco ball of yours or whatever the hell it's called."

"Honestly, I haven't found the time to name it yet." The cousins stared at each other in another tense silence until Halsey couldn't keep up the solemn mood after the way Brigham had ceded to her plan. "You know, I actually kinda like the sound of that."

With another heavy sigh, he crossed his arms and glared at her. "Of what?"

"Asshole disco…" She snorted, pulled herself together, then added a strained, "Ball."

He perused her, his lips flickering into a ghost of a smile he didn't want to let her see. He managed to keep a relatively straight face after that. "You're a real piece of work. You know that?"

"Has a nice *ring* to it, don't you think?"

"Seriously? How old are you, four?"

"Same age as you, cuz." Halsey spread her arms and grinned. "Always have been, always will be."

"Then I guess maturity really does have nothing to do with age, huh?"

"What d'ya say, Brigham?" Pursing her lips, she raised her hands over her head and pumped them in an awkward dance with no music to show her the way. "Time for a little Asshole Disco, huh?"

"Stop."

"With the A-Team!"

"Aw, hell. Don't say it like *that*, Hal. That's just—" He grimaced and tried to look away, but now his cousin had turned sideways to give him a full profile view of her butchering attempt at dancing the Running Man. "Jesus Christ. You know that's not even disco, right?"

"Ooh. Big *disco* guru wants to score a few points with Elvis…"

"Totally wrong decade."

"James Brown?"

"Nope." Fervently shaking his head, Brigham stalked around the closest end of the table until he'd reached her side of it. By the time he approached her, her terrible dancing had devolved into Pushing the Cart. "Stop. I'm serious. No movement. No disco, just—damn it, Hal. Cut it out already!"

He'd shouted due to a lack of any better ideas, but a strangled laugh wormed its way into his words as he snatched her wrists in his hands and forced at least her upper body to stop making a fool of itself. Laughing, Halsey didn't try to fight from his grasp. She bobbed her head in a jerky rhythm to some made-up tune only she could hear.

"You know you suck at dancing, right?"

She shrugged, and he released her hands. "You know what I *am* good at?"

Brigham looked her over from the corner of his eye. "Enlighten me."

"This." At this point, she'd sidled up to him closely enough that when she lifted the copper orb under her face, it also happened to be fairly close to her cousin's face.

He instinctively flinched away with a hiss but surprisingly didn't jump across the room or try to bat her hand away. "Really?"

"I'm good at *this*, Brigham. I didn't know how it was gonna work with these potions because I wasn't thinking about it the right way. But trust me, it'll work. If nothing else, I'm good at knowing when this thing is gonna work."

"Yeah, but that's bullshit. You're good at everything else you've ever done. You don't even have to try." He took one sidestep away from her, then sniggered. "Except dancing. We can scratch that off the list."

"I thought we already did. Like, a *long* time ago."

"Well, thanks so much for the reminder." They both laughed as the burden of this mission's final step lifted from their shoulders again, if only for a few minutes. Then Brigham dared a longer, more scrutinizing look at the copper ball and grunted in distrust. "Fine. So how the hell are we supposed to heal all these people with a fake antidote and a piece of freaky magical metal?"

Halsey grinned. "I'll take care of that part. You make sure everybody in that recovery room gets their party drinks."

"So enticing." Brigham picked up the glass she'd set down, gave it a tentative sniff, and brandished the thing like it was filled with wildly expensive sipping scotch instead. "You know, you really have a way with words."

"Bite me."

CHAPTER FOURTEEN

Half an hour later, the last golden filament of light snaked away from the copper orb in Halsey's hands and dropped gently into the last tall glass of liquid. It didn't make a sound as it hit the surface and sank to the bottom of the glass like all the others before disappearing into the greenish glow. The surface of the water hardly moved beneath the final piece of her magic blended with the magic of the sphere.

When the golden light faded, and the filament disappeared into the water, leaving no indication that something extra had been added to the pretend potion, Halsey let herself blink. She released a massive sigh and nodded. "There. That's the last one."

"Damn." Brigham bent over to peer at sixty-seven new antidote tonics on the conference table, his nose inches from the closest glass. "If Mauve was gonna unlock the door and walk in on us, I'm glad it was during our little water fight and not, you know…the last half-hour. A few splashes here and there can be explained, but how do you even come up with a semi-convincing reason for all *that*?"

"We can't." She scanned the glasses covering the surface of the table and felt spread oddly thin. Like a thousand little pieces of her had been scattered on the wind, each of them pulling her in a different direction. "I think this is the last—"

A wave of dizziness overwhelmed her, joined by sudden nausea that inexplicably made her feel like she was about to burst into sobs. Halsey staggered backward, swaying on her feet, and tightened her grip on the copper ball.

"Whoa, whoa. Hey." Brigham leapt toward her and caught her arm to keep her steady. "You good?"

"I'm good." When she looked at her cousin, they were both surprised to find a shimmering layer of unshed tears in her eyes. His face blurred in her vision.

"Uh...that doesn't *look* good, Hal. Is it the disco ball? Does it hurt?"

"No, actually." Blinking back the tears to keep them where they belonged, she drew a deep breath and rolled her shoulders. "Doesn't hurt. There's no pain, I promise. I think I'm just..." Halsey scrunched up her face, trying to put a finger on exactly what was happening inside her now that they'd come this far and only had one more step ahead of them before completing this mission. "I think I'm *feeling* things."

He snorted. "It's called being human, cuz. We may have magic, but otherwise, we're still as human as the rest of them."

"Things that don't belong to me." She met her cousin's gaze again, her vision cleared of the blurring tears this time, and studied his reaction. *He's either gonna brush it off or freak out. But that's the best way I can describe it.*

Brigham stared at her with wide eyes. Then he released her, stepped back, and glanced at the copper orb in her hand. "You know, maybe this wasn't such a good idea."

Great. He went with freaking out.

She shook her head. "That's not what I'm saying."

"I knew this was a bad idea." He backed farther away from her and pointed a condemning finger at the orb. "That thing's a fucking loose cannon."

"Brigham, I said I'm fine."

"Oh, sure. You say a lot of things, Hal, but that doesn't mean they're always true, does it?"

Halsey opened her mouth for a quick retort. Yet someone else's emotional turmoil raging inside her, along with the fact that she was still keeping some hard and scary truths from her best friend, made it impossible for her to say anything.

Brigham must have taken the stunned look on her face as an indication that he'd gone too far because he sighed heavily and ran a hand through his hair. "Look, I'm sorry. That was harsh. I went overboard."

"It's fine."

It took him a minute to look back up at her again, and when he did, she found another surprising mix of worry, fear, determination, and regret all mingling together on his features. "I appreciate that, but I respectfully disagree. It's not cool to talk to you like that. I'm just... Shit, Hal. Making a weapon that looks like a toy out of leftover magic is one thing. When you start feeling someone else's shit that doesn't belong to you? Like actual *feelings*? Unless you tell me right now that's not what you meant, I'm gonna say that's freaky as hell. Not a good sign. You feel me on that, right?"

"Of course."

"I'm not the one *actually* losing my mind, right? Getting all misty-eyed because you're feeling shit that doesn't belong to you… That's a pretty big red flag."

Halsey let a tired smile flicker across her lips. "Some people call it being an empath."

"Ha, ha. So hilarious," he replied flatly without an ounce of humor. "We're talking about magic, and you're trying to write it off as a sudden oversensitivity to other people's emotions? You. Halsey Ambrosius. The badass. Come on."

It wasn't only an oversensitivity to other people's emotions, and both cousins were confident in that assessment. Halsey had known from the moment she'd felt the powerful energy emanating from the scattered piles of sand that the magic inside it had belonged to someone else. Technically, when she'd transmuted the copper orb, she'd been manipulating another person's magic too. Her intentions that day had been only to make the sand easier to transport so she could bring it back and ask Meemaw what it was. Which turned out to be fruitless, anyway.

She'd never intended to grow so attached to the orb or the insane amount of power inside it. The power she wielded whenever she used it.

Somewhere along the way, as she'd used the orb's magic to do what she couldn't have done on her own, her magic had rubbed against the leftover sand's power.

Now they're…what? Connected? The same? Jumbled up until

I can't tell what's mine and what belonged to the person who left the magical sand behind? That's insane.

"Hal?" Brigham had stepped toward her again and set a gentle hand on her shoulder in concern.

She blinked up at him and shook her head. "I'm good."

"Bullshit. What happens if you push this thing too far, huh? We have no idea what that thing is or everything it's capable of or even where it—"

"We know it's already saved our lives more than once," she interrupted, clenching the orb in both fists and intently holding her cousin's gaze. "And we know it can heal all those people out there. My guess is it's the only thing that can, or at least the only thing available to us. I don't wanna go off on another wild magic chase to find another way. We *know* this way works. You're literally living proof of that, which is good enough for me."

"Yeah, but at what cost, huh? Let's be real here."

They stared at each other, and Halsey wasn't even aware of the tears welling again in her eyes or the one that slipped free until her cousin brushed it off her cheek with a knuckle.

Whatever these tears are about, they're not mine. Not really. I've spent a lifetime carrying my family's shit on my shoulders without knowing what it was, either. If I have to carry this too, fine. Maybe it's part of the job now.

"It's not gonna kill me, Brigham," she murmured before a quick sniff and blinking the tears away again.

"That's great and all, but there *are* worse things than death, Hal. I'm living proof of that too."

Halsey nodded toward the conference room door. "Every single person lying in a bed out there is gonna be living proof of it too when we're done. This thing?" She looked back down at the sphere, and while her cousin clenched his jaw in distaste, he didn't back away again. "It's creepy, yeah. I don't understand it, and that can be a wild card sometimes. So far, the wild card's done nothing but help us."

"Until it doesn't."

"I'm not gonna think about that right now, okay? Listen." She took another deep breath to collect herself and felt the roiling emotions that weren't hers ease under her manufactured calm. "I'm the one who made this thing. I'm the one who's using it. I'm the one who's dealing with the consequences of using it, whatever they might be in the future, other than freaking us both out."

Brigham snorted as a tiny smile flickered at the corner of his mouth.

"I know it's insanely powerful, I know it can get the job done, and those are pretty much the only requirements for knowing we *have* to do it. I'm going Spiderman with this thing. My mind's made up."

He frowned and tilted his head. "Spiderman?"

Now it was her turn to let herself smile. "Yeah. 'With great power…'"

"'Comes great responsibility.' Yeah, I get it."

"Oh good." She exaggerated an eye roll and pretended to sigh and relief. "For a second there, I thought I was gonna have to explain it to you. But seriously, cuz. That's what this is. I've got the means and the ability, and I don't think I could keep calling myself a good person if I didn't move forward with this plan and help all those people and finish our mission so we can get back home. Not sure I'd be able to call myself a good monster-hunter, either."

"All right, well, don't take it *that* far. Damn." They both laughed, then Brigham glanced at the orb again before turning to gaze at the glasses of fake potion, each with a tiny, seeded filament of the sphere resting somewhere within. "Fine. You wanna play hero."

"Yeah, that's *exactly* why I'm doing this. Wow. I'm so glad I have you around, cuz. You know me."

"Uh-huh." He ignored her sarcasm in lieu of moving on to the next step in their already precarious plan. His smile faded, and they were back to looking at each other in all seriousness because neither one of them knew what would happen after this. "I'm with you on this, Hal. I don't like it, but I'm with you."

"Thanks."

"Naw, don't get all mushy on me now." He pointed at the orb again. "But when you do this… If that thing hurts you, or blows you up or whatever, or this shit goes haywire faster than we can fix it, you lock that thing up like I wanted you to in the beginning, yeah? For real this time."

Halsey nodded slowly, then held the orb fully in her left hand so she could extend her right hand toward him. "I can deal with that."

"Great." Brigham clasped her hand in a strong grip, and though he held her gaze and nodded as they shook, she still felt a tiny tremor go through him.

What, he can't stand to touch the hand that's been touching the disco ball? Fine. At least he's willing to push through it.

It hadn't escaped her notice, either, that her cousin hadn't listed "emotional damage" with the other items constituting their newest deal. Halsey was fairly certain the copper ball wouldn't act up in a way that would get them or anyone else hurt in the process. Not while she was the one wielding it.

But if I go too far, whatever I'm feeling right now that almost made me cry someone else's tears is gonna get a whole lot stronger than this. Not the worst thing I've been through in my life. And it's not like I'm a big crier anyway. This should be fine.

With another firm nod, Brigham released her hand, then sighed as he turned to face the conference room door. "Okay. I'll go get our buddy the acting chairman of Coningsby. Tell him we're ready to get this show on the road. Get some people in here to start handing out the healing juice."

"Hold on a sec." She tucked the orb in her pocket and headed after him, grabbing one of the glasses of antidote water on her way. "I think we should do a test run first."

"I thought *I* was the test run."

"Yeah, with being able to heal barghest wounds up close and personal. Not from drinking down a fake potion while I take care of the rest from the sidelines. I want to make sure this thing works. And what it's gonna be like for me to heal one person like this."

"Why? You don't think it's gonna work?"

"Because I'd rather not break down into a quivering puddle of sobbing, Brigham. Okay? And that's the whole point of science experiments, right?" She headed toward the door with a smile. "Testing a theory's pretty important."

"I'm gonna pretend like I didn't hear you call this a theory after you've been saying this whole time that you *know* it'll work."

"Cool." With a shrug, she stopped by the door and waited for him to catch up with her.

"And in case you forgot, this isn't a science experiment. This is magic."

"Eh..." Halsey wrinkled her nose as her cousin unlocked and opened the door for her. "Plenty of people used to think science *was* magic back in the day. I'd say it's both."

CHAPTER FIFTEEN

After spending so many hours in the conference room waiting for their supplies, then filling up all the glasses, then hashing out how they both *felt* about the situation, Halsey had almost forgotten how intense the sight of the recovery center was. Lines of beds covered almost every available inch of open floor space save for a three-foot-wide perimeter around the room, allowing those who hadn't been attacked to move freely. Healthy villagers knelt or sat beside their bedridden friends and loved ones. While the stink of decaying flesh and unmoving sickness still permeated the air, Halsey was able to push it all from her mind.

This is it. Putting my magic where my mouth is, right? Showtime.

Before the cousins could get anywhere near one of the as-yet untreatable patients, Remus Hornbull caught sight of them from the front of the room and hastily excused himself from his current conversation with two men whose names he hadn't been able to remember even after speaking with them several times over the last few days. "I'd love to pick this back up at a later time, gentlemen, if we may. Please excuse me."

Then he hurried down the side of the room in his business suit and well-shined loafers toward Halsey and Brigham standing outside the conference room door. Not wanting to alarm anyone, he cleared his throat and raised a hand slightly higher than his shoulder. "Agents. Agents! Just a moment!"

Halsey turned first to see the chairman bustling toward them, his loafers squeaking across the floor as he moved somewhere between a powerwalk and a jog. "Mr. Chairman," she exclaimed with a smile. "Is everything all right?"

"Ah, well." Remus cleared his throat again as he slowed, then tugged on the hem of his suit jacket and fiddled with the middle button. His gaze fell on the glass in her hand. "I could ask you the very same, Agent."

Halsey wanted so badly to correct the man and tell him to stop calling them "agent," but they were too close to the end of this to start clearing up the misconception now. "Everything's fine," she told him politely.

"Is that it?" He looked around them, then leaned closer and lowered his voice. "Is that the cure?"

"As far as we know," Brigham replied with a chuckle.

Remus' eyes widened in horror. "You said—"

"I'm kidding, Remus." The younger man clapped a hand on the inexperienced leader's shoulder and gave him a reassuring shake. "Just pulling your leg."

"I see."

"This is it," Halsey confirmed, slightly lifting the glass for all three of them to clearly see but keeping it low enough that it was less likely to draw attention from everyone else in the enormous room. "But just in case, we'd like to try it on one person first. To see if we need to tweak the recipe, right?"

"I don't understand." Remus looked between the cousins, his frown deepening the whole time. "You said you could do this. That you knew it would work."

"It *will* work." Halsey lowered the glass again and swept her gaze across all the beds and all the wounded, suffering people in them. "We know that for a fact. But to be perfectly honest, we haven't had to administer cures for a barghest wound to so many people at the same time, especially while working with what limited supplies we brought with us."

Brigham nodded. "Believe it or not, Mr. Chairman, Coningsby's a special place. Takes the global record for highest number of victims after a barghest sighting."

The man's eyes bulged before he shouted, "You mean there's—" Realizing the need for subtlety, he cleared his throat and lowered his voice to a harsh whisper that was only slighter quieter. "You mean to tell me there are more of those…*things* out there? All over the world?"

Brigham laughed. "Well, if this were the only one in the history of humankind, the good people of Coningsby wouldn't have known what the hell to call that thing, would they? Where do you think all the stories come from?"

Remus paused to consider those implications, opened his mouth soundlessly, then frowned even deeper when more realizations struck him harder than he was prepared to handle. "What about all the other stories? Trolls? Sprites? The kraken? Are *those* real too—"

"Let's stay focused on the task at hand, Remus." Halsey nodded politely, hoping they weren't about to break this man's mental capacities for a second time. Plus, it would be harder to cover up standing in the recovery center like they were with so many witnesses to the acting chairman's mental deterioration. "If you have any other questions after we've finished our work here, we may be able to answer them."

Brigham shot her a quick sidelong glance and barely shook his head.

"But," she continued, her smile growing tight, "I should preface that by saying the answers to most of your questions are probably classified."

"*Highly* classified," her cousin added.

"We're authorized to reveal whatever information's necessary to garner aid from the locals here. And you, of course." She gestured toward Remus with the tall glass, which made him lean back in alarm before she quickly lowered it again. "It's hard to clean up a situation like this one without offering a viable explanation to those involved."

"And we can't pull out something that looks like a pen, press a button, and wipe everyone's memories," Brigham added with another chuckle. "That's only in the movies."

"Well, that's… I…" Remus clearly didn't have a clue how to respond to such a strange remark from a "secret agent," so he clamped his mouth shut and nodded with a sense of finality worthy of his temporary position. "Very well, then. After it's all finished, and only if you're authorized to divulge information that may enlighten me further. I would…very much appreciate that."

"Perfect." Brigham stuck his hands on his hips and grinned.

They all stood there a moment longer, sharing looks and waiting for someone else to restart the conversation again before Remus finally remembered why they were all here. "Ah, yes. You wanted to…have a go at one of the sick people?"

"Eh, I wouldn't say that's what we're looking for," Brigham murmured.

Halsey elbowed him in the ribs to shut him up, and he fought back a laugh.

"A trial run," she added. "Just to make sure we've hit the right specifications."

"Yes. Of course. Anyone you like." Remus turned slightly and gestured toward the entire room filled with willing participants. "I can't imagine anyone here would refuse the opportunity. Unless of course…" He grimaced and leaned back toward the cousins. "Unless you're expecting negative side effects."

"Not at all." Halsey raised the glass again, but this time, she made sure to do so away from the man to not startle him all over again. "The cure doesn't have any negative side effects."

"Which is why it's called a cure," Brigham added.

"We want to make sure we've gotten the proportions right. You know, that it's strong enough to be completely effective. So we don't disappoint a whole lot of people by having to go back to the drawing board."

"Yes, yes. Excellent idea." Remus stroked his chin,

nodded, then nervously laughed as he gestured toward them again. "Of course it is. You're the professionals here. Shall I call for volunteers? Or perhaps you might—"

"Actually, I think it's better if we pick someone quietly," Halsey interrupted. "Without getting anyone else too involved. The victims here won't cause much of a fuss, for obvious reasons, but I imagine the families might have quite a lot to say about who gets to go first, for lack of a better term."

"Quite right. Yes, quite right. I'll leave it in your capable hands, then, Agents. Again." The man pressed his palms together before bringing his fingertips to the underside of his chin. He stared blankly across the room, running through any number of possible scenarios he might have to deal with as acting chairman should something else go wrong.

Halsey turned toward Brigham, nudged his arm with the back of her hand holding the glass of barghest-venom "antidote," and nodded at the row of beds closest to the small stage on this side of the large room. He nodded, then she took off toward the one victim she'd had at the front of her mind this whole time.

Brigham clapped his hands together, startling Remus from his deep contemplation. "Mr. Chairman."

"Yes?" The man blinked furiously as his gaze darted all over the place. "What's this, now?"

"Just a thought. While we're checking and double-checking our final product to give it the green light, why don't you go call in a group of folks who might wanna help us out with this last part, huh? Halsey and I only have two hands each, and there are a lot more than four cures to carry out of that conference room. The more hands on the deck, the faster we can get all these wounded people what we need, hopefully without anybody's eagerness getting the better of them." He leaned toward Remus and shot the man a quick, subtle wink. "And the faster we can all get back to our regular lives and put this whole thing behind us."

The man's eyes widened, and he broke into a beaming grin before instantly forcing it back down into a semblance of seriousness far more appropriate for the current circumstances. "Regular lives. Normalcy. Yes, Agent, that's exactly the thing."

"Good man."

"I'll find Mauve. She gets the word out better than anyone else in the village."

"Yeah, I bet."

"When you give the word to start handing out those cures, Agent, we'll be ready." Without another word, the acting chairman spun and hurried across the recovery center, nodding and smiling encouragingly to those who met his gaze while he searched for Mauve and any other volunteers he could find to help the Ambrosius cousins hand out their cure.

Chuckling to himself, Brigham turned toward the row of beds closest to the stage and searched for his cousin.

He found her almost instantly, kneeling beside one of the beds in that first row that looked empty save for a bunched, bundled nest of blankets and pillows. So he headed that way to join her, wondering why an empty bed had drawn her attention and how in the world the victim who'd been in it had managed to get up on their feet and walk away.

Only when he approached the bed he realized it wasn't empty.

Jesus, she's only a kid.

The six-year-old girl with stringy hair and bones like a bird had somehow gathered enough strength and energy to look up at Halsey with wide, intensely lucid eyes despite her paleness and lack of strength and the fact that she looked like she was at death's door anyway.

A woman sat on the edge of the girl's cot, holding one frail little hand between both of hers and gently patting it. Tears glistened in the woman's eyes as she stared at Halsey, slowly nodding.

That's what hope looks like right there, Brigham thought. *Enough to keep her going but not so much that her world comes crashing down around her again if this somehow doesn't work out.*

He studied the compassion and confidence in Halsey's expression as she finished explaining to the little girl what they were about to try.

Who am I kidding? Of course this is gonna work. That's why we're the best, right? That's why we're here instead of some other militia team. Nobody else would've tried anywhere near this hard to help these people if they'd been in our mission shoes instead.

A wave of pride washed through him at the reminder of how valuable of an asset he and Halsey were to the Ambrosius Clan, to the Council, to their entire militia. Of how capable they truly were of making a difference. Only this time, they were making a difference in the lives of normal humans and actually being recognized for it.

Don't let it go to your head, man. It's a job. Sure, the praise is nice, but this ain't gonna happen on every mission from here on out. One-time thing. It sure as hell better be.

"So I wanted to ask you first, Makayla," Halsey finished as she held the little girl's gaze. Then she glanced up at the woman sitting on the cot and nodded in acknowledgment. "And your mom too, of course."

The woman returned the nod and patted her daughter's hand again, tears in her eyes and a small, exhausted smile on her lips.

Then Makayla noticed Brigham standing slightly off to the side, and she lifted her other hand from the blankets to point at him. "Mummy, who's that?"

Halsey shot her cousin a glance. "Oh. This is my cousin Brigham."

With a kind smile, he raised a knuckle toward his forehead and mimed tipping the brim of a hat in her direction. "Ma'am."

The girl frowned, but her mom's smile grew.

"Makayla is one of the bravest people I know," Halsey added, speaking to her cousin this time.

"Is she, now?"

"Uh-huh."

"Well, that's saying somethin'." He smiled at the little girl and pointed toward his cousin. "Halsey's the bravest person *I* know."

"Really?" Makayla's voice was scratchy and hoarse as if it hurt her to keep talking through the agony of her systemic supernatural wound. That seemed likely judging by the streaks of black creeping up her neck and halfway up her sunken cheeks to her wide, still-curious eyes.

"Absolutely." Brigham tilted his head toward his cousin, then looked at the girl's mother. "I'd follow her anywhere. And I trust her with my life."

Makayla's mom swallowed thickly but didn't say a word.

"So what do you say, kiddo?" Halsey dipped her head toward the thin girl buried in all the blankets. "Wanna be the first hero who comes out of this thing on the other side?"

Makayla craned her fragile neck to look up at her mother, asking without having to say a word. The woman smiled and gingerly wiped a few strands of stringy, matted hair from the child's black-streaked face. "It's entirely up to you, sweetheart."

"But Mummy, we don't *know* them," the girl whispered.

"True." The woman met each of the cousins' gazes in turn, then grabbed her daughter's hand in hers again. "I believe them, though. I believe in what they're doing. That they can help us. And I believe in you. So there—" Her voice broke as more tears shimmered in her eyes, but she swallowed and quickly recovered herself. "So there you have it."

"Don't cry, Mummy." Makayla comforted her mother with a few gentle strokes of her hand on the woman's arm. She reached out to draw the woman into an embrace before turning toward the Ambrosius cousins. Her glistening brown eyes flicked toward Brigham, then landed on Halsey again. "Okay."

"Okay?"

"I'll do it."

"See? What did I tell ya?" Halsey grinned at her cousin. "Bravest person I know."

"Well, now I'm convinced."

Now that they had their volunteer, Halsey lifted the glass toward the girl's tiny body buried in blankets and held it until Makayla had grasped the drink with both hands. Even two-handed, the girl almost didn't have enough strength to raise the entire glass to her lips. Her hands shook, and the green-glowing water sloshed around. Then she paused. After staring at the cure for several seconds, she flicked her gaze toward Halsey and wrinkled her nose. "This won't turn me into a toad, will it?"

Brigham barked a laugh and quickly covered it with a forced cough.

Halsey exaggerated a sheepish grimace. "Why?" she asked, lowering her voice. "You didn't *want* to be a toad, did you?"

Makayla scoffed indignantly. "Absolutely not."

"Whew. Then we're all good here."

The girl looked dubiously down at the water again, then finally settled the glass against her lips and drank.

It took her longer to suck down the whole thing than if she'd been at the prime of her health, and her mother had to help her tip the glass to get every last drop through her open, chapped lips. When nothing remained in the glass, Brigham reached down to gently take it from her.

Makayla smacked her lips a few times, then grimaced. "It takes like broccoli."

"Well, *there's* a good reminder to always eat your vegetables, huh?" Halsey shared a knowing smile with the girl's mom as everyone had a light laugh about it.

"What do we do now?" the woman asked, looking far healthier and full of vitality herself now that the possibility of a cure had finally been delivered.

Halsey nodded. "Now we wait. Makayla, I don't mean to be rude, but would you mind if I sat right here with you for a few minutes? I'd like to see it with my own eyes when this works."

"I don't mind," the girl replied matter-of-factly.

"Thank you."

"Just don't try to take my blankets."

Everyone laughed again, and Halsey lowered herself off her knees before drawing both legs up beneath her to sit cross-legged in front of the cot. "I wouldn't dream of it."

CHAPTER SIXTEEN

After offering the girl's mother another reassuring look, Halsey inhaled deeply, slipped her hand into her pocket, and closed her eyes.

"Mummy," Makayla whispered now that she wasn't being diligently watched. "She said *when* it works."

"I heard, love. It's good to be positive."

"It's going to work. I know it."

Halsey forced back the new wave of emotions threatening to overwhelm her. That foreign sadness and anxiety she'd felt from the orb mixed with her own feelings around having to heal a kid in the first place. Not to mention being the one responsible for reassuring the little girl's mother and watching them go through this whole ordeal together.

This isn't about me, though. I didn't have my mom. Makayla does. And she'll turn out better for it as long as I can get this last little piece to work the way I want it to.

So she set all thoughts of her absent mother and the compassionate empathy she felt for all these people aside, and she focused on the next steps.

Through the maelstrom of emotions that didn't belong to her, Halsey searched for the energy of that powerful foreign magic not in the copper sphere resting beneath her hand in her pocket but now inside a brave little girl named Makayla.

If she thought about it too hard, it was easy to feel uncomfortable using her magic to feel around inside someone else. The life force of natural elements was one thing. The life force in a living human being was something else entirely. The difference was made even greater by the fact that this child was a regular human, without magic, who trusted Halsey to heal her as much as Brigham, with all his knowledge of the supernatural world, had trusted her.

So don't think about the bigger picture, she reminded herself. *Go smaller. Find it.*

There was no way to tell exactly where the tiny, invisible speck of magic was inside the little girl's body, but Halsey's magic felt it and connected with it all the same.

With her hand tightly gripping the orb in her pocket now, Halsey breathed slowly and evenly, fueling her focus. That way, she was able to move the piece of the orb's magic around, duplicating it, making it grow, making it spread.

Makayla sucked in a sharp breath.

"What is it?" her mother asked in concern.

"I'm hot..."

"Is that a good sign?"

Knowing his cousin was preoccupied, Brigham answered for her. "It could be."

The little girl kicked the blankets off before settling

into stillness again. Eventually, she grabbed her mother's arm and rested her head on the woman's shoulder.

The orb beneath Halsey's hand grew hot again. Not nearly as hot as when she'd used it to heal her cousin, but hot enough to notice. She didn't move her hand, and she didn't stop her healing work because she wasn't quite finished.

Now her magic surged away from her, caught in the grasp of the sphere's power and responding to her commands in the same way. Magic that was hers but not hers. Not elemental, not anything she knew she'd had until earlier today when it had emerged to save her cousin's life. She had to call on it now.

The hand clamped around the hot ball in her pocket trembled.

"Oh my God," Makayla's mother whispered. "Sweetheart, look at me. Oh my God. It's working."

"Well, look at that," Brigham added softly, though the awed approval in his voice was unmistakable.

"Mummy, my leg itches."

"Can we look?" her mother asked.

He chuckled. "It's her leg."

Mother and daughter worked together to free the girl's itchy leg in question from the nest of blankets. The woman gasped. Makayla giggled. Brigham pressed his lips together and said nothing.

"In all my days..." the woman breathed, awestruck.

Almost... Halsey tilted her head, half-aware of the very positive feedback she was hearing while she focused on finishing her work.

Knowing what she knew now about the barghest's

unhealable wounds and the copper orb's effectiveness in curing those effects, this time around didn't feel like nearly as much of an emergency as it had when Brigham was the one lying on the ground and needing seriously powerful magic to make him whole again. She was able to take her time, to pay attention, to learn from whatever this odd new ability was, so maybe she wouldn't be so easily blindsided by what she and the sphere could do together next time.

Then the orb buzzed furiously under her hand, and her eyes flew open in surprise.

Right there in front of her was Makayla's thin, pale leg, the bottom half of it nearly having been destroyed by the monster that had attacked her and put her in this bed. But now, the decaying black edges of the gaping wound had already cleared over halfway. The black streaks racing beneath the girl's flesh from head to toe were nearly gone and quickly fading the rest of the way.

Halsey's eyes welled with tears again. It was finished.

Time to come home...

It was a ridiculously strange thought to have in a moment like this, especially when she realized it was a command given to the speck of magic she'd placed in the little girl's potion. However, now wasn't the time to worry about why she'd thought that.

She had to wrap this up so they would know whether it had actually worked.

Soon, it was perfectly clear it had.

The wound on Makayla's leg had healed to healthy, if still open and bleeding, flesh. The black streaks were entirely gone. The color had returned not only to her face but to her entire body. Her smile lit up the room as she stared at her leg in astonishment.

Then the piece of magic the girl had washed down with a glass of green-tinted water complied with Halsey's command and "came home." Whatever that meant.

Only when she saw the thread of golden, glowing light emerge from the healing wound in the child's leg did Halsey realize they hadn't made a contingency plan for this phenomenon. The Ambrosius cousins could create a cover story on the spot with the best of them. They could make plausible excuses for flying water. They could pretend to be secret agents from a nameless government organization who'd come to fight off monsters and protect the general public in their own homes.

Yet they couldn't hide the glowing thread of magic lazily undulating toward Halsey.

She sucked in a sharp breath and looked at Brigham. He'd noticed the glowing strand worming its way through the air. He fixed her with a wide-eyed look that said everything she was already thinking.

How the hell are we supposed to explain that?

However, Makayla and her mother didn't look like they'd seen a thing. Either they were too caught up in the healing process, which they thought was the result of a top-secret, highly advanced, medically proven cure and not pure *magic*, or they didn't think a glowing thread of light was strange compared to watching a deep laceration seal itself like someone had pressed the fast-forward button on the laws of time.

Or they literally can't see it. The way no one saw the sand or the orb in Dublin. To them, it doesn't exist.

The golden thread slithered over Halsey's lap, then dove down into the pocket where she'd been holding the copper orb. There, it reattached itself to its source. While the sensation was small, a mere drop in the magical bucket, she felt that one speck of the orb's power return to the whole. The weight of those foreign emotions that weren't hers lessened a touch.

She exhaled a long, slow sigh, then bowed her head.

The sphere's heat faded quickly.

At first, no one said a thing.

Then Makayla turned toward her mother, bouncing on the cot. "Mummy, it worked! She was right!"

"How do you feel now, kiddo?" Brigham asked.

"I feel amazing!" The child's shout echoed through the whole recovery center, which caught the attention of everyone else in the room who was lucid enough to hear the cry and recognize what it meant.

Makayla threw her blankets off, then jumped from the cot and barreled into her mother's arms.

"It's a miracle." The woman laughed, tears streaming down her face as she hugged her daughter back.

"Something like that, yeah," Brigham muttered.

The girl's mother met Halsey's gaze as she stroked her daughter's hair and whispered, "Thank you."

All Halsey could offer in reply was a small smile and a nod. Her cousin squatted beside her and murmured in her ear, "You good?"

"Yep."

He grabbed her forearm and helped her to her feet while the quickly growing murmur of curiosity and renewed hope spread among all the wounded patients and their loved ones at their sides. "Good. 'Cause now we need to get this party started before we get ambushed. And the way people are looking at us right now, I'm not so sure a hopeful mob is that much better than an angry one."

"Relax, Brigham," she muttered, fighting not to sway on her feet or let herself be distracted quite yet from the first small victory right there in front of them. "We're not gonna get mowed down by a hopeful mob. Or any mob. But I *would* say now's the perfect time to tell our friend Remus that we're ready for help with the handouts. Because it worked."

"It fucking *worked*," he echoed in a hushed but jubilant tone, his voice slightly breaking on the last word. "Okay, let's get you outta the way. As soon as people start noticing that this is the end of all their problems, you're gonna be one very popular secret agent."

Halsey snorted and let him lead her away from the cot toward the corner of the recovery center again and the door to the conference room. "Speaking of…"

"Uh-huh." Brigham caught Remus' gaze and nodded for the man to start telling his people it was time to hand out cures to all the sick and wounded.

"I'm gonna need you to run interference on that for me."

"What?" He regarded her with a playful frown, then his eyes widened. "Shit, are you okay?"

"I'm fine. Only a little dizzy. Kinda tired. That's it."

When they reached the conference room door, they had to stop beside it. A flurry of activity moved in and out of the open door as the acting chairman's volunteers hustled to grab their two glasses each, deliver them to patients, and return for more.

"Okay..." Brigham watched the activity, then turned his attention to his cousin again. "*Kinda tired* never stopped you before. What's with the request?"

Holding onto her cousin's arm for support now, Halsey chuckled softly and had no idea why she thought this was suddenly so funny. "Because that was from one little piece, Brigham. In one glass. I'm about to heal all these people at the same time without a single one of them knowing it."

"Oh. Huh." He thought over what she'd told him, then clicked his tongue. "Shit. Hey, Remus? Remus? Chairman Hornbull, right. Where is he? Remus! Can we get a chair out here for my partner? Thanks."

Oh, sure, that *won't make anyone suspicious.*

But as she waited for one of the volunteers to bring her a chair so she could sit right outside the conference room and watch all these victims get their "cures," Halsey realized there couldn't have been a better moment for her to feel under the weather and have it go relatively unnoticed by everyone around her.

These people would be so overjoyed to see their friends and loved ones healed and whole again, with life in their eyes and strength in their limbs, that one random stranger from across the ocean who seemed tired and possibly unwell wouldn't be strange enough to grab their attention. Brigham would know, but Brigham was in this with her.

I've given up plenty of other things to be the best Ambrosius monster-hunter out there. What's a bit of my energy and magic, right?

It was all well and good to joke about the personal

sacrifice for the purposes of helping these people and completing their overly complicated mission at the same time. Yet the foreign and overwhelming grief inside her, coupled with the energy it had taken to heal the wound on Makayla's leg, made her collapse into the requested chair the second it was provided.

CHAPTER SEVENTEEN

Fortunately, the volunteers moved so quickly and eagerly that none of the victims had to wait that long for the healing effects of their "cure" to show themselves. By the time the last of the wounded villagers had received their miracle antidote and downed every last drop of glowing green water, Halsey had already started working her magic around, within, and through every sliver of the copper orb she'd delicately added to each tall glass.

At first, the feeling of so many different parts of herself —no, of the *orb*—filled her with a dark elation that would have scared her if she'd had enough awareness to pay attention to it. Yet she was too focused on feeling every filament, knowing every location, reaching out to connect with every little piece that had to be precisely instructed.

The knowledge of how to perform magic like this, to heal dozens of victims all at the same time without touching any of them, came as naturally as her previous understanding of what the sphere could do.

She simply *knew*.

That didn't particularly make it easy, but at least she didn't have to worry about whether or not she was doing it correctly.

With her eyes closed and her hand on the copper ball as she sat in the provided chair, Halsey drew a deep breath and locked onto every piece of the magical signature that would get the job done.

There you all are. The thought was hers, but not *entirely* hers. Like the magic that had healed Brigham and Makayla and was about to heal everyone else was hers but not quite. *Each one of you has a job to do. So do it, then come home.*

It briefly occurred to her that maybe she'd worked herself too hard with this mission, stretched herself too thin by healing two unhealable wounds in the same day, and now trying to do it again with an entire roomful. Still, now that she'd started the process, she couldn't stop.

Not that she chose to continue.

Halsey couldn't stop even if she'd tried.

At one point, she did try. With her eyes closed and her full concentration on moving the dozens of copper orb specks through dozens of bodies toward the source of the magical sickness inside them, the first shout of awe and surprise from across the recovery center sounded like a scream. Several others followed. Then the entire room erupted into a cacophony of voices, shouts, snarls, screaming, and wailing.

At least, that was what it sounded like to Halsey through her concentration.

She wanted to open her eyes, but they wouldn't respond. She wanted to jerk her hand from her jacket pocket to break her contact with the orb but found she couldn't move.

Oh, no. Shit. Something's wrong. I ruined it. I screwed up. This isn't right...

Then she felt the approaching presence of one of those hair-thin, golden-glowing strands of the orb's magic. Even with her eyes closed, she knew exactly where it was as it finally left the body of a barghest victim and sailed back toward its home and its master.

Toward her.

When the glowing thread dove into her jacket pocket like the last one, a burst of overwhelming relief flooded through her. It was small but powerful. One of many, part of the whole. The moment she felt the thread returning, her panic eased.

You're overthinking it, Halsey. Keep going.

She settled into the feeling, along with her inability to open her eyes, move her body, or speak to her cousin. She put everything she had into healing these people with magic that had undeniably become hers somewhere along the way.

Not that Brigham would have been able to hold an intelligent discussion at the moment.

The barghest's victims and their families watched what they thought were the healing effects of the consumed antidote, smiling and laughing and hugging each other because they finally saw the light at the end of the tunnel. However, Halsey's cousin stood awestruck by the sight before him.

Watching dozens of open wounds that had already started to rot reverse the damage of the barghest's poison was unbelievable enough. Then came the smiles, the strength and energy, the healthy color and vitality. He could believe all that. Every villager in Coningsby could believe it after what they'd seen here today.

What happened next was something directly out of a fairy tale, even for an elemental monster-hunter who literally based his life's work on fairy tales.

Thin, undulating threads of golden light rose from every body lying in a bed, drawn from the victims like threads of yarn from a sweater. They emerged from necks, legs, torsos, and arms. The golden filaments effortlessly pulled themselves from the clueless humans, mere whispers on the wind, though the air in the recovery center was as still as it could get.

Flitting above cots, between bodies, and over the heads of villagers hugging and jumping and laughing for joy, all those golden threads converged toward a single location in the far corner of the room. Their pulsing light filled the room with an otherworldly aura.

While Brigham had never personally gone after fairies during his time in the militia, he knew they were real. He guessed walking into a fairy ring looked a lot like this.

Only when the golden threads had all made it to his side of the room did he remember where they were going and why. He backed up in amazement, certain he wouldn't be able to look away from all the lights. But then he managed to stagger sideways and forced himself to look down at Halsey.

She was still in the chair, fortunately. Her eyes were open wide, her lips slightly parted, and her back perfectly straight instead of slumped against the chair in exhaustion like the last time he'd checked on her. She'd taken her hand from her jacket pocket, which would have been worrisome if she hadn't been holding the sphere in both hands, settled primly in the center of her lap.

When did she take that thing out? I didn't see her move.

Clearly, he'd been much too preoccupied with the beautiful sight of hope and life and celebration that had made its way through the entire recovery center and would soon make its way through the entire village, no doubt.

Seeing Halsey now, though, his gut churned.

Shit. We're gonna have so many questions after this. And she wants me to run interference? I can't even lie convincingly enough to myself about that damn disco ball. How am I supposed to...

His mind went blank when he realized he'd been worrying himself for no reason. There was nothing here to worry about.

Half the golden threads had made it back into the copper orb in Halsey's hands, the other half on this side of the room now and following the rest. But not a single villager of Coningsby stopped what they were doing to stare at the spectacle. They didn't even look at the Ambrosius cousins, which was a massive relief in and of itself.

They can't see any of it. Only me and Hal can. Holy shit, it actually worked!

Brigham leapt toward his cousin again but stopped short to avoid contact with the last of the golden threads. Then he realized he'd heard the noise all along but hadn't been aware enough to question what it was until now.

It was the sound of his cousin choking.

The orb glowed, the golden light tinged with a deep

blood-red that made the thing look like it had been hauled from a blazing fire. Halsey's hands clamped around the thing so tightly that her arms shook. Her body trembled violently, and the look in her wide eyes was vacant. Lost.

As if Halsey had gone too far using the damn thing, and now the orb had seized its chance to take over.

"Hal." He lunged for her, then thought better of it and quickly pulled himself back together. If he caused a scene now, there might be enough suspicion among these villagers for them to gang up and start asking the questions that were *really* difficult to answer. He didn't want to draw attention, and he didn't particularly want to touch the copper orb, either. Yet he had no doubt that if he didn't act quickly, something terrible would happen to his cousin.

He dropped to his knees at her side and kept his voice low but firm. "Hal, can you hear me?"

Choking noises were Halsey's only response. Two more golden threads of light remained in the air, making their lazy, undulating way toward her and the copper orb. Taking their damn sweet time. Brigham fought against the sudden urge to bat those threads of light away from his cousin like they were blood flies or mosquitos. But that seemed like a terrible idea too.

The damn copper orb was doing this to her, and there was a good chance it would stop when all the pieces of itself had returned.

So he waited, willing the last two threads to hurry the hell up.

"Hal, if you can hear me, it worked. You did it. Whatever happens next—"

The glowing orb hummed when the final floating

threads settled into the object. The sound rose in pitch for a split second, then the thing released a brilliant flash of golden light with a *crack* that made Brigham's ears pop.

None of the normies noticed any of it. Without magic, they were blind to the orb, the strings of light, and anything else about the strange power Halsey Ambrosius now wielded. Some of them did notice Brigham kneeling at his cousin's side while she stared blankly ahead, her hands in her lap and her entire body trembling.

Others saw him reach for her shoulder in concern, then jerk his hand back the second he touched her before shaking it out in alarm.

"What the hell?" Brigham looked at his fingers, which didn't show any signs of having been injured by the jolt of power that had crackled from Halsey's shoulder and into his hand. Like he'd touched a live electric fence instead of his cousin. "Hal, are you in there? Come on, man. You gotta say *something*. Hal!"

His terrified shout drew the attention of everyone in the recovery room. The healed victims, their families and friends, the volunteers who'd cared for them, and all the self-appointed village officials.

Then Halsey Ambrosius' eyes rolled back in her head before she went limp and crumpled sideways from the chair.

CHAPTER EIGHTEEN

Halsey woke in a room she didn't recognize, surrounded by someone else's things, and had a much harder time than she should have figuring out where she was.

It was the tall, clear glass on the nightstand beside the bed that jogged her memory.

Oh shit. Brigham's gonna kill me.

She bolted upright in the bed only to immediately sink back onto the pillow when her head lurched and spun. She desperately wished for a trashcan. Being sick in a stranger's bedroom all over their things wasn't an admirable move, even if she was the one who'd saved the victims and the village.

Eventually, though, she managed to quell the dizzying nausea enough to reach for the glass.

This one didn't have any drops of Florence Ambrosius' bunk healing potion in it. Nothing but water. It was cool and sweet on Halsey's lips as she drank as much as she could stomach. Then lay flat on her back to stare at the ceiling and tried to remember how she'd gotten here.

It was working. It did work. I used the orb to heal all those people. I was sinking down into it, letting it happen, and...

The rest was blank. Nothing remained in her memory between the moment she'd convinced herself to relax into the orb's power and the moment she'd opened her eyes in a completely different room, most likely on a completely different day.

Not good.

At best, she expected to get a ranting tirade from her cousin about how careless she'd been, how she'd almost given him a heart attack, how they'd almost blown their cover because "secret agents" generally didn't pass out from sitting in a chair while the civilians they'd come to help got their lives back. At worst, Brigham would count this little episode as a complete violation of the terms of their agreement back in the conference room. Then he would expect her to live up to her end of that deal. To put the copper orb away, lock it up somewhere safe where no one could get to it, including her, and move on with her life as an Ambrosius militia operative.

Back to the beginning.

Back to doing things the way Halsey and Brigham had been doing things together for the last five years in the field.

Back to doing things the way the Ambrosius Clan had been doing them for generation upon generation.

That wouldn't work, though. It was the whole point of all the extra effort Halsey had put into trying to find the silver coffin. Into researching her family's history and solving a massively insane puzzle that pointed to the Mother of Monsters' return.

She couldn't lock up the orb after this. Not now. It was too important, and Halsey had too many unanswered questions, and if she could somehow get her cousin to see the truth in that and the importance of not giving up until this whole crazy nightmare was over—

A brisk knock at the door startled her from her thoughts.

Halsey jolted in the bed and tried to call out, but her voice didn't work. So she quickly cleared her throat and tried again. "Come in."

Her voice sounded almost as raw and dry as Makayla's before she'd taken the potion. But the reason for that was something entirely different, and the worst part was that Halsey didn't even know what had happened.

There was a pause outside. Then the doorknob turned sharply, and the door swung inward. Brigham's face popped into the bedroom, his eyes wide. "Holy shit. You're awake!"

"Well yeah." She gave him a weak shrug. "Kinda hard to say, 'Come in,' if I'm passed out."

"Goddamnit, Hal." He looked over his shoulder, then hurried into the room and closed the door behind him as quickly and quietly as possible. Brigham stalked so quickly across the small bedroom that Halsey briefly wondered if he would start picking things up and chucking them at the walls or out the window behind the nightstand.

Instead, he dropped without warning onto the edge of the bed and wrapped her up in a desperately tight hug.

"Whoa…" Halsey released a self-conscious chuckle. With the hug mostly pinning her arms at her sides, she managed to reach up and gently pat his lower back. "We're hugging now. Okay."

"That's what people do," he called over her shoulder, still holding on for dear life. "Especially when they thought their best friend might be about to hit the dirt. You know, like, forever. So deal with it."

Brigham ended the hug with a final squeeze that almost choked the air from her lungs, then he released her and scooted away on the edge of the bed to give her space. There might have been tears in his eyes.

Then again, those tears might have belonged to Halsey instead. It was hard to tell the difference.

"I'm okay, cuz," she told him gently. "Really. See? Not even a little dirt."

"That's not funny."

"It's kinda funny." The only response she got to her crooked, tired half-smile was a very serious frown from her cousin, so Halsey decided it best to leave the jokes at the door and get down to business. Jokes were mostly Brigham's thing, anyway. "It worked, right? Healing all those—"

"Yeah, it fucking worked." He scoffed but wouldn't look away from her. "Everybody drank the Kool-Aid, the barghest venom disappeared, and now they can all live happily-ever-after. Hurray…"

"That's great, Brigham. That means—"

"I thought I was gonna lose you, Hal. For real. I thought you were…I don't know." With a sniff, Brigham finally lowered his gaze to his lap. "You told me it was all gonna work out, and I believed you. But all that back there? That was… Shit." He sighed and shook his head. "What *was* that?"

"Honestly? I have no idea."

"Right." He nodded slowly, his expression oscillating between rage and relief. "You did a thing, you don't know how it happened or why, and that's gonna have to be good enough for me, huh? Pretty much par for the course at this point."

"Not as in I can't explain it," she began. "More like I… don't remember."

"Huh?"

"As in I passed out, dude. One second, I had my eyes closed in that chair, focusing on the magic until people started shouting all over the place. Next thing I know, I'm waking up in this bed with no idea how I got here. By the way, where even *is* here?"

Brigham searched her gaze, his hazel eyes moving fast as he bit the inside of his cheek. At first, she thought he was trying to figure out whether or not to tell her, but then she realized he was trying to hold back a smile. "Believe it or not, this lovely little room is nestled in the back of Mauve's guesthouse."

"*Guesthouse.*" Halsey laughed. "Well, isn't that the most hospitable, neighborly thing?"

"That's what *I* told her." He scratched the back of his head and wrinkled his nose. "More or less."

The room fell silent. Where Halsey's curiosity normally would have gotten the better of her, she discovered she wasn't that worried about what happened during those moments she couldn't remember. Still, she could tell her cousin needed to talk about it. That seemed like the least she could do for him right now.

"So." She slapped the bedcovers on either side of her and turned to face him, crossing her legs beneath her. "First things first, right? The cure worked. The victims are healed. Any bad-news bears still roaming around that I should know about?"

Brigham snorted. "Not when it comes to the villagers of Coningsby and one hell of a successfully completed mission. No."

"Good." She rubbed her hands across the sheets. Not because there was anything on them but because it seemed to warm up her body, which felt like it had been hit by a train. "Item number two, then. You wanna tell me what happened out there? Everything I apparently missed?"

"You sure you wanna hear it?"

"We have plenty of time, cuz. And look at me. I'm sitting up on my own, my brain's functioning the way it's supposed to, and I don't feel any extra limbs popping up from my..." Scowling, she reached over her shoulder to experimentally pat the top of her back.

"What?" Brigham lurched toward her, reaching toward her back as well. "What's wrong?"

Halsey froze, her eyes wide, then broke into a gleaming grin. "Other than the fact that my partner's totally paranoid? Nothing much."

Rolling his eyes, Brigham puffed a sigh that ended in a wry laugh. "Asshole."

"Not my fault you're so gullible, cuz."

"Yeah, well, if you'd seen what I saw, you'd be pretty gullible too. Trust me."

"Okay." She folded her hands in her lap and shrugged, giving him her full attention. "So tell me what you saw. I can take it. Promise."

So he did.

The tale wasn't very long and didn't take much time despite how much detail Brigham put into recounting the events of Halsey's magical seizure and everything that had happened after she'd lost control. When he was done, she still had absolutely no idea how she'd lost herself to such a concerning blackout like that one, why the copper orb had rendered her unconscious afterward, or what might happen next now that they officially knew using the transmuted magic came with certain dangers and no way to predict what they would be.

She might have taken it too far, but they didn't discuss that possibility. It was too fresh. Brigham was simply glad she was okay, and the village of Coningsby was in a fantastic mood. All thanks to the Agents Ambrosius, who had rid them of the demon-dog barghest and healed its sick and wounded victims.

"Mauve said we can stay as long as we want," Brigham added, moving onto the less-important points now that they'd covered the more unsettling topics.

Halsey laughed. "All the better to ply us with good food and maybe a few pints and see how much more information she can wheedle out of two foreign secret agents, huh? She's crafty. I'll give her that."

"Tell me about it." Another awkward silence filled the room, then Brigham sighed. "You hungry?"

"Not really." It was already dark outside, and Halsey was exhausted enough to lay back down and get a full night's sleep again, even after only having been awake for about an hour. "I think I'm gonna catch some more sleep. Rest up."

"Yeah, yeah. Sure. Mauve said something about a full English breakfast in the morning, so that'll be good. And I'm, uh…right across the hall. If you need anything."

"Thanks."

"Sure." He shot her a tight smile, then stood quickly from the edge of the bed. "Okay. I'm gonna go stuff myself, so…" With another wry chuckle, Brigham playfully nudged his cousin's shoulder and shook his head. "Don't pull that shit on me again, huh? It was terrifying."

"Well, you know *me*. I'm only doing it for the laughs."

"Jerk." They both laughed, then Brigham headed out of the room, pausing when he was halfway through the entrance. "Night, Hal."

"Goodnight."

"I'm glad you're not dead."

Halsey chortled. "Ditto, cuz."

Then he slipped into the hall and shut the door, his footsteps creaking noisily across the floor of Mauve's guesthouse, and Halsey was left alone in a strange room, in a strange village, with a lot of strange new information to ponder.

He didn't say anything about our deal or *what he wants me to do with the orb. Which means I really did almost give him a heart attack.*

Still, she expected her cousin to bring up the safety issues concerning her transmuted copper tool at some point in the near future. Even Halsey couldn't deny the fact that her physical safety, at the very least, was now an official concern if she wanted to continue using the thing. But that was a conversation for a different day.

Right now, she only wanted to go to sleep, get some rest, and head back home tomorrow with one more successfully completed mission under her belt. One thing at a time was always the best way to handle things, even when it felt like new problems and unsolved mysteries kept piling themselves on top of her and Brigham.

No matter how hard she tried to drift back to sleep, she couldn't. Halsey's mind raced through what their stupefying mission had become. From a barghest hunt to a preposterous undercover story about being secret agents who'd come to fight the monster and heal the wounded victims who otherwise would have stayed in bed for who knew how long, never recovering and never dying. She'd used the orb not only to destroy an indestructible monster but to heal nearly a hundred innocent villagers. And Brigham.

Worst of all, Halsey didn't like having lost those hours between fully committing to the orb's magic mixed with hers and waking up in Mauve's guesthouse. Her memories had always been fully intact, and having an almost photographic memory had been one of the things she'd prided herself on from the moment she'd learned it was a rare skill.

If anything terrible had happened, Brigham would've told me about it. This is no more than a little blackout. A fugue. Probably because I plugged into too much power trying to heal all those people at the same time.

Would it have been safer for her personally to heal the victims in smaller groups? Probably. Although that would have raised a whole new set of questions from the citizens of Coningsby that she didn't think either she or her cousin could have answered.

I made the right call. And now I know where my limits are, probably. So that's a good thing.

Even that train of positive thought didn't calm her enough to drift back to sleep, though. After what felt like lying in bed for hours, Halsey finally switched on the lamp on the nightstand, crawled out from under the covers again, and walked to the small desk and chair on the other side of the cozy room.

CHAPTER NINETEEN

Her weapons bag was on the floor by the chair, her canvas jacket hanging over the back of the chair. Everything looked neat and tidy, exactly the way she would have set it all up if she'd walked herself into this room fully conscious. When she reached the chair, though, her stomach flipped with anticipation and more worry than she was used to carrying around with her.

Before her blackout, she'd been holding the copper orb in her lap, apparently. Then she'd fainted, fallen from the chair in the recovery center, and was most likely brought here on a stretcher.

She had to make sure, though.

She reached slowly into her jacket pocket and released a massive sigh when she felt the cold, smooth surface of the cobber orb resting there. That's where she'd wanted to keep it. That's where she *had* kept it, hidden away from the villagers of Coningsby on the off-chance that coming face-to-face with a real-life barghest and proof that at least one monster was real had somehow given them the ability to see more than they'd previously been capable of seeing. Like magic, to start.

Brigham had assured her that none of the normies in the recovery center had seen the golden threads of the orb's power mixed with her new healing magic. They'd all bought the story that these two young "agents" had been able to duplicate the antidote to make enough for nearly one hundred victims, and that was that. No one had seen the copper ball, no one knew who Halsey and Brigham Ambrosius actually were or what they were capable of, and there was nothing to worry about on that front.

He picked it up and put it in my pocket. She frowned as she brushed her fingers one more time against the orb's surface, then broke into a smile. *He doesn't like this thing, but he took the time to make sure I had it again. Brigham touched the disco ball with his bare hands and didn't say a word about it. Looks like he's coming around, even if he doesn't want to admit it.*

Having gotten this close to the sphere was all the relief she needed. The transmuted magic that had recently helped her squeeze out of so many tight spots thrummed with reassuring energy. It felt whole and at peace.

Halsey felt whole. No longer broken into pieces she'd yearned to have restored immediately after she'd slipped the magic into those potion glasses.

When she realized how strange it was to equate her emotions with the energetic state of a magical tool she didn't understand, she removed her hand from her pocket and drew a deep breath.

That part's new. And creepy. If I start using this thing as an emotional crutch and not only a massive asset for carrying out our missions, I'm asking for trouble.

Brushing off her hands but still staring at her jacket pocket where the orb would stay for the night, she headed back toward the bed. A muted buzz made her stop, and the blue-white light of her phone flashed through the left pocket of her jacket. Frowning, she retrieved her phone to see it was 11:48 p.m. and she'd received a new text.

From Seamus Havalon.

"It's a little late for casual texting, don't you think?" she muttered, then broke into another smile when she realized it was 5:48 p.m. in Texas. The tall, dark, handsome son of the Havalon Clan's Council head had every reason to believe Halsey was back in Texas, where she lived, or at least still in the U.S.

With her phone in hand, she climbed into bed and opened his text.

> *Evening, Hal. It's been a while. Figured I'd pop you a message and say hi. Been thinking about you. If you're ever on this side of the pond again, let me know. Maybe we can meet up.*

Halsey almost laughed as she read over the text several times. She hadn't spoken to any of the Havalons since the day she and Brigham had driven off the family's property to head home. Since she'd killed the silverback alpha who had once been a Viking man named Rolfr Magnusson.

Apparently, Seamus thought now was a great time to reach out and say he'd been thinking about her. Nothing about monsters. Nothing about elementals or family feuds. Nothing about the looming threat of the Blood Matriarch's return and what might be required of every elemental still alive today when they figured out how to approach the monster changes and the war with their family's age-old nemesis.

The woman who'd started it all.

The woman who was supposed to be trapped for eternity in a silver coffin at the bottom of the ocean.

Thinking through those infinite possibilities made Halsey's stomach clench, and her head hurt.

Not now. I can't get into this right now.

She would have loved to reply to Seamus' text, but she had a feeling she might end up blurting out everything that had happened over the last few days without any filter. He hadn't extended an invitation for a venting session. Not that Halsey needed those often, but she'd been through a lot recently. There was still so much more she needed to discover about the orb, her own magic, and what the hell was happening to her before she could talk about it with someone who wasn't already in the know.

Even though she was on Seamus' side of the pond, now didn't feel like the right time for a casual meet-up with a decent chance of turning into a date.

Maybe later, Seamus. Sorry.

She decided she'd text him back tomorrow after she'd gotten some sleep and had enough brainpower to figure out how to best respond. The thought of lying to him about where she was and what she'd been doing wasn't appealing, but casually glossing over her myriad problems right now in a text was all she had the bandwidth for.

Tomorrow.

Yet, with her phone in her hand, she couldn't stop

thinking about the conversations she'd eventually need to have about this particular mission. Their debriefing with Cavanaugh when they returned, another chat with Meemaw, maybe even a call to her dad or a private in-person visit with him to gauge how much of the situation the Council needed to know.

Leaving out a few core details about exactly how she and Brigham had defeated the chimera in Turkey was one thing. Telling the Council that Florence's healing potion had worked without a hitch, letting the Council think their methods were still working so she could keep the orb a secret...

That was dangerous.

At the very least, I can tell them it's mission accomplished over here and that Brigham and I are coming home.

She opened her emails, meaning to draft a quick status update to send to the Council, but she didn't get that far. Her gaze fell on a familiar name in bold letters in the "sender" column.

Halil Aydem.

Four other recent emails were stacked above it in her inbox. Promotions, spam, and subscription email newsletters, but nothing important. Nothing from the Council. Halsey considered no news to be good news when it came to the Ambrosius Clan unless they were actively trying to keep secrets from her. But news from Aydem?

His little henchman in Turkey told us Aydem was too busy for a chat, and I was too unprepared. Now he's sending me personal emails?

Her curiosity was far too strong to push aside, especially when she opened the email and saw she was the message's only recipient. No other addresses copied in, not even Brigham. Part of her was surprised, seeing as the mysterious Halil Aydem of the Order of Skrár seemed to know plenty about their family, that he'd made the discovery of certain Ambrosius Clan secrets a prerequisite for meeting each other in person.

She shouldn't have been instantly angered by the man's unexpected outreach attempt. She'd been going behind her cousin's back this whole time and had set up her first secret meetings with Aydem. That had been a wash after Brigham had found her in that tea shop in the Grand Bazaar a few minutes too early. But that had been on *her* terms.

Having the man contact her first, with only the two of them involved, was different. It felt like Halsey was being forced into covert communications, where the privacy of an email without any other receiving addresses forced her between a rock and a hard place. And until now, she hadn't even considered the possibility of having to make that impossible choice again because she'd thought her chances to meet with Aydem were up.

Though it hadn't been overtly spelled out for them in the waiting room of Yusuf Burakgazi's enormous Turkish estate, Halsey had been fairly certain that when Aydem's elderly assistant said his employer wouldn't speak with them, the man had actually been referring only to Brigham. Her cousin had no reason to catch onto that little detail. Brigham hadn't known about her first attempt to meet the man in the Grand Bazaar, so he naturally hadn't known about the stipulation that she meet with Mr. Aydem alone. Without backup or a bodyguard to keep her company. Bringing her cousin along wasn't allowed.

Now, apparently, Aydem was attempting to contact her while once more specifically excluding Brigham. After Burakgazi had set up their little meeting with the Order of Skrár's representative in his home, Aydem must have noticed Halsey wasn't there alone. Plus, the Order was supposed to know everything about every member of every elemental family for the entire span of magical history. He *had* to know who Brigham was and why Halsey would want her mission partner to join her. At least the second time.

No matter what the man truly knew, he clearly only wanted Halsey in on this little correspondence.

After staring at the subject line that read "A Moment of Your Time," she sighed and read the rest of the email.

Greetings, Miss Ambrosius.

Please do accept my humblest apologies for not having been able to make a second meeting between us work in Turkey. I was called away by an urgent matter, though my assistant Highford reported that he delivered the message in my stead. As is often the case in my line of work, there are many moving parts in constant motion at all times, and this requires a certain level of flexibility to respond appropriately at any given moment.

Fortunately, the business that took me away from Turkey wrapped up significantly faster than I'd anticipated, and I now find my schedule unexpectedly open for the next several days.

I fly into London midday tomorrow and plan to stay at least until the week's end. In the hopes of finally realizing this continuously postponed meeting of ours, I do hope you'll manage to get away from your no doubt numerous other pressing responsibilities and obligations to meet me in London.

If I haven't provided you enough advanced notice, I understand. However, I cannot say with any certainty that I will have this much of an opening in my schedule again for quite some time. And I am very much still looking forward to meeting you in person and answering the many questions referenced in your original correspondence.

Should you find yourself in London before this coming Sunday, I'll be staying at the Windladge Estate just outside London proper. Address and other contact information to follow below. The telephone number is for the guard at the estate's gatehouse. No need to send a committed response. If we haven't met face-to-face before Sunday, I can safely assume you have been as busy with your own important work as I have been with mine.

Regards,
Halil Aydem

"Wow." She had to read the email two more times to make sure she saw the right words on the screen.

It was finally happening. Halil Aydem was ready and willing to meet with her, but only on *his* terms. Alone. In London. With an incredibly small window of only a few days in which he expected her to drop everything and have this meeting she'd been trying to make happen for weeks.

First, he set our meeting at the Grand Bazaar in Turkey. Then he oh-so-conveniently showed up at Yusef Burakgazi's massive estate because the man of the house gave him a call for us. And now he happens *to be in England at the same time we are, with only a few days left to get this show on the road.*

Halsey scowled at the email. It all seemed way too coincidental, but she'd never even met the man. If he'd been keeping tabs on her this whole time, she would have known.

The Order of Skrár's been keeping tabs on every single monster and elemental since the beginning of magical time, and none of us have a clue what they've got locked away in their "living records."

Though the email seemed personable enough, without so much as a hint of danger or foreboding in the man's words, she couldn't help the feeling that something still wasn't right about this situation.

Because Brigham still wasn't invited.

No, that part hadn't been explicitly stated in the email. But she knew.

Her first meeting had been canceled because Brigham had come storming into that teashop in the Grand Bazaar, berating her for losing him along the busy streets and winding passageways. The second meeting had been called off verbally by Aydem's assistant, who'd all but spelled it out for them that his employer didn't *want* to speak with Brigham. And now?

Now, Halsey was being summoned to a private location where Aydem was physically staying for the next few days while in London. Not a chance meeting in a public place. Not a coincidental sharing of the same client in Yusef Burakgazi. This was an open invitation without the need for a date or time so long as it fell within Aydem's timeframe of *before Sunday*.

She could come clean tomorrow, tell Brigham about the whole thing and ask him to come with her as backup. Like he always did. Then she'd run the risk of this third, and what felt like a final, attempt at this in-person meeting being called off yet again because she'd failed to come alone.

That was what the man wanted, even if he hadn't said as much.

And if she chose to go into this alone? To take on the entire meeting and whatever she found out from Aydem on her own? Well, he was a member of the Order of Skrár. The protectors of magical knowledge. The slightly magical beings were not human, not elemental, and not blood-human, but clearly something else. They'd been keeping tabs on people, places, and events since long before the great war if everything Greta said about them was true.

It was safe to meet with the man alone. He hadn't harmed her, nor had he made any real threats. The only thing Aydem had done to cause Halsey any real concern was refuse to meet with her when anyone else was present. Maybe that was how the Order of Skrár operated.

Halsey didn't have any other choice. She had to do it. She needed answers about what her copper ball actually was, what it could do, and why it had been affecting her magic.

She had to find out *what* that magic was and why she was the only elemental in the history of her kind to develop something that definitely was *not* elemental magic.

Brigham wouldn't like it. Then again, Brigham didn't like a lot of things, and neither of them could change the fact that he wasn't invited to the private meeting where she *would* get all her answers.

He'll get over it eventually. I'll come home, tell him what I learned and apologize for keeping it from him. He'll be so relieved to have an explanation for the magical disco ball that he won't hold it against me. Not for too long, anyway. We can keep going, and I can arm us both with the new knowledge Aydem gives me. I can arm us all.

With those thoughts racing through her head, Halsey set her phone on the small nightstand beside her bed, put the screen to sleep, and fell asleep almost immediately because now she had a plan. No, it wasn't the best plan in the world, and she didn't feel amazing about keeping one more secret from her cousin. Yet it was all she had right now.

In the end, when she was finished, she had no doubt it would all be worth it.

CHAPTER TWENTY

She woke the next morning to the clanking and banging around of what could only have been Mauve bustling around in the kitchen. It made sense that their eager-to-please busybody of a hostess would wake up so early to fix her two "foreign secret agent" guests a hearty breakfast.

But then Halsey remembered the full scope of where she was and frowned as she blinked the sleep from her eyes and reached for her phone.

This is her guesthouse. Isn't that supposed to mean the guests get their privacy until they decide to join everybody else later?

Then again, after everything she'd learned about Mauve in such a short expanse of time, she wasn't all that surprised that Mauve had taken it upon herself to make her guests breakfast in the same building she'd given them rooms for the night.

Halsey got out of bed and headed for the attached bathroom shared by the next bedroom over. Clean towels were folded and stacked on a shelf beside the sink, and the water was instantly hot and perfect for a wake-me-up cleanse.

By the time she'd dried off and dressed in one of the two extra changes of clothes she'd brought with her for this particular mission, the smell of bacon, toast, eggs, and something baked and sweet had already made its way through the guesthouse toward her room.

Then someone knocked on the door.

"Hold on. I'm coming," Halsey called as she headed across the small room with a smirk. "You know, cuz, I'm actually impressed you managed to get up this early and—"

She opened the door and stopped. It wasn't Brigham standing on the other side but Mauve.

The woman's eyes widened with curiosity, and she plastered on a winning smile the instant Halsey stopped talking. "Well, good morning to you too, love. Though I must say, I've been up since before sunrise. And you seem to have slept in, haven't you?"

"I..." Halsey huffed a laugh. "Sorry. I thought you were Brigham."

"Oh, of *course* not." Mauve placed a hand on her chest in mock surprise and giggled. "No, your partner's downstairs in front of the breakfast table. I've already made him his tea."

"Tea, huh?" It was difficult to imagine Brigham requesting a cup of tea with anything he ate, but then again, they *were* in England.

"Quite." Mauve leaned slightly to the side to peer past her guest into the small bedroom beyond. "Asked for a cup of *coffee*, he did. Of all the things..." When Halsey leaned as well to catch the woman's gaze again, her hostess leaned in the opposite direction. "Don't care for the stuff personally. Too bitter. Too *dark*. Can't drink coffee at whatever time of day you please for any and all occasions. I'll tell you that much."

"I'm sure the tea's perfect." Finally deciding to end the back-and-forth with the woman playing Sneak a Peek Inside the Room, Halsey spread both her arms across the doorway and grinned. "Can I help you with something, Mauve?"

"Hmm? Oh. No, of course not. What a silly thing to ask." The woman giggled again, this time rolling her eyes and brushing the whole thing off. "You're staying in *my* guest house. What could I possibly need from *you*?"

"I was wondering the same thing, actually."

"Aye, well..." It looked a whole lot like the middle-aged know-it-all was trying desperately to come up with a believable reason for wanting to snoop around inside her guest's room, but then a grin of realization spread across Mauve's face and lit up her eyes. "I'd told your partner last night about all your accommodations here in the guest house, including the full English I've prepared. Realized this morning that I hadn't had a chance to tell *you* anything, I did, so I said to myself, I said, 'Mauve, that bright young woman's like to be appalled at your hosting skills if you don't tell her about the full English, she will.' And I can't have *that*, of course. So I thought it best to inform you of the situation myself. In person."

When she finished, she made one more attempt to sneak another peek past the young elemental standing in front of her.

Halsey kept smiling and nodded. "Well, thank you for telling me. I'll be down in a few minutes—"

"Why not *now*?" This time, the woman seemed oblivious to how intrusive her questioning might have come across.

If she's looking for another weird, magical indoor water park, she's gonna be disappointed.

Halsey pointed at her own head. "I still have to brush my hair."

"Oh, aye!" Mauve's face lit up again as she finally focused on her guest's person instead of what existed behind her. "Of course."

"Wouldn't wanna kick off the day with such bad manners, right?"

"No, no. Absolutely not." Mauve pointed at her. "Do *not* come to the breakfast nook until you're entirely fixed up for the day, Agent, and not a second before. You hear me?"

It took everything Halsey had to fight back a laugh. "Yes, ma'am."

"And if you need anything, absolutely *anything*..."

The bedroom door began to close as Halsey backed away into the room. "I don't think I'll need anything else, Mauve. You've been very considerate."

"You let me know all the same." The woman wagged a finger and stood her ground despite a growing length of wooden door closing between them. "The last thing I want is for word to get round that Mauve McRahl doesn't know how to properly provide for her guests. Especially guests as important and vital as two secret agents fighting *monsters*—"

"If anyone asks, we'll tell them you're the best." Halsey

blurted out the words, trying not to be overly rude while also wanting to get the woman out of her face for a moment of peace. "You should open up a bed-and-breakfast, even. Here in the guesthouse."

"Aye? You think so?"

"Absolutely. I'll be down in a bit, Mauve. Thanks for stopping by." The door shut with a soft click, and Halsey froze there on the other side, her hand hovering above the knob as if it would turn and the door would fly open again at any second.

Out in the narrow hallway, Mauve hummed in consideration, then tittered. "A bed-and-breakfast. Would you listen to that? And Mary Whitehall thought it was a terrible idea, did she? Ooh, just *wait* 'til I tell her Agent Ambrosius, Coningsby's lauded heroine, suggested the very same. That'll piss in her hedges, it will. Ha!"

The woman's voice faded incrementally down the hall as she jabbered to herself, and Halsey sighed. Still, she waited a moment longer to be sure Mauve hadn't forgotten something "important" that compelled her to return. The woman was clearly the type to do so.

Yet after her hostess' chipper voice and light, bustling footsteps disappeared, it seemed the woman was far more preoccupied with this notion of proving Mary Whitehall wrong about the bed-and-breakfast idea. For a few minutes at least, Halsey was alone with a little peace and quiet.

She burst out laughing.

We kill the barghest terrorizing a small village, heal every single victim with magic no one can see, convince the population we're foreign special agents authorized to hunt monsters all over the world, and dealing with one busybody queen of village gossip is the hardest part of the whole mission. I wonder how Brigham's dealing with all this.

The thought of her cousin sitting stiffly at the breakfast table, trying to stuff his face while Mauve blabbered on about everything under the sun without letting him get a word in edgewise, made her laugh even more. She decided to take a few more minutes than she needed to brush her hair before joining them in the guesthouse kitchen.

Finding the aforementioned "breakfast nook" in Mauve's guesthouse turned out to be rather simple. The bedrooms were situated at the back of the medium-sized cottage in which she counted four bedrooms rooms and two bathrooms. The narrow hallway led to a beautiful, open living area with floor-to-ceiling windows on both sides of the house, flooding the space with soothing morning sunlight. Several windows had been opened to let in the fresh, crisp air and the sound of birds happily twittering toward the end of summer.

Halsey almost would have preferred to stay here in this room, with the simple but tasteful couches and armchairs in light, soft colors amid the dark wood of the floor, tables, and sparse bookshelves. It felt like a new start. The complete opposite of the way the village had first appeared when the Ambrosius cousins drove past the welcome sign and down the small community's main road.

But Mauve's nonstop chattering echoed from the other side of the living area, where the mouthwatering scents of a freshly cooked breakfast grew stronger. Halsey was forced to follow her stomach instead, and she moved quietly across the guesthouse until the open entryway on the left gave way to a small, neat kitchen. Against the far wall to the right of the counter was an extended bay window housing a table large enough for six. A bench had been built into the wall beneath the window on one side, and four well-oiled wooden chairs surrounded the other open seats at the table.

Brigham sat on the bench with a massive plate of food in front of him. Fried eggs, fried bread, fried ham, baked beans, blood sausage, fried mushrooms, and tomatoes, and a mound of seasoned fingerling potatoes. He ate ravenously, chewing and nodding at all the right intervals and occasionally looking up from his stuffed plate to eye the woman sitting across the table from him.

Mauve kept blabbering away, talking about anything and everything in one constant stream of thought. The only time she paused was to take a delicate sip of tea or to ask Brigham about the food.

"Oh, you're out of tea, dear. Here, let me. Can't have you running empty. Enjoying the blood sausage, are you? Aye, that's something of a specialty. No, no. It isn't *toast*, love. Never call it that. Fried bread is something entirely different. Well, I can't tell you *how*. Special family recipe, that. I'm thrilled you enjoyed it all so much. More beans? Don't say a thing. There's plenty right here, and after the ordeal the two of you've been through over the last several days, you'll need your strength back. There. That should be enough to suit you."

The whole time, Brigham ate and drank and accepted

the food with gusto, nodding and wordlessly engaging their hostess with all the right sounds of agreement and interest. Instead of being overwhelmed by the woman's incessant talking, he was in heaven.

Halsey choked back a laugh and continued across the kitchen toward the breakfast nook. *Should've known a good meal with bottomless servings is the best way to make him feel like everything's right with the world again.*

She moved slowly across the kitchen until her cousin finally noticed the movement.

Brigham whipped his head up to look at her, widened his eyes, and exclaimed around a mouthful, "Hal! You made it! Get in here, dude. You gotta try this."

Mauve spun around in her chair and grinned at the young woman heading toward her. "I was starting to wonder if you were ever coming down, love. This one right here's well on his way to eating the whole meal on his own!"

The woman tittered at her own joke, and Brigham fixed his cousin with a sheepish smile and a shrug.

"Right here, love. Already set a place for you, I have." Mauve stood with a light scrape of her chair legs across the floor and pulled out one of the end chairs. A plate, silverware, teacup, saucer, and cloth napkin had already been laid out, and the woman waved Halsey urgently toward it. "Come. Sit. Eat. You must be famished, poor thing. Would you fancy a cuppa? Aye, of course you would. There's cream and sugar on the table. Lemon as well. I'll fix you a plate."

Halsey didn't have an opportunity to say, "Yes, please," or, "No, thank you," either way, but she plopped down into the provided seat and grabbed the cloth napkin to place on her lap while Mauve poured her a steaming cup of black tea before turning to the food.

It was hard enough to get her cousin's attention when Brigham was so enthusiastically smitten by the incredible meal their hostess had prepared. The fact that Mauve narrated her every move as she fixed up Halsey's plate from the dishes on the table, spooning up a rather large helping of everything without waiting for her guest's preference for any of them, made it impossible for Halsey to address her cousin directly. When her plate was set down in front of her, she almost apologized preemptively for knowing she wouldn't be able to eat the entire thing, but Mauve didn't give her a chance.

The woman plopped back down into her seat, grabbed the teapot to refill her cup, and babbled away like she hadn't taken a break from her one-sided conversation with Brigham to set up one more guest at the table. "The vegetables are all grown right here in Coningsby. Plenty of back gardens in this place, there are. And you won't find a finer tomato plant than what Angus Talworth grows so lovingly season after season. Man's a right saint, he is. That's why his tomatoes are so good, you know. And so *big*."

Halsey stared at her cousin as she sipped her incredibly strong black tea until Brigham finally noticed her gaze on him. While Mauve continued talking to herself, Halsey darted a gaze toward the woman and raised her eyebrows. Brigham smirked as he chewed, shrugged, and tapped his plate with the side of his fork before digging in again.

Yeah. Food's great. Conversation's nonstop. Wouldn't surprise me if I didn't get a chance to actually talk to him until we're all packed up and on our way out.

"But enough about our gardens." With another little giggle, Mauve shifted in her chair to face Halsey and fixed her with an intensely curious gaze. "Why don't you talk to me about that bed-and-breakfast idea of yours, Agent?"

Halsey nearly choked before she'd even taken her first bite. "Um…what about it?"

"Bed-and-breakfast, huh?" Brigham mumbled around a mouthful.

"Oh, aye. Said so just this morning when I went back to fetch her for breakfast." Mauve nodded enthusiastically. "I tell you what, I've been saying the same thing for years, I have. *Years.* But Mary Whitehall… She's head of the library committee, and apparently, that makes her head of everyone else's business, as I'm sure you could tell. *She's* the one who's been telling me the whole time that this guest-house of mine would simply never do as a successful or even appropriate bed-and-breakfast because of the various *amenities* it already lacks. Can you believe that? What amenities? This place has everything a person could possibly want in a nice, cozy little cottage for a private holiday, don't you think?"

"Everything's been great so far," Brigham replied quickly before shoveling another forkful of eggs into his mouth.

"That's what I said, too," Halsey replied. "There's plenty of room—"

"Exactly." Mauve pointed at her, then raised her tea to her lips again for another polite sip. "And to think, all the time and energy I've let go to such a tragic waste because I didn't have the common sense to tell the woman I know what I'm talking about. The guesthouse is perfect for renting out. Such a quaint little holiday spot. Folks come through Coningsby all the time on their way to other places. Why not make this a bit of a destination stop along the way? Of course, the place would need sprucing up beforehand. Liven things up a bit. I was thinking..."

Then the woman continued yet another long diatribe of everything she'd wanted to do with her guesthouse cottage and everything Mary Whitehall had assured her would be a terrible idea. And she didn't stop.

After the first few minutes of slowly eating and waiting for a pause in the one-sided conversation so either of the Ambrosius cousins might offer a different topic over breakfast, Halsey finally had to accept that the pause wasn't going to happen. She followed Brigham's lead and focused on her breakfast instead.

Everything was delicious, naturally, and she surprised herself by clearing her plate much faster than she'd thought possible before eagerly agreeing to second helpings of everything, even though she didn't have a choice.

With a good meal, bright sunshine streaming in through the bay window behind Brigham, and the happy chattering of their hostess, who was unaware of the possibility that anyone around her might not be fully interested in every little thing she had to say, Halsey felt like she was being fully recharged. All the frustration, surprise, and taxing endeavors of the day before that had taken more out of her than she cared to admit settled farther into the past.

They'd completed their mission. They'd cleaned up the collateral as best they could after taking out the barghest.

They could start over fresh with new endeavors when they left Coningsby. Only the Ambrosius cousins wouldn't be leaving together for those new endeavors, which was the one wrench left in the gears.

I have to get him away from her for at least a bit so we can talk. And whatever happens after that, we'll deal with it then. Assuming Mauve doesn't sneak after us trying to eavesdrop on the whole thing.

CHAPTER TWENTY-ONE

After a long, delicious, and thoroughly filling breakfast, Mauve insisted her two guests take their time to relax and use their downtime wisely while she cleaned up. Brigham offered to help, which seemed to insult her more than anything. Then she practically kicked them out of the kitchen.

Halsey jumped on the opportunity to get her cousin alone and away from curious ears, always listening for new information to add to the woman's arsenal of gossip, facts, and confidential information. As Brigham sat on the couch in the living room with a sigh, his cousin called toward the kitchen, "Mauve? We're going for a walk."

He looked at her with wide eyes. "We are?"

"Of course, love. You do as you please. I'll be in here. Mind you don't stray too close to the brambles, though. They're sharp as needlepoints this time of year, they are. And don't go past the river. That's Jenson Blackmill's land on the other side, and he pulls a shotgun on the *birds* landing in his grass. I'd hate to see what he does to people, I would."

"Don't cross the river. Got it. Thanks." Dropping her voice into a low whisper, Halsey bent toward her cousin on the couch and raised her eyebrows. "Come on. I gotta get out of this house."

Brigham smirked. "Sounds more like a *you* problem, Hal."

"I told her *we're* going on a walk. You and me. There's no one else."

"Okay. It's not like we can't change our minds. You go for a walk. I'll stay here. Maybe take a nap. That breakfast…" He released a massive belch, then slapped his belly and groaned in satisfaction. "Best meal I've had in a while, know what I'm saying? I don't even know if I *can* walk."

"Well, maybe you shouldn't have eaten so much." She waved him forward and off the couch. "'Cause we're taking that walk right now."

The clanging of dishes and running water in the sink proved Mauve had already gotten to work on tidying up after breakfast, which was the only reason Halsey felt like it was safe to say anything at the moment.

Her cousin didn't look convinced as he scowled at her. "Hal. We finished the mission. Job's done. I don't see any harm in sitting back and relaxing until we get riled up to go again. Hell, you could probably use more rest after yesterday."

"I passed out and slept the rest of the day, Brigham. I don't need more rest. I *do* need to talk to you about a few things, and I'd rather do it somewhere our fantastically dedicated host can't overhear and repeat it to every single person she talks to in the next twenty-four hours, okay?"

His scowl only deepened.

"Please?"

"Hal." A defeated sigh escaped him, followed by a much smaller burp. "I just sat down…"

"Look, I know there's not a lot that's more important to you than your digestive system after a good meal, but this is one of those things. Give me half an hour, okay?"

"Outside?"

"Yes, outside." Halsey rolled her eyes. "Fresh air and sunshine. And walking after a giant meal is supposed to be good for you. Especially after the five thousand calories you crammed into your face."

A dreamy smile spread across his lips. "And all of them were so, *so* delicious."

"Let's *go*." She grabbed his wrist and hauled him off the couch before he could make any more excuses.

"Okay, okay! Damn." Brigham ripped his wrist free, rubbed it as if she'd actually hurt him, then pushed to his feet and glared at her. "Half an hour. And no hills."

Halsey fixed him with an exasperated look, then chuckled and rolled her eyes as she headed across the living area toward the glass door that opened onto the side patio. "Deal."

The morning was absolutely gorgeous, the sun shining warmly down on the open field behind Mauve's guesthouse beneath an uncharacteristically blue English sky studded with puffy white clouds. A line of trees cut across the swath of open land where the river formed a border between their hostess' property and the next, and Halsey led her cousin that way to get as far away from the guesthouse as possible without making Mauve think they'd abandoned her.

She took deep breaths of the cool air sweetened with the scent of freshly mowed grass and a hint of someone's smokey cookfire on the breeze. "We haven't had a lot of time to enjoy places like this, have we? I mean, without a mission attached to it."

"Which is exactly what I was trying to do on that insanely comfy couch you pulled me off," Brigham muttered dejectedly.

With a snort, Halsey elbowed him in the side. "You can pass out on the couch for the rest of the day after this if you want. As long as Mauve doesn't sit down and keep you awake with her constant talking."

"Actually, if I'm not eating anything, I'm pretty sure her talking would only *help* me fall asleep." They shared a laugh at their hostess' odd quirks, then Brigham shot his cousin a sidelong glance as he kicked a dirt clod away from him across the grass. "So what's this important thing you had to talk to me about ASAP, huh? Something happen?"

"What? No. I don't think so."

"Was it that asshole disco ball again? 'Cause look, I know you're pretty attached to the thing or whatever, but I swear, Hal. If it's only making shit worse for you in the long run, I'm not gonna sit around and watch it take over again and again and again."

"It's not that."

"All I'm saying is there's gotta be a line." He shrugged. "If it were *my* line, that freaky-ass thing would've crossed it a long time ago, and we wouldn't even be having this conversation. But it's yours, and you're not me, so I guess I have to suck it up and—"

"Brigham." Halsey laughed and stopped in her tracks to face him in the open meadow. "It's not the orb, okay?"

"Right." He scanned her, wrinkled his nose, then glanced all around the empty land behind Mauve's home and guesthouse before meeting his cousin's gaze again. "Then what is it?"

"I actually wanted to talk to you about what happens next after Coningsby." She said it casually, as if it wasn't that big of a deal, and kept walking toward the tree line along the river.

"What happens next?" Scoffing, Brigham skipped forward across the grass to catch up with her, then slid both hands into the pockets of his jeans. "We go home. That's what happens next. One more mission under the A-Team's belt, right?"

Halsey pulled a grimace and shook her head. "A-Team? Still?"

"Hey, you said you were on board with the whole thing. Unless you're lying to me about the name growing on you to get me to shut up about it."

He'd clearly meant it as a joke, but the reference to her lying to her cousin hit harder than it should have. Even a tiny white lie like pretending to be okay with the ridiculous name he wanted to give their two-person monster-hunting team.

I can't say anything about meeting with Aydem until it's

over. He'd never let me go on my own, and this meeting has to happen. I have to know what the Order of Skrár knows about my magic and this orb. Then when I come home and finally tell him everything, he'll see it was the right call in the end. It sucks now, but I'm doing it to help all of us.

"Hal?" Her cousin chuckled uncertainly and leaned forward to catch her gaze. "It was a joke, cuz."

"Yeah, I know."

"So we're good on the name, right? A-Team is pretty badass."

"When we're actually out on active missions, sure." Halsey cleared her throat and shrugged. "Maybe keep it to mission talk, though, okay? 'Cause when we're not doing militia stuff, I honestly like us better as only Halsey and Brigham, you know?"

"Brigham and Halsey? Yeah. Sure. I guess I can get behind that." Then he noticed there was still something his mission partner wasn't saying out loud, and his curiosity made it too hard not to press her further. "I still have a hard time believing you brought me out here to talk about what we call ourselves when we're not secret special agents or on a hunt. Right?"

"Ha. Good to know your extrasensory perception's still working at a hundred percent."

"All right, Hal. Spit it out." They reached the tree line, and Brigham stopped to face her. "What comes next after Coningsby that you're being so weird about telling me? It's not, like…another secret side mission off the books or anything like that, right?"

Halsey fought back a laugh. "No, it's not a secret side

mission. Though you gotta admit, those've turned out to be pretty awesome."

"With disappearing silver coffins, weird-ass sand you suddenly like turning into a round little creep show, and talking alpha werewolves begging you to kill 'em? Yeah. Totally fucking awesome, cuz."

"Actually, I was talking more about our last time in Ireland. Meeting the Havalons. Helping clean up the mess *we* left when we thought we were doing our jobs. Starting to mend a few little rifts between the Clans... That kinda thing."

"Oh." Brigham scanned the tree line, then shrugged. "I guess that all turned out pretty okay in the end. Except we didn't actually find anything about that coffin or who took it, so I don't know how much I'm into *more* solo investigations, you know?"

"Totally fair. Only that's, uh... That's not what this is, to be clear."

"Okay..." He stared at her intently. When Halsey wasn't forthcoming with more, he pulled his hands from his pockets, spread his arms, and huffed a wry laugh. "Then what the hell *is* it, Hal? I'm startin' to think I should be more concerned—"

"No, it's nothing *bad*. Chill out. It's this thing..." When he raised a skeptical eyebrow, Halsey realized it would probably be easier and slightly less embarrassing to show him instead of trying to explain. So she pulled her phone from her jacket pocket, opened the text Seamus had sent her last night, and shoved her phone toward her cousin. "There. It's this."

Pursing his lips and squinting, Brigham silently read

the message. Then he glanced at Halsey, looked back at her phone, and snorted. "'Maybe we can meet up'? *That's* the line he went with?"

"Oh, come on." She put her phone to sleep with a soft click and tucked it back in her pocket. "He sent that to me last night."

"Uh-huh. And you haven't gotten back to him, I see."

"Well, I wanted to talk to you first before I made a decision one way or the other," she snapped and instantly felt bad for how much genuine emotion she was putting into this and for how much she was twisting the truth. "So I'm talking to you."

"Yep. You sure are." He looked at her jacket pocket as if he could see through the canvas to eye Seamus' text one more time, then clicked his tongue. "So…what? You want me to block his number for you? Call him up and tell the guy to quit harassing my cousin? I can do all that, sure, but I'm not going to meet him in person, Hal. The dude's a giant. And I'm, you know…not all that into starting fistfights. Especially with a guy I actually think is okay, which is totally what this would turn into. Using magic for a thing like this is asking for a whole lot more."

"Seriously?"

"Yeah. That's what happens. I know *you've* never had to do it before. You're a chick—"

"Brigham, I'm not asking you to protect my honor or whatever. That's ridiculous." Halsey sighed in exasperation and shook her head. "I'm telling you, Seamus basically invited me to come see him in Ireland. And we're already on *this side of the pond*…"

Her cousin studied her face with a blank expression,

blinked a few times, then shrugged. "What? You want my permission?"

"No..."

"Good. 'Cause if *I'm* the only person you ever ask for permission, we've got a whole bunch of other problems. Like the Council figuring it out and turning me into some kinda Halsey Ambrosius handler so at least *someone* can rein you in. And I'll tell you right now, I'm not gonna be that guy. Or person. Or whatever. We're a team, not a messed-up...stupid..."

Halsey heaved a massive sigh and decided it was best to go for it. "I'm saying I wanna go to Ireland and see Seamus for a few days. By myself. And I'm telling you now so you don't think I disappeared on you when I'm not heading in the same direction."

"Right." A deep frown darkened his features, and he narrowed his eyes at her. "And what am I supposed to do?"

"Go home?" She shrugged. "Enjoy a little time off by yourself where you don't have to worry about me 'cause you'll know I'm safe with the Havalons. Or at least with Seamus."

"Go home. By myself." He clicked his tongue. "Are you for real?"

"Well, it doesn't make any sense for me to go home with you only to fly all the way back out here, does it?"

"Doesn't make any sense for me to go back home and sit down for a shitshow debriefing with Cavanaugh all by *myself* to tell him how *you* managed to shoot the barghest with a shotgun and heal the whole village with that *goddamn ball*—"

"You don't have to tell him any of that, okay?"

Brigham tossed his hands up into the air and spun away from her in half a circle. "Then what the hell am I supposed to tell him?"

"You tell him the same thing we told everyone here. Minus the foreign-secret-agent part, obviously." Halsey sniggered at how this little story of theirs had stuck so well with the locals that the Ambrosius cousins had actually become "agents" in Coningsby. Her cousin wasn't nearly as amused. "Tell him we handled the barghest like normal, no problem, and we had to improvise to duplicate Florence's healing potion when we found way more victims than we expected. Easy hunt, easy cleanup, and make sure you cover the part about the barghest looking like a weird werewolf hybrid or something.

"Obviously, we still have to report monsters that aren't acting the way they're supposed to. That'll be enough, plus the fact that *this* barghest got to a village full of civilians before we put a stop to it. That doesn't happen, either. You just…leave out the part where you got hurt, and I healed you. Also, the part where I healed everyone else with the orb. Then it's basically the same story."

"Except it's not the *actual* story, Hal."

"We can't tell Cavanaugh or anyone else on the Council the *actual* story." With no idea why her cousin couldn't see the truth and determined to help him get there, Halsey spread her arms and added, "We didn't say a thing about the orb when we debriefed after Turkey. As far as anyone else knows, we took down the chimera with a few well-placed hits, and that's it."

"So you want me to lie to him." Brigham stepped back from her and tilted his head. "Again."

"*Yes*, Brigham! I want you to lie to him, okay? Tell Cavanagh whatever you think will be enough for him to accept the story and write up his report, then go to your apartment and do what you normally do until we get our next mission. I'll go to Ireland for a few days, not very long, and we can regroup when I get back."

"Regroup."

She stuck a hand on her hip and tried to laugh, but it came out sounding bitter and unamused. "Now you're just repeating everything I say."

"Uh-huh." For a minute, it looked like he would explode on her and start popping off about all the ways her plan was the worst plan ever. He didn't, though. Instead, Brigham shrugged and muttered, "Whatever." A slow smile spread across his lips. "So, this thing with you and Seamus Havalon…"

"There's no thing." She couldn't keep a straight face, which instantly alerted them both that her statement hadn't been entirely accurate.

"Oh, yes, there is." Her cousin wagged a finger at her and chuckled. "I think somebody's blushing."

"No, I just—"

"Hey, of the two of us, I'm the only one who can see your face right now. You're blushing." Brigham shoved his hands back into his pockets, and they headed back across the field together toward the guesthouse again. "No problem, cuz. I get it. If I were you, I'd probably want a break from me too. Especially if your break includes a tall, dark, weirdly handsome Irish dude who's always grinning and loves going against what his Clan tells him to do as much as *you* do. It's actually pretty perfect."

"We're just friends, Brigham."

"Uh-huh. Totally. Except your *friend* didn't invite both of us. Only you." When she shot him another concerned frown, he burst out laughing. "I totally get it, Hal. You don't have to worry about me. I'll go home and lie my ass off to Cavanaugh at our debriefing, and you can…go to Ireland to unwind. Or whatever. Hey, I don't wanna hear anything about it, but you should know I'm still telling Cavanaugh why you didn't come back with me. Unless you want me to make shit up about that, too, but then you're *really* gonna owe me one."

"You can tell him whatever you want." Halsey drew a deep breath and nodded. "Just as long as you don't mention the orb or my weird magic issues. Not yet. Deal?" She stuck her hand out toward him, and he eyed it like it was covered in goo.

"Not my favorite, but fine. You got yourself a deal."

They shook on it, and a massive weight lifted from Halsey's shoulders at that moment.

No, she didn't exactly feel proud about telling Brigham, and through him the entire Havalon Clan, that she'd be spending the next few days in Ireland with Seamus. Not when she actually intended to meet Halil Aydem at a private estate in London for the answers to her magical questions.

At least no one would be worried about her while she was there. When she came back, she'd have plenty of information to help her explain why she'd done it in the first place.

She simply had to get there first.

CHAPTER TWENTY-TWO

Halsey and Brigham stayed in Coningsby through that day and into the next because one of the local mechanics in the village had offered to fix up their rental car as best he could to get them back on the road again. All free, of course, as a thank you for everything the Ambrosius cousin "agents" had done for the quiet little community.

The village citizens didn't throw any parties or make grand gestures, and that was fine. Mauve made up for it with her elaborately prepared meals. Lunch, afternoon tea, *and* dinner, in addition to a full breakfast. Halsey had a feeling that Coningsby's citizens were willing to let Mauve McRahl take up the monster hunters' attention. It meant the woman's neighbors wouldn't have to deal with her in *their* business until the American visitors left.

That gave Halsey and Brigham plenty of time to settle in and let themselves relax while the rental was being repaired. They didn't talk about Halsey's plans to pop over to Ireland first or exactly how Brigham would describe the ins and outs of their latest successful mission when asked back in the debriefing room at the Ambrosius estate. Instead, they spent their time silently, side by side or across from each other on the peaceful side porch or on different sides of the guesthouse. It gave them both plenty of time to get their heads screwed back on straight after the odd discoveries they'd made.

When their rental was finally finished and ready to go the next morning, a small but friendly procession of Coningsby citizens emerged to thank the Agents Ambrosius one last time for saving their village and to wish the young cousins well. It wasn't anything formal or fancy. Merely a few handshakes, hugs, and grateful smiles.

The only person who had anything more to say was the little girl, Makayla. Halsey's first willing and successful "test subject." She and her mother had stood in line for a few minutes to get to the agents and say their goodbyes. When it was finally her turn, Makayla ran at Halsey without warning.

She was a tiny thing, but speed and fierce gratitude still packed a punch when she ran into the young elemental and wrapped her arms around Halsey's middle as tightly as she could.

"Whoa." Chuckling in surprise, Halsey gently placed her hands on the girl's back to return the hug as best she could, looking up at the girl's mother for approval. The woman smiled knowingly and nodded. "Hey, kid. You're a good hugger. Everything's gonna be okay now, all right? You keep taking care of your momma like you have been."

When Makayla craned her neck to look up, her arms still wrapped around Halsey's waist, Halsey winked at her. The girl grinned. "Thank you," she whispered.

"Aw, hey. You bet. Thank *you* for being so brave. You helped a lot of people by choosing to be the first one. That takes guts."

The pride and joy couldn't have been more clear on the girl's face. But when Makayla released the incredibly tight hug, she beckoned Halsey closer with a wave.

After shooting Brigham a quick look that made him shrug as he laughed at her discomfort, Halsey had to bend at the waist and prop her hands on her thighs to make it down to Makayla's level.

The girl slowly walked toward her to whisper in the elemental's ear. "Did you see her?"

Halsey tried not to laugh so she could play along with this awesome kid a little longer. "See who, kiddo?"

"The barefoot woman."

A bolt of recognition and foreboding lanced through Halsey's entire awareness, but she succeeded in hiding it as she leaned back to look the girl in the eye and slowly shook her head. "I don't think so... What did she look like?"

Makayla looked over her shoulder at her mother, then turned again to whisper one more time in Halsey's ear. "She was beautiful with long black hair. And she wore a white dress and no shoes. She kind of looked like *you*, but I don't think she wanted to help us very much. I'm glad *you* did."

There was no sign on the girl's face that she'd said anything remotely alarming. When she backed away, she offered the kind of wide, joyful grin only possible at such a young age, then spun and practically skipped back toward her mother.

Halsey's heart fluttered. She tried to keep a straight face

and an easy smile as she scanned Coningsby's main street and the villagers gathered around them. Of course she wouldn't find a dark-haired, barefoot woman in a white dress wandering the village out in the open. That was ridiculous. She couldn't help looking all the same.

That's exactly what one of Patrick's guys said he saw through his back window. The woman in white. It's either a coincidence or that little girl saw the Mother of Monsters walking around out here and had no idea what was happening. It needs to stay that way.

After the villagers had said their goodbyes and stood back to let the cousins climb into their mostly fixed rental, Brigham stepped up beside her and elbowed her in the ribs before raising his other arm to wave. "They're expecting *something*, Hal. Smile and wave. That's how this works, right?"

Gritting her teeth, Halsey mimicked his motion before walking around the front of the car and getting in on the passenger side. After both front doors were shut and seatbelts were buckled, the engine started far more easily than it had when they'd picked the thing up at the Heathrow airport.

Brigham grinned and smacked the center console. "Look at that. It's like new."

"I hope you got insurance."

"On *this* thing? Ha. Come on. They won't even notice it got smashed to pieces and put right back together again, trust me." He shifted into drive and pulled slowly forward down Coningsby's main street, heading away from the village and back toward London. Then he gave his cousin a double-take and snorted. "What's going on with you, cuz? You look freaked the hell out."

"That little girl Makayla. The first one we healed?"

"Kinda hard to forget, yeah. What about her?"

Halsey drew a long, deep breath and found the girl standing front and center with her mom in the side mirror's reflection, both of them waving their arms high in farewell like everyone else. "She asked me if I'd seen the barefoot woman."

"Okay..."

"With black hair, in a white dress, who looked like me but wasn't here to help her or the other villagers."

"Well, that's a *little* weird, but it's..." Brigham sat quickly back against the driver's seat as he kept rolling them slowly down the main street. His eyes widened as it dawned on him, then he released a weary sigh. "Oh. *That* barefoot woman."

"Yeah. That one. So now we've had two different sightings in the U.K. Which probably means she's still here and hasn't, you know...spread to anywhere else. Yet."

"Not in person. But the monsters are still wonky as hell." He swallowed thickly and shook his head. "And I could've done without *that* kinda reminder, thanks."

"Just sharing a creepy little interaction, cuz. That's all."

"Well, until we figure out how the hell we're gonna stand against the Blood Matriarch and actually win, not to mention how we're supposed to find her, I'd rather not add her face to the list of things that keep me up at night, thanks."

She turned her head to frown at him. "Stuff's been keeping you up at night?"

"What? No. I sleep like a baby. But if something *was* gonna keep me up at night, it'd be that. I'm not gonna think about it, and you should probably do the same thing until we're prepared enough to handle it for real. Right?"

"Right." Halsey nodded and couldn't hold back a soft chuckle as she gazed through the windshield and their mostly straight shot across the English countryside back toward London. "Keeping my mouth shut from here on out. About *that*, anyway."

"Well, obviously. You can't keep your mouth shut about *everything*, Hal. We both know that's impossible."

Their drive back to London was fortunately as uneventful as it had been on their way into Coningsby. Brigham had already bought his ticket back to Texas the night before, but Halsey told him she planned to wait to see if she could snag any last-minute deals. Otherwise, she might take a few buses and a ferry to get to Seamus.

She stuck with her cousin until he'd returned the rental and checked into his flight, then she had to leave him outside security so he could go on without her. When the time came, they hugged each other fiercely, and Brigham clapped her on the shoulder with a laugh when he released her. "Don't do anything stupid, yeah?"

"Wow. Thanks, dude. I'm flattered you think I'd even consider such a thing."

"Ha. Please. I mean Seamus. He looks like the kinda guy who does stupid crap all the time. So don't, like, follow him off a cliff or anything."

Halsey laughed and spread her arms. "That's me. Halsey Ambrosius the elemental *lemming*."

"You know what I mean." He punched her playfully in the shoulder, started to turn toward security, then stopped to look back at her with a frown. "If you guys run into anything crazy while you're there, you'll let me know, right?"

"We probably won't. At least not anything crazy Seamus and I couldn't handle on our own…"

"Hal. I'm serious."

She wiped all amusement from her face and nodded. "Yeah, of course I'd tell you. And thanks again for being cool about this. And handling all the report stuff with Cavanaugh on your own."

"Well, someone's gotta do it. Doesn't mean I like it, FYI."

"I'll make it up to you."

"Uh-huh. See ya." This time he did turn fully around and took off toward the security checkpoint. He didn't turn around once to look back at her, and Halsey figured it was better if she made herself scarce.

Brigham was trying to be gracious about the whole thing, but she could tell he was pissed. Not only because she was sending him home alone or because he now had to shoulder the entirety of their mission report and debriefing with Cavanagh the second he made it back onto the Ambrosius Clan estate. There was something else.

He'd asked her to let him know if she ran into any trouble, and she'd agreed without pause. That was her natural response because why wouldn't she let him know?

Yet the look he'd given her didn't make it seem that

simple. For a moment, it had looked like he didn't believe her.

That's your own mind playing tricks on you, Halsey. How could he know? He doesn't. And you're a grown-ass adult. If you want a few days' vacation with an Irishman, that's your business, not his.

She could tell herself these things all she wanted, but it didn't change the fact that she didn't have any intention of going to Ireland to see Seamus. Halsey needed a viable reason to stay on this side of the ocean for a few more days, and Seamus happened to be it.

I'll text him back after I'm done talking to Aydem. We'll see what happens then, but one Havalon isn't my main focus right now. Gotta keep your eyes on the prize, right?

That felt a lot easier said than done, but at this point, Halsey was willing to do whatever it took to get what she needed. And apparently, she could justify the hell out of almost anything.

After driving back to London from Coningsby, seeing Brigham off at the airport, and catching public transportation to the heart of London to find a place with decent Wi-Fi so she could plan her next steps, Halsey had little time left in the day. The little coffee shop she stopped at for an afternoon hit of caffeine and a snack became her base of solo operations for the next hour while she looked up the address Aydem had left for her in his email. She didn't have nearly enough time to get her bearings again, figure out exactly what she wanted to say to the man, and get herself to the estate where he was staying before 11:00 p.m., so she decided to stay in the heart of the city for now and grab a hotel room for the night.

Then, if everything worked out the way she hoped it would, she could call a cab early the next morning to take her to this meeting that was finally going to happen, and the whole thing would be over and done with.

What she didn't want was more time than absolutely necessary to sit around and think about what had happened, what she still had to do, and what might or might not happen in the future if she was wrong about what Halil Aydem could offer her.

So she busied herself finding the closest available hotel at the best price that would still let her book an available room at such short notice. Then she packed up her single duffel bag, which still held all the gear she'd brought to battle the barghest and only two changes of clothes, before getting a taxi to the hotel.

Brigham probably would have balked at the price and the condition of the room she let herself into, especially after their oh-so-fun experience being put up in an elaborate and luxurious Turkish suite by their one and only paying client. Thinking about her cousin's reaction made her laugh as she closed the door and hauled her bag onto the small, built-in desk across the room from the single queen-sized bed.

That laughter was short-lived, because the reality was that Brigham *wasn't* here. He wasn't even halfway through the incredibly long direct flight from London to Houston, and he'd still be on his way home to his apartment in Lufkin before Halsey woke up the next morning.

It's one international trip, Halsey. He can handle himself. I need to handle my business here so I don't have this thing hanging over my head for the rest of forever.

The hotel was still nice enough to offer room service, so she ordered a small pasta dinner and two beers for herself, which she quickly consumed while sitting in front of the flatscreen TV mounted on the wall. She didn't pay attention to the show, but it was enough to keep her distracted from what was coming next.

Then there was nothing else to do but turn down the sheets, climb into bed, and get a good night's sleep.

She didn't think she'd be able to sleep well with her meeting the next morning looming over her, but sleep came quickly and easily. Maybe it was the heavily sauced pasta or the beers. Maybe she was still recovering from the immense amounts of energy it had taken to heal an entire community center full of barghest victims. Or maybe she was exhausted from the constant day-to-day of knowing something had to be done but still not getting the answers she needed.

Either way, as soon as her head hit the pillow, Halsey had enough awareness left to think about how nice that pillow felt before she was out cold. Which was what she would have preferred.

The next morning, her alarm went off at exactly 5:00 a.m. Halsey leapt out of bed, wide-eyed with her pulse racing as if she were already late. A quick shower, an even quicker pack of her duffel bag after pulling out only a change of clothes, and a brief stop at the café in the hotel's lobby for a to-go cup of coffee and a pastry were all she needed to feel well and truly ready for what came next.

By 6:00 a.m., as the last of the night's complete darkness gave way to the gray-blue glow before dawn, the taxi the hotel concierge had called for her pulled up to the curb outside the hotel and had no problem whatsoever with driving her out to the address of the estate Aydem had provided in his email.

Sitting in the back of that taxi and nursing her coffee was probably the hardest part of the whole ordeal before actually meeting face-to-face with the Order of Skrár's one member willing to speak with her. It meant she had nothing to do, nothing to check or take action on, and nothing to think about beyond rehearsing over and over the questions she meant to ask the mysterious Halil Aydem when he finally stood in front of her.

She'd only checked her phone once since leaving the hotel. No new messages, notifications, or missed calls, and her email inbox was as clean and empty as she liked to keep it. After that, Halsey couldn't bring herself to keep checking. It would only be another frustrating distraction she didn't need while preparing for this clandestine meeting that was finally happening.

Brigham hadn't sent her a thing. Why would he? Her cousin was probably either landing in Texas or working on getting a ride back to his apartment before passing out in his own bed, surrounded by his own things. Plus, she'd told him exactly where she would be, even though where she said wasn't anywhere close to the old, pristinely kept estate the taxi was taking her to now.

You said you'd be with Seamus. Done and done. If Brigham is still awake, he's probably more worried about blowing up my phone and invading my privacy than checking in and letting me know he made it back. Which is considerate. There are zero problems to fix right now, Halsey, so quit trying to make something up and leave it alone.

The drive took around half an hour, and though she wasn't particularly excited about the rather steep fee for a taxi ride, she wouldn't argue about it. The driver had even asked if she wanted him to drop her off at the estate's entrance gates before what looked like a very long private drive stretching across the center of the manicured lawns stretching out in every direction. And she'd told him she'd pay the fee. It didn't matter. Just keep driving.

They had to stop at the closed gates anyway, and Halsey dialed the number Aydem had given in his email. As the man had claimed, the number went straight to the gatehouse, and a gruff, gravelly male voice with an incredibly thick Cockney accent answered.

"Ringin' from the hack outside, are ya?"

"Um...yeah. Hi." Halsey cleared her throat and pretended she didn't notice the cab driver raising an eyebrow at her in the rearview mirror's reflection. "I'm here to meet with Halil Aydem. He told me he was staying here and gave me this number to call when I got here—"

"Name?"

"Halsey Ambrosius."

"Tell the cabbie there's a tight ten minutes to get up to the big 'ouse and back. Any longer'n that, and 'e won't be 'appy wiff it."

"Got it. Thank y—" The line clicked, the call ended, and

Halsey heaved a sigh as she stared at the home screen of her phone. Then she did look up into the rearview mirror and nodded at the driver. "He's gonna open the gates. And he said you have ten minutes to drop me off and get back through the gates."

"Right." The driver cleared his throat and adjusted the cap on his head as the muffled sound of the large iron gates' motorized mechanisms whirred to life, and the gates slowly swung away from them toward the property. "That'll cost extra."

"Totally fine."

Halsey tried to get a good look through the gatehouse window at the brusque guard she'd spoken with, but the bright sunrise starting to light up that side of the property reflected too harshly against the glass, making it impossible to see anything but a bright glare and a quick reflection of the taxi moving slowly past until the gatehouse was behind her.

Fortunately for the cab driver, it only took another three minutes to get to the circular drive at the front of the massive, sprawling estate house. Halsey didn't waste any time paying for the ride with her card and quickly exited the vehicle with her duffel bag slung over her shoulder. The second she shut the car door, the cab driver floored the gas as if he were driving a getaway car instead.

A spray of gravel and dirt kicked up behind the taxi's rear tires, and the vehicle fishtailed as the driver steered tightly around the circular drive. Then he was off in a puff of dust and a roar of the engine that was clearly more accustomed to making quick trips in the city and not long country roads in the middle of nowhere with a firm time limit.

Halsey watched the taxi race away until it disappeared over the rise of the first hill heading away from the estate house. Then she spent another five seconds watching the plume of dust settle over the top of the hill before turning around to face the estate house.

Okay. The guard let me through the gates. I'm here. So how does it work now? Do I walk right up to the giant front door and knock, or...

Before she could finish the thought, that giant front door set within an old but still incredibly sturdy frame of stone gave a heavy metallic *clunk*. The door swung slowly open with a creak that spoke of the estate's immense age, and a warm yellow light spilled onto the front stoop's intricately worked stone steps.

CHAPTER TWENTY-THREE

At first, she couldn't see anything but the glow of that light from the foyer, but she did hear the murmur of two low voices in quick conversation before either of them said anything intelligible.

"...take it from here, Collins. Thank you."

"Very good, sir."

Then a man's silhouette appeared in the doorway, the golden light seeming to radiate from all around him and blocking out all the details of his features. Slow, steady footsteps brought the silhouette out onto the front stoop, then the enormous front door closed from the inside, cutting off the warm light.

Without that glow behind the figure, the faint light of the rising sun was plenty to make out the man's physical appearance now. Standing at around six-two, he looked neither thin nor especially muscular, but his tailored business suit fit him snugly enough to show he was in decent shape for his age. Halsey placed him somewhere in his early to mid-fifties, which was made instantly apparent by the uniform gray of his short hair that had still retained the darkness of its youth at the man's temples.

He stood perfectly erect and poised as if he'd been groomed to live and work and handle business matters in places like this very same estate. Though Halsey couldn't be sure with so much distance between them as she stood off the circular drive at the bottom of the stairs, she noticed the man's perfect posture and lack of facial hair or visible wrinkles.

Distinguished. Important. Yeah, that's the image he's been keeping up this whole time, isn't it? Guess the Order of Skrár takes care of its members. Or the guy's done all this on his own.

The man stood there on the top step, his hands at his sides, as he smiled casually down at Halsey. Probably sizing her up based on what he was seeing in front of him. It felt like way too long of a wordless appraisal, and her urgency forced her to break the silence.

"Mr. Aydem?"

"Miss Ambrosius." The man's smile widened. "How wonderful to see you've made it."

The man's English was perfect, with no trace of an accent or any other indication this wasn't his first language.

Halsey hadn't known until seeing him for the first time that she'd expected someone completely different. Someone more like Yusef Burakgazi, for instance, or the older gentleman serving as Aydem's personal assistant who'd walked into the meeting room at Burakgazi's enormous Turkish estate to tell the Ambrosius cousins that Mr. Aydem couldn't meet with them that day.

A tiny part of her had also expected recognition when

the man she'd been trying to meet for weeks finally showed himself. Now that she was looking at him, she realized she'd been holding onto the suspicion that she'd seen him before. That Halil Aydem had been the bald man she'd seen fleeing from the teashop in the Grand Bazaar after she and Brigham hastily made their exit empty-handed.

The same bald man with a bright-red tattoo on the back of his neck that *could* have been a blood rune if Halsey had let her imagination run away from her without studying the tattoo's design first. He'd covered up the whole thing with his dark hood before she could.

Before he'd shot her one final, surprised glance through the crowds milling around the bazaar and disappeared into them.

That wasn't this man, though.

Halil Aydem was someone entirely new. Someone she'd never seen before, who looked very much like he belonged at this estate outside London's city proper. He could have been anyone she'd passed hundreds of times on the street, sat next to on an airplane, or steered her shopping cart away from at the grocery store.

Guess that's the whole point of the Order of Skrár, right? Hiding in plain sight. Keeping eyes and ears open on everything related to magic and monsters and elementals and whatever else exists between them.

It felt like a letdown to realize this meeting might not bring her a grand realization or automatically put together the puzzle pieces she'd been trying to wrangle since the day she and Brigham found that damn silver coffin in Moher.

The day everything started to change.

Aydem finally looked away from her to gauge the brightening sunrise beyond the last hill of the estate and inhaled deeply through his nose. "Beautiful morning, wouldn't you say? I must admit I'm surprised someone your age would have the determination and willpower to be up and on your way to see me at such an early hour…"

"Sorry if it's too early," Halsey blurted, not wanting to send the wrong impression and have him turn her away again. "Your email said to stop by whenever I could, so I assumed—"

"That you wouldn't wake me with a call to the guardhouse?" The man chuckled softly, and even *that* sounded friendlier than she'd expected. "You assumed correctly. I don't sleep much these days, believe it or not. So don't preoccupy yourself with worrying about my beauty sleep or any other factor you imagine might somehow determine the outcome of this meeting between us. I prefer early morning, to be honest. And you've picked a fine day for it."

Then he stood there and took in the view of the slowly lightening sky beyond the horizon of what the one hill in front of the estate house provided. He didn't look at Halsey for what felt like an incredibly long time after that, and she didn't move or say anything for fear it might distract him from his thought and make him change his mind about seeing her.

I have no idea what I'm supposed to do now. He can't expect us to talk about everything I came here to talk about while we're standing here in front of this giant house...

But the man didn't give any indication that he intended

to be anywhere except the estate's front stoop. The fact that he'd let the door close behind him made it clear he didn't intend to bring her inside.

"Well, then." Aydem's voice in the relative silence of dawn almost made Halsey jump, and she blinked before instantly corralling her immediate response into something that looked calm and composed, even if it didn't feel like it. When the man returned his gaze to her, his smile widened even more and made him look like a kind, soft-spoken, unassuming middle-aged man in whose presence anyone would easily feel comfortable.

Even when he slowly walked down the wide steps curving around the front entrance of the estate house, it seemed impossible that he might be capable of anything beyond a friendly conversation that would hopefully answer all the questions with which Halsey had armed herself today. It briefly occurred to her that she didn't feel even a flicker of apprehension or wariness as he moved toward her, and that had to be a good sign.

"I enjoy a good walk in the morning, Miss Ambrosius," he added as his well-shined black loafers crunched across the circular gravel drive toward her. "Gets the blood flowing and clears the mind. Do you mind if we walk for a bit before we get started?"

The question took her by surprise, which made her forget for a split second that he'd asked her a question and expected to receive a response. After swallowing thickly, she shook her head and offered him as much of a smile as she could manage. "No, not at all. Walks are great."

"Excellent. I'm sure you noticed the impeccable landscaping on your way in, but I can assure you the rest of the property is even more breathtaking. We'll cut back this way, and I'll show you some of my favorite installations." Aydem didn't walk toward her but turned right along the gravel drive to head toward the south end of the enormous estate house.

Halsey paused to watch him until it became clear the man wouldn't slow down or wait for her. So she readjusted the strap of her duffel bag over her shoulder, took one final look at the front of the estate house that didn't look to be occupied by anyone else, and hurried to catch up with the man she was finally about to talk to in person.

Now, she'd get her questions answered by someone whose literal purpose was to have all the answers in the first place.

The entirety of her walk with Aydem was uneventful, leisurely, and filled with silence. The only thing he said to her before he found the area on the estate grounds where he wanted to stop for their conversation after they'd rounded the back of the estate house. The man gestured toward a stone patio separated from the back of the house and all the patio furniture laid out there beneath a huge awning that would provide shade when the sun rose high enough to shine behind the estate house and light up the western side of the property.

"Feel free to leave your belongings here," he offered without turning around to look at her. "You have my word no one will touch them. We have a bit of a stroll ahead of us, and there's no reason to burden yourself with luggage all the way there and back."

Halsey didn't think twice about taking the opportunity to lighten the load. Her weapons bag had quickly started to feel heavier than usual, and it wasn't like she'd need any of her weapons where she and Aydem were going. He was a member of the Order of Skrár. The one supernatural organization unrelated to elementals or blood-humans and responsible for keeping updated records on all of it.

Aydem wasn't armed. He didn't look like a man who'd had training in hand-to-hand combat, so what was there for Halsey to protect herself against? Her grandmother had suggested meeting with someone from the Order to "ask the living records" anyway, which meant anyone Halsey met with would be safe.

Men like Aydem watched and took notes, as they'd apparently been doing for millennia. They certainly didn't fight. For now, there were no other threats Halsey needed to protect herself from. After she dropped her weapons bag on one of the white-painted metal patio chairs, she felt instantly lighter.

Free.

More capable of finally wrapping up this part of her path as a monster-hunter, an Ambrosius elemental, and a girl with a new and different type of magic before she moved on to all the other pressing matters. Those other matters concerned all three remaining elemental Clans *and* the Order of Skrár. For now, though, she finally had the opportunity to focus on herself.

She did double-check that she still had the sphere in her right pocket. Its weight reassured her as she patted her jacket. She needed to keep it with her because what she was about to discuss with Aydem wouldn't be convincing or revealing if she didn't have the orb to provide a demonstration. She doubted she'd need more than a quick show of the orb and a few flashes of light to make the point that she wasn't playing around anymore. That she meant business.

That whatever he knew, he could tell her because she'd figured out so much more about the orb and herself than the last time they'd planned to meet and didn't.

She hurried to catch up with the man, who hadn't slowed to wait for her. They kept walking together in an expectant silence that felt a lot more peaceful now that she didn't have to lug her gear around with her.

The surrounding birdsong grew louder by the second as morning arrived in full swing. A cool, refreshing breeze blew across the immaculate lawn, though the sun still hadn't risen high enough to bring Halsey and Aydem out of the shadow of the estate house. That was fine by her. She reveled in how good it felt to walk in an open expanse of nature with no immediate worries or concerns. Even the questions she'd mentally amassed quieted enough for her to drink in the present moment without constantly wondering what was coming next.

Halsey knew what was coming. Soon enough, she'd have her answers.

They came to a well-kept garden on the other side of the open grounds, though Halsey doubted this marked the end of the property for an estate like this one. Large trees loomed up in front of them, pruned and shapely, and she followed Aydem beneath an archway covered in vines and ivy and small, budding blue flowers.

After they passed through the archway surrounded by trees, the space beyond opened into a small, circular courtyard of perfectly cut grass and blossoming flowerbeds lining the entire area. In the center of the courtyard-garden was a large pond made to look natural but was too perfectly round not to be manmade. White stone benches large enough to seat at least three people were situated tastefully around the pond, and the birdsong was even louder here now that they were surrounded by trees, hedges, and flowerbeds.

Aydem walked straight toward the closest bench without a word, then stopped beside it and clasped his hands behind his back to stare contemplatively out at the surface of the pond.

Not knowing whether it was better to go sit on the bench or wait for him to invite her to do so, Halsey figured stopping beside him with a good five feet between them was the best way to go. And she didn't want to copy his posture in a way that might end up making her look desperate. So when she stopped at the same distance away from the pool as he had, she slid both hands into her jacket pockets and waited.

I seriously hope he doesn't expect me to know exactly how to start this conversation...

Now that she was here, getting to the point where they actually talked to each other about all the unknowns in Halsey's life felt like an insurmountable obstacle, harder even than walking blindly into a new mission against a monster that had inevitably changed in a way no elemental on the planet could predict anymore.

They stood at the edge of the pond, listening to the birds and the wind, watching a few ripples moving across the water's surface. Halsey thought she could even see the bottom of the pool lined with rocks and sand, but she didn't have enough time to double-check it for herself. Her host for the morning, fortunately, didn't keep her waiting much longer.

"So," Aydem began without looking at her. "You have questions."

"I do," she murmured, forcing herself not to laugh. He'd stated the most obvious thing either of them could have said right now.

"And you believe the Order of Skrár has the answers you seek."

"If anyone does, it's the Order." Halsey looked up when a pair of birds flittered from their perch in one of the trees across the pond and tracked them flying over the garden. With the sun not yet risen high enough to spill light into the hidden courtyard, she could watch them longer without having to look away. She hadn't come here for birdwatching, though. She dropped her gaze to the water and added, "I need to know what's happening to me, too."

"This is a personal matter, then?" Aydem turned his head slightly toward her, but he didn't look away from the pond.

"Only part of it." She didn't think she would know what to say after that, but the words flowed effortlessly from her now that she'd gotten started. "But the personal part of it is something I need to figure out before I can help my family and the other Clans get ready for what's coming next."

"Ah, yes. The impending *war*. That's the overarching theme occupying your mind lately, isn't it?"

Halsey nodded. "Assuming there will be another one, yeah." She turned her head slightly to catch a glimpse of his profile, but if Aydem felt her gaze on him, he gave no indication whatsoever he'd noticed. "Which I'm guessing the Order knows a whole lot about too."

The man slowly dipped his head. "Ask your questions, then, Miss Ambrosius."

She'd traveled all this way, had lied to her cousin and to her Council, had fought desperately to get this one chance meeting with a "living record" from the Order of Skrár, and had been so prepared to ask everything she needed to ask so she could fully understand what the ball of copper was, why it only responded to her, and what it was doing to her magic. She'd prepared for *that* to be the topic of her first question and probably the majority of all the others that followed.

Yet instead of inquiring about the orb out the gate, she asked Aydem something she hadn't anticipated putting so bluntly, let alone having it serve as the official start to their meeting. "There *is* going to be another war, isn't there?"

The man breathed deeply through his nose again and nodded. "Yes."

"Because the Mother of Monsters has returned. Hasn't she?"

His pause was only slightly longer than the first. "She has."

A mixture of relief, fear, conviction, and determination

flooded through her. This was only one of the answers she'd hoped to receive, though she couldn't possibly have anticipated what it would feel like to hear it spoken out loud by a member of the supernatural Order whose sole purpose was to know everything that happened within the secret world normal humans were never allowed to see and could never fully understand.

I knew it. She's been here the whole time since we found the coffin, and that's why all the monsters are changing. Now we need to figure out how to defeat her this time without destroying the entire world and killing almost everything in it merely to put her away again. For good.

That seemed like the only logical thing to ask next, so she did. "How do we defeat the Blood Matriarch this time, Mr. Aydem?"

The man's eyes moved slowly as he scanned the surface of the pond, the muscles of his jaw working visibly. Then he shook his head. "The Order of Skrár holds the living records for all of us, from the beginning of time to the present moment. But we cannot provide answers to questions about the future, Miss Ambrosius. Only in regard to the past, recent or ancient. And from *those* answers must each person's individual projections of the future be extrapolated."

Halsey's heart sank at the words, even though she'd known it was a longshot. "Meaning you have no idea."

"Just so." He lifted his chin and smiled again, still without looking at her. "I do hope your other questions do not focus entirely on what has yet to pass."

"That was only the beginning." Quelling her disappointment at the Order's lack of future-telling abilities, which she hadn't expected anyway, she collected her thoughts and mentally reordered her questions from most important to least. Aydem didn't quite give her as much time as she needed before prompting her again.

"You mentioned a copper orb in your first email correspondence to me. Transmuted from a pile of sand with its own unique magical signature. Do you still wish to ask about the creation of yours and the purpose you now carry with such an item in your possession?"

So the living records can read minds now too, huh?

This time, she failed to hold back a wry laugh as she realized there was very little she could keep from this man. "Yeah. That's the next thing. What is it? The orb, I mean."

Aydem took so long to reply that she almost thought he hadn't heard her. Then he slowly turned his head toward her and scanned the sky instead of her face, as if he wasn't willing to look her in the eye. "Before I provide you with *that* answer, I would very much like to see this object for myself."

"Right. Good thing I keep it on me pretty much all the time." Halsey's fingers closed around the cool, smooth surface of the orb in her pocket. She quickly drew it out so he could see the thing and they could move on to the part where he told her what she was dealing with.

Aydem finally looked at her, but his dark eyes merely grazed across her face before dropping toward the sphere resting in her slightly outstretched palm. His expression had been completely unreadable. Now the man's eyes widened, and the stoic lines of his lips spread into a surprisingly eager grin. "Interesting."

"Yeah, I already know *that* part." She released a self-conscious chuckle, but her attempt at a joke fell flat. "I'm hoping you can tell me more about it than the fact that it's interesting."

Tilting his head, Aydem studied the orb with more intensity than anything else he'd done so far. His dark eyes moved rapidly across the surface of the orb. The whole time, he kept beaming at the thing as if she'd brought him a precious gift or offering instead of a mystery she'd been trying to unravel since day one. "It is so much more than that, yes. I assume you've learned more about its capabilities since you first reached out to me."

"That's one way of putting it, yeah."

"Then by all means, do share." His eyes widened slightly, then he flicked his gaze up to meet hers and raised his eyebrows. "Please."

"I thought *I* was supposed to be the one asking questions and *you* were the one answering them."

"It is important both for you to say it out loud and for me to hear it coming from you. Then I will answer your questions, I assure you."

"Okay..." Swallowing thickly, Halsey regarded the orb and turned it over a few times in her hands. She hadn't expected to reveal her entire story to the man. The living records were supposed to know everything she'd done with it and everything she'd discovered about both the orb's magic and her own, whether or not Halsey had shared the full scope of that information with anyone else before now.

If he wants to dangle a carrot on a stick in front of me, fine. I'm not leaving this meeting until I've heard what I need to hear.

So she decided to go with the abridged version of her

exploits with the copper orb over the last several months and all the ways the thing had come in particularly handy during her missions and monster hunts with Brigham. Her focus remained on recounting what the orb had done for her when nothing else in the Ambrosius cousins' repertoire of battle tactics, magical attacks, or arsenal of elemental surprises had worked. Tearing a chimera into three separate animals. Healing the unhealable barghest wounds on Brigham and all the other victims in Coningsby. Halsey's ability to separate fragments of the orb into fake potions to heal them while no one saw the magic flowing through all the normies and back into her.

She even described the way the sphere seemed more tuned to her and her magic than anything else, that it responded to her emotions and desires and intentions sometimes even before she was fully aware of them herself. She told him about unlocking the orb's new latent abilities piece by piece, as each new circumstance warranted, without knowing what it was capable of beyond the present moment or how it was able to provide exactly what she needed at exactly the right time.

And, throwing all caution to the wind, she told him that since the day she'd transmuted the orb and had taken to carrying it around with her wherever she went, the object had affected her magic too.

She gazed thoughtfully at the orb in her hands. "When I healed my cousin from the barghest wound, it wasn't only this thing's magic anymore. It was *mine* too. Like this thing…unlocked something new inside me I never realized I had. It's not elemental magic, Mr. Aydem. I can tell you that with one hundred percent certainty. Brigham felt it, too."

"I'm certain he did." Aydem kept staring at the orb, and though his smile had faded a bit, he didn't seem any less enthusiastic about the sight in front of him as he'd been when she'd pulled the thing from her pocket. "You've unlocked something incredibly powerful in your use of this item. And such control over such a small amount of time."

"Thanks." It sounded strange coming from her own lips, but Halsey shook off any notion of being embarrassed before the feeling could make her lose her nerve. "So now you know what it can do and what *I* can do now, apparently. But I still need to know what it *is*. Please."

"Yes. Of course you do." The man spoke as if he was already lost in a daydream, musing about what each of them did or didn't know like they had all the time in the world to discuss philosophy and hypotheticals instead of true answers and solutions to very real and palpable problems. He took another long, deep breath and didn't take his eyes away from the orb. "To put it quite simply, Miss Ambrosius, this item in your possession, crafted by and from your own magic, is *you*."

She froze, holding her breath and waiting for him to go into more detail as to why he thought that was an acceptable response. He said nothing else, though. "I'm sorry, but... I mean, that's not really an answer—"

"It's the only answer that truly matters."

"No, it's not. Saying it's *me* doesn't explain why I can do things I shouldn't be able to do."

Aydem pressed his lips together, then turned back

toward the lake to study the water's calm surface instead of the copper orb or the face of the young, mystified elemental standing right there beside him. "That, Miss Ambrosius, is simply because you are coming at the issue from the wrong direction. And, as a result, you have not yet asked the *right* questions."

This is ridiculous. More riddles and talking me around in circles, huh? I'm not gonna be able to hold it together much longer if he keeps this up.

She slowly inhaled and tried to steady her rising anger. "What questions should I be asking, then?"

A soft chuckle escaped him. "Not *that* one."

"Then I..." She sighed and slid the orb dejectedly back into her pocket. "Then I don't know what you want me to say, here. I need to know these things, and you agreed you would answer my questions."

"You *do* know what to say," he snapped, his voice sharp and barbed despite his posture and expression remaining calm and serene. "You simply haven't given yourself permission to go where you need to go. To be who and what you need to be. To ask the *right* questions from the *right* direction. You must be blunt. Straightforward. Charging through the things you are terrified to even consider, because *that* is where your answers lie. Waiting for you to find them."

"That doesn't help me."

"Well you'll have to help yourself with this one, I'm afraid."

"Really?" Halsey gaped at the man, who kept gazing at the lake as if their conversations hadn't gone entirely sideways without warning. But he was absolutely serious. And she had to be too if she wanted to get past this sudden wall he'd put up between "the way she asked her questions" and what she needed to know. "Fine. What about the changes to all my magic? The...*new* things I can do? The part that *isn't* elemental like the rest of my family? Like every other elemental in the history of our kind? Why is the orb doing that?"

"Close." Aydem tilted his head from side to side before letting out a noncommittal hum. "But not quite."

"Then I have no goddamn clue what you want from me!" Her shout rang out across the pond, startling several more birds from the trees on the other side. Aydem gave no reaction whatsoever. After quickly pulling herself together, Halsey scanned the garden but didn't truly see any of it. *What does he mean close but not quite? What kind of questions am I supposed to ask when all the ones I've already thought of apparently aren't good enough for him?*

Then she remembered that brief and unelaborated-upon conversation with Brigham after she'd healed his barghest wound. Her cousin had known she'd used the orb's magic along with her own, but at that moment, her magic hadn't been elemental by any stretch of the imagination.

Then what the hell is it?

CHAPTER TWENTY-FOUR

"What kind of magic did I use to heal my cousin?" Halsey finally asked, her voice low and barely loud enough for him to hear. "What kind of new magic did the orb give me?"

Bowing his head, Aydem closed his eyes and sighed. "You're almost there, Miss Ambrosius. You're on the right track. However, I'm afraid you aren't paying close enough attention to what I've already told you."

"What, that the orb I transmuted from someone else's magic is actually *me*?" A bitter laugh escaped her. "That's impossible. I *made* it with my magic, but someone else left that pile of sand behind in a storage unit, and it wasn't me. I'd know."

He was silent again for another long moment that stretched into eternity, then cleared his throat. "I was under the impression that my assistant Highford made it perfectly clear how ill-equipped you were to handle this form of conversation when he canceled our last-minute meeting in Turkey on my behalf. The second one."

"He didn't make anything clear. Only that I needed to find answers about my own past and where I came from on my own before you would even agree to see me."

"Just so. And I had assumed, with all this new information you've brought to our discussion today, that you followed that advice and sought many of those answers within your own family…"

"Ha. Yeah. I found answers, all right." With even more frustration and anger bubbling up inside her now, it was impossible to keep everything that flooded her mind from spewing out of her mouth. "I found out my entire family's been lying to me for the last twenty years. I found out none of them actually believe my grandmother's crazy and that they only kicked her off the Council and banished her into the woods because they only wanted to cover up the truth they all knew but didn't want to accept.

"Worse, I found out that my mom *wasn't* insane, that she *didn't* die from losing her mind one day out of the blue. She *killed* herself! The whole time, instead of telling me the truth, my entire Clan had been feeding me one giant lie. Everyone I looked up to, trained under, and was supposed to admire and respect. They made me think *I* was insane, like her, but she never was! And none of that tells me a damn thing about this orb or why I can suddenly heal people or split monsters apart by thinking about it!"

Her voice crashed across the garden this time, startling more birds into flight and echoed much longer than her last outburst. Halsey thought she saw a different kind of shadow flicker across the surface of the pond, but with her fists clenched tightly at her sides and her breath heaving, it was hard to pay much attention to anything else, let alone a few moving shadows.

Then she waited for the man from the Order of Skrár to say something, anything, that wouldn't automatically translate into a new potential reality that she'd screwed up this meeting, again. This time beyond repair.

Aydem didn't say a word. But he did take a step back away from the pond before slowly turning to face her head-on. His eyes were closed, and he took another deep, calming breath before nearly driving her crazy all over again. "Oh, dear…"

Shit. I screwed this up. And now I threw my chance at answers down the toilet because I can't get a grip on my anger issues.

Halsey pressed her lips together and watched him intently, not daring to say another word in case one more thing from her mouth pushed him into calling off the entire meeting before it had even truly begun.

"It seems," the man continued softly, "that my previous message was not entirely clear when presented through Highford. Which is unfortunate, to say the least."

"But I did what you wanted," she inserted, her voice barely rising above a whisper. "I went digging into my own family, and I found exactly what everyone's been keeping from me my whole life. I found out who I am—"

"You've done nothing of the sort." His eyes flew open as he barked this last correction at her, and Halsey could have sworn a dark light flashed across his eyes as he did so. She wrote it off as a trick of the rising sunlight, the reflection of the water, and the fact that she was almost too angry and irritated to see straight. "You went digging in the right place, but once again, Miss Ambrosius, you failed to use the proper tools. You have learned nothing of how to ask the appropriate questions, the *only* questions that truly matter, and until you rectify that mistake of your own doing, there is *nothing* I tell you that will aid you in your endeavors. You simply aren't ready for the truth."

His words hit her like a physical blow, and her mouth ran instantly dry. "No. I'm…I'm sorry I yelled at you, Mr. Aydem. I didn't mean—"

"It has nothing to do with your tone of voice." The corner of his lips flickered again, but he didn't smile this time. "I rather enjoy watching such an intense passion flaring up within you. But passion will only get you so far."

"Please. I'm ready for the truth. I really am." She almost stepped toward him, part of her ready to beg and plead and fall to her knees in front of him if that was what she had to do. The other part of her, the stronger part of her, was too proud to stoop that low. She had to fix this, right now. She only needed more time to figure out exactly how to do that. "If you could give me another chance, Mr. Aydem. To start looking at things the right way and ask the right questions, like you said."

Aydem lifted a hand to stop her and raised an eyebrow.

Halsey's gaze instantly went to the man's open palm and the cuff of his suit jacket below it, where the tip of a dark, crimson shape peeked out from under his clothing, right on the inside of his wrist.

Like the mark she'd seen on Yusuf Burakgazi's wrist before he'd covered it up.

"You may think yourself sufficiently prepared," Aydem

stated before lowering his hand. "However, you clearly are in need of more guidance in that regard. A little more... practice and experience, we might call it."

"Mr. Aydem—"

"I am willing to aid you in this next step of the process, Miss Ambrosius."

She stopped trying to argue with him, and her mouth popped open in surprise instead. From the corner of her eye, something else stirred over the surface of the lake, but she could hardly think of that now.

He was giving her another chance.

She hadn't screwed everything up, after all.

"Provided that you are willing to see this through to the *very* end. Because what you will discover is the kind of knowledge from which you can never return. Which you can never forget. Which changes everything entirely, with no hope of your life or your perception of reality ever going back to the way it was. Even if that is how you think you prefer it. Do you understand?"

"Yes." Halsey nodded vigorously, no longer trying to hold herself together until this man's attention because she was finally getting what she wanted. "Absolutely, I understand. I'll do whatever it takes, Mr. Aydem. I swear."

"Good." He dipped his head, then motioned across the surface of the pond one more time. "Then tell me what you see. Really, *truly* look at what is in front of you. Wait for the knowledge to reveal itself, Halsey. And when it does, then you will understand every aspect of your capabilities. Every aspect of who and *what* you are and always have been."

Still nodding, she turned briskly back toward the pond

and studied its surface. Halsey had no idea what she was looking for, but she was done trying to guess before anything happened. A member of the Order of Skrár was telling her to look for the knowledge she needed in the pond, and that was exactly what she would do.

Whatever it takes...

She had no idea how long she stood there staring at the water, but it couldn't have been long before something materialized below the surface. A dark thing moving swiftly through the water. Then another blurred shape made of shadow, and another. Still, she watched the pond, not daring to ask any more questions for fear of missing what was very clearly her last chance to find what she needed to know.

Aydem didn't say a word. After she'd turned toward the pond, the man had faded in the background of her awareness, blending in with the garden like he was simply part of the scenery. Only when Halsey denied her fierce urge to turn around to gauge her success by his expression did she realize the garden had grown considerably quieter.

Too quiet, almost.

The birds had stopped singing. The breeze that had kept them cool and had felt like such a refreshing, feathery touch against her face had all but died.

In fact, she heard nothing but the sound of her own breath and the rushing of her pulse in her ears.

Keep watching the water. Don't think about anything else. This has to be some kinda test, and I'll be damned if I don't pass it with flying fucking colors now...

Then she *did* see something in the water, though she

couldn't believe what it was until it had almost left the wavering shallows of the pool right there in front of her.

The first sign that something was incredibly wrong appeared as a flash of two glowing green orbs below the water's surface. Like eyes. Then they *were* eyes. Enormous, buggy eyes within a squashed, oblong face covered in bumpy flesh. The creature to which the eyes belonged clawed its way from the pond. Long, thin, webbed fingers tipped in sharp claws. Gangling limbs emerging from the water. The whole time, the creature stared at her like she was the only reason it had chosen to show itself.

Because she was.

What the hell is a grindylow doing in there?

It was the only thought she had time for before the creature leapt to its feet at the edge of the pond and scuttled toward her.

Halsey reacted on instinct and reached out with her elemental magic to call on the life force of the trees around the garden. A thick root erupted from the ground in front of her at her command, spraying dirt and grass everywhere as it lashed back and forth. She hurtled it toward the jabbering, grumbling grindylow that scrambled toward her. The root hit the three-foot monster with a wet smack and sent the creature sailing over the pond to crash into the trees on the other side of the garden.

By the time the grindylow was off its feet, the surface of the pond had started to bubble. Not with heat, and not with magic.

With the surfacing heads, mangled faces, and glowing green bug-eyes of a dozen more grindylows. Then two dozen. Then three.

Halsey lost count after that.

Hissing, she pulled another tree root from the ground and sent both of them smacking across the surface of the pond. They caught a few grunting grindylows off guard, but the rest merely dove beneath the surface to avoid the attack before coming right back up again and heading toward her.

The first six who'd managed to claw their way up onto dry land scuttled toward her, and Halsey stepped back before connecting with the earth itself beneath her. Enormous rocks hidden under the top layer of earth for centuries rumbled and pulled themselves free. She drew her hand back before launching it toward the first wave of grindylows, and the giant boulders smashed into them a second later, cutting off their war cries and making it harder for the creatures behind them to leave the pond and head for the lone elemental in their midst.

How the hell are there so many in one tiny-ass pond? And where the hell did they come from?

Then she remembered she'd come here not to fight monsters but to have an important conversation with a member of the Order of Skrár. A man who did not possess the kind of elemental magic that would protect himself or help Halsey.

While more grindylows clambered over the crushed boulders and the bodies of their pancaked kind beneath, Halsey spun around and reached toward where she'd thought Halil Aydem still stood. "Mr. Aydem! Get back. There's too many—"

The words stuck in her throat when she realized the

man wasn't where she'd expected him to be. He stood beneath the archway covered in vines and small blue flowers with his arms spread, wearing the most malevolent grin she'd ever seen on another human face.

"This is how you learn what you can *really* do, Halsey."

"What?" She launched another boulder straight into the pond this time, catching several grindylows beneath the enormous weight, but they just kept coming.

"Should you succeed, I very much look forward to our next encounter," he added with a chuckle.

His growing laughter filled the air, then his voice faded away.

"Are you fucking *kidding* me?" she shrieked in fury, then had to spin around in time to avoid getting clawed in the face by a single grindylow who'd made it past the front lines. It sailed toward her, its mouth open to dual rows of glittering, razor-sharp teeth in an unnatural wide snarl.

Halsey cocked a fist and pummeled the thing to the ground with one blow, coating herself with a layer of thick, viscous green slime. "Aydem!"

She tried to look back and find the man again, only catching a glimpse of the archway between the trees that was now completely empty.

Halil Aydem was gone.

But she didn't have any time to think about how much that sucked, because bitingly sharp claws dug into her left calf, and Halsey screamed.

She kicked at the creature latching onto her flesh and sent the thing sailing backward into the air. The gangly green body disappeared into the pond that wasn't even a pond anymore but had now become a roiling swarm of grindylows all fighting to get to Halsey Ambrosius first.

Calling on the calm air around the garden, Halsey funneled the life force magic of the wind and shoved it out in front of her with both hands. The conjured vortex tossed grindylows into the air like scattered bowling pins, but still, the things kept coming.

They were relentless.

They were legion, spilling from the pool in a single-minded mass that couldn't be stopped or even slowed, which made itself perfectly clear as the swarm continued toward her. Grindylows snarled and scrabbled and raced toward her, tiny fangs bared and claws extended like they were tiny green toddlers running toward a hug instead of monsters intent on tearing her down.

If it had been one or two of them, Halsey could have handled it. Hell, if it had been a normal-sized swarm of eight to ten, she would have been fine.

But this was over a hundred, and she was all alone.

She kicked at another grindylow that had somehow gotten its gross little mouth around the toe of her boot. Another volley of gusting wind cleared a momentary path through the swarm, but more of the grotesque vermin took its places. Something sharp and painful nicked the back of her neck. Halsey cried out before slapping away the grindylow that had clamped down on her with its vicious claws.

One of them dug its way up her leg until she batted it away. Another leapt onto her shoulder and tugged at her hair.

Halsey clutched her elemental magic and tried to draw more tree roots from the ground, but the grindylows leapt on her only other source of defense and bashed the roots back to the ground. The healthy wood was ripped to shreds in second.

Whether she'd tripped over a rock, a slight bump in the grass, or a grindylow that had rushed behind her, she had no idea. She only knew she was going down, and after she did, the odds of ever getting back up again were slim to none.

That didn't mean she didn't fight back with everything she had as the closest grindylows leapt toward her. More kept spilling from the pond that couldn't possibly have any water left in it. She grabbed the nasty little creatures by their heads, arms, legs, webbed feet and hands, snarling and scratching and kicking back with all her strength.

Every bit of her exposed flesh and even the parts of her covered by her clothing burned incessantly as hundreds of tiny, needle-sharp claws pierced her like daggers. The swarm hadn't managed to pin her down quite yet, but they would if she didn't think of something soon.

Halsey scrambled to regain her feet, to press her boots against something solid that would hold against her weight so she could stand again, but everything she touched was a grindylow. Everywhere she looked, the creatures yapped, grunted, and snapped at her, yet somehow, she hadn't managed to lose a finger or a hand. She hadn't been pressed against the ground by their combined weight until she suffocated.

Not yet.

But soon.

She knew it in her bones.

Halsey Ambrosius was going to die here in this private garden in England, fighting an impossibly huge swarm of grindylows on her own, and no one would ever know.

This was it.

I'm so sorry.

That was the first real thought racing through her mind as she kept fighting back, trying to claw free from the swarm. It was an apology to herself, to Brigham, to her entire family for having been so stupid in thinking she could do this alone.

It was an apology for all the unrealized things her life should have been. For wasting her chances. For not knowing enough about herself and what she could do to make this one more epic fight for Halsey Ambrosius the monster-hunter to stick under her belt.

This was the end.

One of the grindylows clinging to her hip released a squeaking, curdling victory cry as it lifted something shiny and metallic into the air for all to see.

Her copper orb.

Bleeding, bruised, and battling all the grindylows she could reach with her feet and one hand, Halsey snatched the creature by the throat and squeezed before tossing into the sea of its monstrous kin. She didn't know how she'd managed it, but with the grindylow gone, she was left holding the sphere. She pulled it toward her center with all her strength to cradle it there and keep it from the creatures about to rip her apart.

Why she could only think to protect the orb and not herself, she would never know.

But the second she clenched her eyes shut and waited for the end, the orb grew agonizingly hot in her hands, flared up through the center of her core, and unleashed a surge of more powerful energy than she'd ever felt from it before. All of it at once.

It felt like the intense magic was bursting through and out of her, shooting from her head and her hands, her bloody legs and from the soles of her boots. A deafening crack echoed across the garden with a flash of golden light, and everything stopped.

Halsey gritted her teeth and clung to the orb with what little strength she had left. She couldn't move at first. She couldn't let herself believe any of this was real, because if she did, she wouldn't be able to face the inevitable end with any sense of dignity. Not that she had any left to begin with, but death apparently wasn't in the cards for her today.

Instead, when she finally pushed past the horror of what she might see and opened her eyes, she realized she was still lying on the ground. Battered, cut, bloody, and out of breath, but still very much alive.

Then she unwrapped herself from the human ball she'd made of her body and looked up.

The entire unnaturally huge grindylow swarm had stopped. Those who'd pulled her to the ground had leapt away, and those standing closest to her did only that.

They were simply standing there. Hundreds of pairs of eyes, all glowing green and all of them staring at her. A few grumbles, grunts, and squeaking clicks echoed across the garden, but those were the only noises beyond Halsey's ragged breath.

Without stopping to think about what she was doing or the implications if it actually worked, she lay on her side and thrust the copper orb as high into the air as she could with one hand. "Leave me the fuck alone!"

For a moment, she felt like a complete idiot. Then the grindylows standing around her bowed low, their gangly bodies folding nearly in half as they scuttled backward and bashed into the others standing behind them.

Slowly, wave after wave, the grindylow swarm repeated the response. Every creature bowed low and scuttled backward, the entire mass of them slipping back into the pond and under the water as if they were a pile of dirt being sucked up by a vacuum hose. They screeched and squealed, but every one obeyed the command.

They were listening to her.

They did exactly as she wanted.

They left her alone.

When the last grindylow backed up toward the edge of the pond, it paused to gaze at her with those enormous, grotesquely buggy eyes. Then it dipped beneath the surface of the perfectly still water and disappeared.

The copper ball kept thrumming in her hand, and now that the danger was unbelievably past, the strength of Halsey's upraised arm gave out entirely. Both her hand and the orb thumped into the grass, then she rolled over onto her back, breathless, and gave herself a moment to stare up at the blue sky above her and the first bits of sunlight finally making their way into the garden from the east.

I'm alive. Holy shit. I'm actually alive. I didn't die. I'm...I can...

Her thoughts wouldn't even continue after that, because Halsey didn't know *what* to think.

She'd walked right into an ambush, thinking she was walking into all the answers to her questions and some sort of enlightenment that would help her fight the coming war. She'd fought an entire grindylow swarm, horribly outnumbered, and hadn't been shredded to bits. Then, with the orb in her hand, she'd stopped the whole thing without so much as a conscious thought before commanding every monster around her to leave.

And the monsters had obeyed.

What the fuck?

That wasn't elemental magic. It wasn't even healing magic or preconceived knowledge about how to split a chimera apart. It wasn't a trick of light and sound to get the attention of a table full of arguing elementals from two different Clans.

It wasn't *her*.

But it *was* her.

She couldn't think about it beyond that, or her mind might explode. Which wouldn't have been anywhere close to the strangest thing that had happened to her this morning.

It took her a moment to find the sphere where she'd dropped it. Then almost the same amount of time to focus on its magic combined with hers so she could heal the cuts, scrapes, and puncture wounds from the swarm that had almost been as deadly as it seemed. Magic, power, and energy heat flared through her again, but it was nothing like the first time today.

It was healing. Soothing. Restorative.

Finishing the healing process on herself took massive amounts of energy, though she hadn't had much to begin with. The orb was apparently powering itself with its own energy now. Still, Halsey was as good as new again in under three minutes.

Physically, at least.

I just commanded hundreds of crazed grindylows. Made them stop. Called them off. They're gone. What the hell does that make me?

She gave herself a few more minutes to lie in the once-perfectly manicured grass of the garden, now torn apart by the battle she'd only narrowly survived. Sweat soaked her clothes, and she didn't know if she would ever catch her breath again. At least she *was* breathing.

What was she supposed to do now?

Without thinking about it, she pulled her cell phone from her other jacket pocket, which somehow had miraculously survived the grindylow fight with her, and found the text from Seamus inviting her to spend time with him if she was ever "on this side of the pond."

If she let herself think too hard about this, Halsey might never type up the message she wanted to send him, let alone hit the actual button to get it from her phone to his. But she needed to *do* something, and this felt like the right thing to do.

She couldn't call Brigham. She couldn't call Greta, either. There was still far too much unsaid between her and her family, for that matter. Everyone would be too busy asking her how she'd ended up like this. She couldn't sit with them and get the comfort she needed from being with another living, breathing, functioning human body. Someone who wouldn't judge her for what she'd done or question her beyond whatever she decided to share.

More than anything, she didn't want to be alone.

Seamus Havalon was so much closer, anyway.

Her fingers shook as she typed up the text, but then she finally got down the words she wanted and sent it off without rereading any of it.

Will today work?

That was all she could manage. And while she waited for his reply, telling herself *that* was the reason she hadn't picked herself up off the ground yet to walk back across the estate for her weapons and off this damn property to call another cab, she couldn't stop thinking about the fact that she was still alive.

She was still here.

If it hadn't been for the copper orb, she wouldn't be. That much was crystal clear.

Halsey wrapped her fingers around the orb again and slid it back into her jacket pocket as her phone vibrated with a very fast, very brief incoming message. Relief flooded her like a raw, gasping breath when she saw it was from Seamus.

Excellent. Let me know when your flight gets in, and I'll be there.

Halsey released a breath, wiped more beads of sweat from her forehead, and forced herself to ignore the massive shitshow she'd walked into. Along with the impossibility of having walked away in one piece.

I told Brigham I was going back to Ireland, and I can't go home. Not right now. Might as well turn the little white lie into the truth, and hopefully that'll buy me enough time to figure out how the hell I'm supposed to deal with this.

More than anything, accepting Seamus' offer might have been the only thing that didn't make Halsey feel like a terrible person she hardly recognized anymore.

It definitely didn't make her feel like a monster.

CHAPTER TWENTY-FIVE

Halsey booked a same-day flight from London Heathrow to Dublin International and spent the entire flight wondering how the hell she was supposed to look Seamus in the eye and tell him she was okay.

Though her fight with the grindylow nest hadn't injured her physically, the psychological and possibly magical upset after that kind of discovery made her start to question everything she knew about who she was.

Halsey Ambrosius the elemental monster-hunter, best of the Ambrosius Clan's militia operatives, might not be the whole truth of her identity.

None of it made sense. Was it the orb? Was it *her*? Was it something else?

She'd shared tea with Halil Aydem, content enough to finally sit down with the man and have their meeting face-to-face. Like she'd been trying to do since Greta had first given her the man's name and contact info. She'd thought she'd made it to the next level of information. Higher security clearance, even, as far as the world of magic and monsters and living records was concerned. Then the man had pulled one hell of a dirty trick on her, simply to watch her squirm.

Aydem's a coward. He talked me around in circles until I didn't know which way was up, then he threw me into the fire. Now he's gone, and I still don't know what this damn orb is or why I'm the only one who can use it!

Being stuck on a plane for an hour and a half, forced to sit quietly and wait, to not make a scene, to not release her anger, frustration, and confusion in a way that would actually make her feel better, seemed like one of the hardest things she'd ever had to do. The whole time, she felt impossibly weighed down by all the burdens she'd been shouldering.

The weight of lying to Brigham again.

The weight of going to another elemental Clan for help before her own family. Again.

The weight of knowing something about her made her different from the rest of her family, though nobody seemed to know what it was.

The weight of having used the copper ball not to strip an invincible monster to pieces or heal her cousin and an entire village of innocent normie victims, but to command an army of grindylows. To command *monsters.* And they'd answered her call.

Her tussle with the obnoxious, razor-toothed little cretins had been messy, yes. The last thing Halsey had expected was to be led right into an ambush, and she'd been gullible enough to trust that her meeting with Aydem was nothing more than that. She'd let her guard down. She'd been fooled, then she'd been…what?

Surprised? Vindicated? Exalted?

The catch-22 played over and over in her mind. If her initial instincts were correct and the grindylows had responded to the orb and to *her*, something was wrong with her. Something dangerous that no one in her family could have recognized, or they wouldn't have brought her into the militia's fold. They would have exiled her onto the massive Ambrosius estate property to make a hermit's life for herself, maybe next to Greta's little bungalow by the river. They would have done whatever they could to shut her up. Even more than they already had.

On the other hand, there was always a chance she was giving herself far more credit than she deserved. That someone else had manipulated her run-in with the grindylows, that it was a manufactured ambush and a manufactured escape on Halsey's part. If she could even call the end of that fight an escape.

The only other person who could have confirmed that for her was Aydem, and he'd fled the scene before she could ask him what the hell was going on. The man who claimed to represent the Order of Skrár might have lured her into that trap and forced the grindylows out of hiding to do their worst, then played out one hell of an elaborate show by calling them off, laughing all the while.

That possibly seemed like a stretch, even after everything she'd been through in the last few days. Yet if it was true, if it hadn't been her magic, the orb's, or a product of anything she'd done, the Ambrosius Clan was in serious trouble. All the Clans were in serious trouble.

If it was true, Halsey had stumbled upon a secret even

bigger than those her family had been desperately hiding from her for her entire life.

It meant the Order of Skrár had been infiltrated by at least one man with enough knowledge of blood magic to arrange such an astounding spectacle. The supposed neutrality of the Order had been compromised, along with all the records of elemental families stretching back for generations, centuries, millennia, and even farther.

It meant Greta Ambrosius had put her faith in the wrong living records, and Halsey's grandmother likely wasn't the only one who'd done so.

It meant the three remaining elemental families on Earth had been betrayed, deceived, and manipulated, and nowhere in the world was safe for any of them.

That seemed like the worst possibility at a glance. Yet when she returned to her part in it, how and why she'd been able to *control monsters,* if that was what happened, blood-humans in the Order of Skrár didn't feel so terrible anymore. An elemental who could fight for and against either side was impossible, yet it had happened. Where would it leave her family if their best operative had to recuse herself from all missions, including the coming war with the Mother of Monsters, because she could no longer be trusted? What would it do to them if she could no longer trust herself?

To top it all off, hard as it was to accept these were her only two options, she couldn't come up with anything else even remotely plausible.

As the plane neared the end of its short flight and began its descent, Halsey also doubted her decision to head to Dublin instead of going directly home. She could have come up with a reasonable explanation for Brigham why she'd cut a fun, frolicking visit with Seamus Havalon short by three days. She could have gone back to her family's estate, directly to Greta's front door, and spilled her guts at the feet of the woman who'd carried the mantle of Ambrosius Family Rebel before the torch had inadvertently been passed to Halsey. She even could have gone to her dad. While Aiden wouldn't have known how to explain the grindylows or what their next steps should be, he'd made it clear the last time they spoke that he was on her side.

Still, what would he have thought of his only child after hearing she'd unintentionally commanded a whole army of nasty little creatures…and those creatures had intentionally obeyed?

The man couldn't handle that kind of loss. No one in her family could.

Jesus, Halsey. You're not dead, and this isn't your damn funeral. What happened to your optimism?

She didn't have an answer for that. She could start with not catastrophizing this new discovery until she had all the pieces and a little advice from someone relatively objective. Like Seamus Havalon.

He liked her enough to be straight with her about plenty of other things. Their families' cold-shoulder battles with each other, her and Brigham's part in the werewolf mess they'd left behind after their first trip to Ireland, and the support the Havalon Clan had offered her if she needed it in the future. However, he didn't know her well enough to take anything she might tell him personally. Or at least not as personally as anyone in *her* family was likely to take it. History had already made it clear how far the Ambrosius Clan would go to cover their tracks when they led to shameful, distasteful places.

With Seamus, she could test the waters of sharing this information. That was exactly what she needed right now, and he'd given her the perfect opportunity.

Halsey's head still reeled when she stood from her airline seat in coach, grabbed her duffel bag from the overhead bin, and hauled it along with her up the aircraft's central aisle. Her pulse thrummed in her head when she entered the terminal through the arrival gate and searched the airport signs to lead her to passenger pickup. The strap of her duffel bag slipped in her clammy hand as she weaved through the hundreds of civilians hurrying back and forth or waiting for their flights or doing their jobs without any idea of what was happening in the supernatural world imposed right over their reality.

And that feeling of being watched returned full-force, raising the hair at the nape of her neck and covering her skin with goosebumps. Every movement caught in the corner of her eye was a possible threat. Every shout, thump, laugh, or banging of trashcans and supplies was a possible distraction.

No, she hadn't heard of monster attacks in crowded international airports, but then again, she'd never heard of an elemental monster-hunter using her magic and a creepy, glowing ball made of someone else's leftovers to control an army of grindylows, either. Or any other creature, for that matter.

Anything seemed possible, and it all loomed over her in a way that made her want to turn and run as fast as she could in the opposite direction.

It made her want to touch the copper orb again, simply for reassurance.

Before she realized what she was doing, Halsey's hand slid into her right jacket pocket only to falter when the familiar smooth curve of the orb's cold metal surface wasn't there.

Bad habits have a tendency to turn into obsessions. Good thing I packed it in my bag. I need my head on straight before I can even look at that thing again.

"Hal!"

The shout came from up ahead, and she froze, fervently scanning the bustling bodies moving in every direction around her.

"Halsey! Over here!"

It took her a moment longer to finally see Seamus standing farther down the terminal, trying to both casually wave and cause enough of a commotion that she noticed him as he leaned from side to side while various normies passed in front of him. His height and wide shoulders would have been hard to miss when he stood at least a head taller than everyone else in the airport. *If* Halsey had been looking for him.

I was looking for monsters instead, wasn't I? Don't be an idiot, Halsey. Being paranoid and being smart are not *the same thing.*

With a curt nod to emphasize the point to herself, she plastered on a smile and took off at a brisk pace toward the only other person she could stand to talk to right now.

Seamus grinned and stopped waving when he realized she'd seen him, and he stayed right where he was in the terminal hallway with his hands slid deep into the pockets of his jeans. When she was only a few feet away, he surprised her by spreading his arms, walking toward her, and wrapping her up in an enormous hug.

Like we've been friends forever, huh? A bit forward, but okay.

Huffing out a laugh, Halsey wrapped her free arm around his waist to hug him back as much as she could, then they released each other. She looked into his luminous blue eyes and realized she was too distracted to hold his gaze. "I thought you were picking me up outside."

"Ah, sure. Lovely to see you too." Seamus chuckled, gazing down at her as she searched the busy terminal. Then his gleaming, perfectly white grin faded into an uncertain half-smile. "Ye doin' all right, there?"

"What, me?" She shot him another quick, distracted glance and shrugged. "I'm fine."

"And I can sniff out a lie as well as any bloodhound." He put a gentle hand on her shoulder and dipped his head, fixing her with the kind of concerned and compassionate gaze that might have made her break down if they hadn't been in public and surrounded by strangers. "Wanna talk about it?"

"Somewhere else, maybe."

"Aye, that suits." Seamus' intense gaze kept boring into her, and though Halsey found it difficult to look directly at him for longer than a few seconds at a time, he slid his hand down her shoulder and the top of her arm as if he already knew his job was to reassure her that everything was okay. "It *is* lovely to see you, Hal. Truly."

That brought a genuine smile to her face, and she finally managed to hold his gaze like someone who wasn't carrying the weight of the world on her shoulders and didn't have anything to hide. Under the current circumstances, flirting with the son of the Havalon Clan's Council head didn't seem nearly as daunting. "It's good to see you too, Seamus. I could use a friendly face right now."

"Well here it is." He released her shoulder and shot her that gleaming grin again. "Ye can have any other part of me ye need or want while ye're in town. No strings attached."

Halsey laughed as her face warmed with all the implications in those two playful sentences. "I'll keep that in mind."

"And I'll hold ye to it. Come on." Without asking or giving her any time to object, Seamus slid her duffel bag off her shoulder and slung it over his own before turning toward the airport exit. "It's a bit of a ride to where I'm staying now. Just outside the city. Ye can start unloadin' yer mind while I drive, then ye can finish over a pint if ye like. What d'ya say?"

As she walked alongside the incredibly tall, handsome, smiling elemental, she had to crane her neck to get a good look at his profile. "I think I'll wait for the pint. Trust me, we're gonna need more than one."

Get sneak peeks, exclusive giveaways, behind the scenes content, and more. PLUS you'll be notified of special **one day only fan pricing** on new releases.

Sign up today to get free stories.

Visit: https://marthacarr.com/read-free-stories/

AUTHOR NOTES - MARTHA CARR

MAY 9, 2023

I've started a project answering questions for my son about my life. I realized after last year's fifth round of cancer, and then chemo this time that he was expecting me to die sooner rather than later. It's been a lot for him to deal with and there isn't much I can do to make it better, except tell him stories that I can leave behind – eventually. Hopefully, a long time from now. I'm going to let you guys listen in as well.

My author notes for this year are going to be answers to questions and all of you can get to know me better, too. Maybe inspire, maybe give you a laugh along the way.

Today's question is: Did you ever get in trouble in school?

All the time in elementary school, and I think it was a good thing. I'm kind of sorry that piece of me got punished out of me and I'm spending a lot of money on therapy to bring it back. I was always getting in trouble for talking. Not talking back to the teacher and not talking while the teacher was talking. I was always looking for small moments to connect with someone, find out a little more about them, talk about the day. I craved connections. But, except for recess and lunch there were no planned times to do that, so I made my own and sometimes got caught at it.

I spent my fair share of time standing outside of the classroom by the door, patiently waiting till the fifteen minutes were up and I could go back inside. If someone wandered by on their way to the bathroom, I quietly talked to them. Why not?

If I was sent to the principal's office I learned to walk very, very slowly and then turn around at the door and walk very, very slowly back. I never actually went inside the principal's office and no teacher ever asked for confirmation. It was a perfect plan.

One year, I think it was third grade, a teacher set up a mini-library in the large closet in the room. We were allowed to wander in there and get books at will. Two things I loved were combined into one event. Books and connecting with friends. I was in that little library every chance I got.

Over time, I ran into teachers who brought their own anger issues with them and cast shame on every kid for everything she saw as a failing. We all probably have a story or two like this one. Eventually, I learned to be very quiet and watchful and just get through the day. I carried that habit into high school and into college and into life.

The conversation I was having on the interior got to be louder, which is not actually a good thing because there's no counter argument, no other reflections and worst of all, no connections. I became more and more self-reliant and that has its upside, but too much independence and I forgot how to ask - and accept - help. All that silence weakened my connection to others. Do it long enough and I forgot how to reverse the practice.

Turns out it's simple but doesn't feel easy. Simple and easy are two different things.

Here's the first big step. Go back to that original joy when I was so young there weren't other belief systems at play yet. Just say hello without wondering what someone else is thinking. Stop trying to pre-sort people or wonder what they're thinking. Just start talking and listen with an open heart and an open mind. Be curious and talk about something fun I'm trying like showing up for running groups. Or be cool if it's someone that doesn't click. Go look for someone else. Connect the dots between that little kid I was and this way-too-serious grownup I've become. It can be done.

I get more and more every year why people who are older long to go back to when they were young. It's not so much about the body that moves without creaking. I can deal with that and push my limits, which is kind of fun. It's because I can see what listening to the wrong grownups can do to the rest of someone's life and I'd know to ignore them and look for better allies, better mentors and just keep going. That's actually my new plan now. Love you. Love, Mom. More adventures to follow.

AUTHOR NOTES - MICHAEL ANDERLE

MAY 2, 2023

First, thank you for not only reading this story, but these author notes in the back as well!

Chasing Big Dreams at 55 vs. Younger Me

As I've reached the age of 55 (56 later this year), I can't help but reflect on the differences in trying to accomplish big goals now compared to when I was physically younger and raising a family.

The challenges of a physically older male body are real, but so were the obstacles I faced when juggling family responsibilities.

For instance, while I no longer have children at home to care for, I find myself dealing with the inevitable medical appointments and tests that come with aging. I've never been a fan of blood tests, but over time, I've become more accustomed to them as a necessary part of staying healthy.

In short, it seems every time I need to see the doc, it's "Go get these blood tests done. See you a week after you make that happen." Why can't we have the Star Trek medical thingamabob real today instead of AI?

Somebody put out the medical scanner, stat!

Here are three more examples of the contrasting challenges between my older self and the physically younger me (who was handsome as @#%!) :

Time management: When I was younger, managing time was all about balancing work and family life. Now, I have more time on my hands, but I also have to be mindful of my energy levels and prioritize tasks accordingly. This means allocating time for rest and self-care, which wasn't as much of a concern when I was younger.

I have lots of "I NEED TO FINISH THIS!" but by later in the afternoon, I find that sometimes I don't give a f#ck. I can work on it in the morning when I'm full of piss and vinegar again.

Physical limitations: As a younger man, I could push myself harder without worrying too much about the consequences. Nowadays, I have to be more cautious and listen to my body. I still aim to accomplish big things, but I need to be more strategic and patient in my approach.

And who thought random bruises showing up on my legs was a good thing? They should be soundly beaten and allowed to have non-random bruises all over their bodies.

Part 2 of that idea. Why is it I don't remember doing whatever caused the random bruises?

Financial considerations: In my younger years, financial decisions were often focused on providing for my family and meeting the next rent check, grocery bill, etc.

Now as an older man, my financial priorities have shifted toward retirement planning and ensuring I have the resources to enjoy my golden years (which often conflicts with trying to grow a business).

Going for big solutions when you are older is different. It's like bootstrapping a business, but with a better food and rent budget.

Ultimately, both stages of life come with their unique challenges, but I believe the stuff I've learned over the years has allowed me to better navigate the obstacles my rebellious streak gets me into…a*ll the damned time!*

But I believe this:

No matter our age, we can still dream big and work towards achieving our goals.

Ad Aeternitatem,

Michael Anderle

MORE STORIES with Michael newsletter HERE: https://michael.beehiiv.com/

BOOKS BY MARTHA CARR

THE LEIRA CHRONICLES
CASE FILES OF AN URBAN WITCH
DIARY OF A DARK MONSTER
THE EVERMORES CHRONICLES
SOUL STONE MAGE
THE KACY CHRONICLES
MIDWEST MAGIC CHRONICLES
THE FAIRHAVEN CHRONICLES
I FEAR NO EVIL
THE DANIEL CODEX SERIES
SCHOOL OF NECESSARY MAGIC
SCHOOL OF NECESSARY MAGIC: RAINE CAMPBELL
ALISON BROWNSTONE
FEDERAL AGENTS OF MAGIC
SCIONS OF MAGIC
THE UNBELIEVABLE MR. BROWNSTONE
DWARF BOUNTY HUNTER
ACADEMY OF NECESSARY MAGIC
MAGIC CITY CHRONICLES
ROGUE AGENTS OF MAGIC
CHRONICLES OF WINLAND UNDERWOOD
WITCH WARRIOR

OTHER BOOKS BY JUDITH BERENS

OTHER BOOKS BY MARTHA CARR

JOIN THE ORICERAN UNIVERSE FAN GROUP ON FACEBOOK!

BOOKS BY MICHAEL ANDERLE

Sign up for the LMBPN email list to be notified of new releases and special deals!

http://lmbpn.com/email/

For a complete list of books by Michael Anderle, please visit:

www.lmbpn.com/ma-books/

CONNECT WITH THE AUTHORS

Martha Carr Social
Website:
http://www.marthacarr.com
Facebook:
https://www.facebook.com/groups/MarthaCarrFans/

Michael Anderle

Website: http://lmbpn.com

Email List: https://michael.beehiiv.com/

https://www.facebook.com/LMBPNPublishing

https://twitter.com/MichaelAnderle

https://www.instagram.com/lmbpn_publishing/

https://www.bookbub.com/authors/michael-anderle

www.ingramcontent.com/pod-product-compliance
Lightning Source LLC
LaVergne TN
LVHW091710070526
838199LV00050B/2338